# Morning Glory

A NOVEL

## Sarah Jio

A PLUME BOOK

PLUME
Published by the Penguin Group
Penguin Group (USA), 375 Hudson Street
New York, New York 10014, USA

USA | Canada | UK | Ireland | Australia | New Zealand | India | South Africa | China
Penguin Books Ltd, Registered Offices: 80 Strand, London WC2R 0RL, England
For more information about the Penguin Group visit penguin.com

First published by Plume, a member of Penguin Group (USA), 2013

REGISTERED TRADEMARK—MARCA REGISTRADA

LIBRARY OF CONGRESS CATALOGING-IN-PUBLICATION DATA
Jio, Sarah.
    Morning glory / Sarah Jio.
        pages cm
    ISBN 978-0-14-219699-1
    1. Artists-Fiction.   2. Boathouses—Fiction.   3. Seattle—Fiction.   I. Title
    PS3610.I6M67 2013
    813'.6—dc23

                                        2013014200

Printed in the United States of America
10  9  8  7  6  5  4  3  2  1

Set in Granjon
Designed by Eve L. Kirch

PUBLISHER'S NOTE
This is a work of fiction. Names, characters, places, and incidents either are the product
of the author's imagination or are used fictitiously, and any resemblance to actual
persons, living or dead, businesses, companies, events, or locales is entirely coincidental.

A PLUME BOOK

# MORNING GLORY

Michelle Moore

SARAH JIO is the *New York Times* and *USA Today* bestselling author of *The Violets of March*, a *Library Journal* Best Book of 2011; *The Bungalow*; *Blackberry Winter*; and *The Last Camellia*. She is also a journalist who has written for *Glamour*; *O, The Oprah Magazine*; *Redbook*; *Real Simple*; and many other publications. Sarah's novels have become book club favorites and have been sold for translation in more than eighteen languages. She lives in Seattle with her husband and their three young boys. Learn more about her at sarahjio.com or facebook.com/sarahjioauthor.

---

### Praise for *The Last Camellia*

"Jio infuses her haunting story of love and loss with an engrossing mystery that will linger long after the final page."          —*Romantic Times*

"The images of the flowers, the landscape, and the manor house are vivid and make for a tantalizing read."          —*Kirkus Reviews*

"An engaging story of two generations trying to move forward despite the powerful pull of the past. A thoughtful examination of history's ability to haunt the present and the power of forgiveness to set things right."
          —*Booklist*

### Praise for *Blackberry Winter*

"Terrific . . . compelling . . . an intoxicating blend of mystery, history, and romance, this book is hard to put down."          —*Real Simple*

"Ingenious . . . imaginative."                                            —*The Seattle Times*

"*Blackberry Winter* never loses momentum. . . . Jio's writing is engaging and fluid."                                                          —*Mystery Scene*

"A fascinating exploration of love, loss, scandal, and redemption."
                                                              —*Publishers Weekly*

"This novel will enchant Jio's fans and make them clamor for her next offering."        —*Kirkus Reviews,* "A Most Anticipated Book of Fall 2012"

"There's no doubt that anyone who picks up this book will instantly fall in love with it and the author."                                        —Brodart

"Sarah Jio's writing is exquisite and engrossing."
                        —Elin Hilderbrand, bestselling author of *Silver Girl*

## Praise for *The Bungalow*

### Pulpwood Queens Book Club, Official Selection 2012

"*The Bungalow* is my favorite book of the year."            —Jen Lancaster

"Jio's first-person Hemingway-ish writing style, like her *The Violets of March* (judged by *Library Journal* as one of the Best Books of 2011), is a pleasure to read. . . . Jio has done a superb job of pulling together the themes of friendship, betrayal, and endearing love. These keep us engrossed in the novel to an unpredictable conclusion."        —*The Historical Novels Review*

"Unabashedly romantic . . . thanks to Jio's deft handling of her plot and characters. Fans of Nicholas Sparks will enjoy this gentle historical love story."                                                          —*Library Journal*

"A captivating tale."                                                    —*Booklist*

"A heartfelt, engaging love story set against the fascinating backdrop of the War in the Pacific."              —Kristin Hannah, author of *Home Front*

"*The Bungalow* is a story as luscious as its exotic setting. Ms. Jio has crafted a wartime story of passion and friendship, loss and mystery. It's also a story of discovery—discovering one's own heart, and of finding a second chance long after all hope is gone. You'll remember the sparkling water and yellow hibiscus long after the last page is turned, and will want to start searching for your own lost bungalow and the parts of yourself you've long since forgotten."                                —Karen White, author of *The Beach Trees*

"Sarah Jio whips romance, history, and a page-turning mystery into one mesmerizing South Sea dream. *The Bungalow* reads smooth as a summer day, but Jio's plot races forward with unexpected twists and timeless, haunting love that make you cheer and cry and ache for more."

—Carol Cassella, author of *Oxygen* and *Healer*

## Praise for *The Violets of March*

### A *Library Journal* Best Book of 2011

"Feed the kids *before* you settle in with journalist Sarah Jio's engrossing first novel, *The Violets of March*. This mystery-slash-love story will have you racing to the end—cries of 'Mom, I'm hungry!' be damned."  —*Redbook*

"A gem . . . True escape fiction that can take you away."  —WGBH-TV

"Masterfully written."  —*The New Jersey Star-Ledger*

"In a sweet debut novel, a divorcee visiting her aunt on gorgeous Bainbridge Island, Washington, finds a diary dating to 1943 that reveals potentially life-changing secrets."  —*Coastal Living*

"The right book finds you at the right time. *The Violets of March* will become a source of healing and comfort for its readers."

—*The Costco Connection*

"In *The Violets of March,* debut author Sarah Jio beautifully blends the stories of two women—one of the past, one of the present—together to create a captivating and enthralling novel of romance, heartbreak, and redemption."  —*Times Record News* (Wichita Falls, Kansas)

"Jio's debut is a rich blend of history, mystery, and romance. Fans of Sarah Blake's *The Postmistress* should enjoy this story."  —*Library Journal*

"[An] endearing tale of past heartbreaks and new beginnings. The story's setting and sentiment are sure to entice readers and keep them captivated page after page."  —*Romantic Times*

"A perfect summer read for an escape into a fictional character's challenges with the charm of a local Northwest setting."  —*425* magazine

"Refreshing . . . lovable."  —*First for Women* magazine

"Mix a love story, history, and a mystery and what takes root? *The Violets of March*, a novel that reminds us how the past comes back to haunt us, and packs a few great surprises for the reader along the way. "
—Jodi Picoult, author of *Sing You Home* and *House Rules*

"*The Violets of March* is a captivating first bloom of a novel, with tangled roots, budding relationships, and plenty of twists and turns. But perhaps the biggest revelation of all is that Sarah Jio is one talented writer!"
—Claire Cook, bestselling author of
*Must Love Dogs* and *Best Staged Plans*

"Sarah Jio's *The Violets of March* is a book for anyone who has ever lost love or lost herself. A fresh, satisfying, resonant debut."
—Allison Winn Scotch, author of *Time of My Life* and
*The Memory of Us*

"An enchanting story of love, betrayal, and the discovery of an old diary that mysteriously links the past to the present. *The Violets of March* is a delightful debut."          —Beth Hoffman, author of *Saving CeeCee Honeycutt*

"A romantic, heartfelt, and richly detailed debut. *The Violets of March* is the story of a woman who needs to step away from her shattered life and into the magic of Bainbridge Island before she can find herself again. Sarah Jio delivers a gem of a book, perfect for reading on the beach or under a cozy quilt."
—Sarah Pekkanen, author of *The Opposite of Me* and *Skipping a Beat*

*In memory of Anna and every other lost and brokenhearted woman.*
*Rainy days aren't forever. May you find your way.*

# Author's Note

As I type this, I'm sitting inside my houseboat, looking out the window to a gray day on Lake Union in Seattle. The rain is falling in great sheets. It pounds on the roof, and the wind splatters it against the windows. These are my favorite days on the lake. I can see ducks swim and boats motor by, as well as the occasional kayaker braving the rain. It's cozy, and I'm content.

When I set out to write this novel, I began with a setting and nothing else: a houseboat on the banks of Lake Union. As a lifelong Seattle-area resident, I've always been fascinated by floating homes (and of course, a little movie called *Sleepless in Seattle* only furthered that fascination). Years ago, as a young journalist, I wrote an article about the houseboat lifestyle, and I'll never forget being invited to tour a floating home for the first time. The woman who graciously welcomed me into her home (through a door with an opening in the bottom for ducks) told me about life on the lake—the way a houseboat sways gently in the wind, how the lake can rock you to sleep, and perhaps most memorable, for me, the way the houseboat community is like a family, helping neighbors in need, keeping secrets like only trusted friends do.

I suppose the very beginning of this novel started that day, when I stepped inside that little floating home. And as time went on, I longed to live in a houseboat of my own. But as our family grew, my husband and I decided that raising three little boys on a houseboat may not be the best choice (imagine playing catch on a small dock). So we set that dream aside, at least until September 2012.

My husband knew I'd begun plotting out an idea for a novel set on a houseboat, and while I'd hoped to find one to rent for a weekend for research purposes, he surprised me with a generous idea. Why not, he suggested, rent a houseboat for an extended period of time? I could use it as my office and really get the feel for life on the lake.

My first instinct was to say no. At first blush, it seemed frivolous, an unnecessary splurge. But then I began to think: How else would I really get to know the houseboat lifestyle, the history of the community, the local personalities and their secrets?

So we went to tour a houseboat for rent, and in the space of 3.5 seconds, I fell head over heels. With a loft bedroom (complete with a working porthole), a rooftop deck with a view of the Space Needle, and a quaint and fully stocked kitchen, this was the houseboat of my dreams. My husband and I quickly signed a lease to rent it for four months.

I could not have written this book without the time I've had on Lake Union. While it's true this is a work of fiction, the months I've spent in the houseboat community have enriched and inspired my writing—from the pair of mallards nesting outside my back deck to the kindness of the neighbors all around me.

We have a few more weeks on the houseboat before our lease runs out. I really hate to go. I've laughed here. I've cried here. I've made new friends and bonded with old ones under this roof. I've felt a great sense of peace here. And mostly, I have fallen in love with the houseboat community.

But it's almost time to say good-bye. For when I turn in the final draft of this novel in the days ahead, I will also be turning in my key and saying farewell to my beloved Boat Street, as I've affectionately called it in real life and in the novel. Even so, the dock, and the story I created here, will forever remain in my heart. Houseboat No. 7. Henrietta and Haines. Little Jimmy. Penny and Collin. Alex and Ada. I feel as if they're all waving good-bye as I make my way up the dock. Years will pass, but I'll always know where to find them.

—SJ

# Morning Glory

# Chapter 1

Seattle, June 12, 2008

I step down onto the old dock and it creaks beneath my feet, as if letting out a deep sigh. It's dark out, but the string lights that dangle overhead illuminate my path.

What did the woman from the rental office say on the phone? Seventh houseboat on the left? Yes. *I think.* I grasp my suitcase tighter and walk ahead slowly. A sailboat sways gently in the water where it's tethered to an adjoining houseboat, a two-story, with a rooftop deck and cedar shingle siding weathered to a gray-brown. A lantern flickers on a table on the front deck, but seconds later its flame is extinguished, maybe by the breeze, maybe by someone lingering in the shadows. I imagine the residents of the dock peering through their darkened windows, watching me, whispering. "There she is," one says to another. "The new neighbor." Someone smirks. "I hear she's from *New York.*"

I hate the hushed exchanges, the looks. The crush of curiosity drove me from New York. "The poor thing," I overheard someone utter as she stepped out of the office elevator a month ago. "I don't know how she even manages to get out of bed every morning after *what happened*. If it were me, I don't know how I'd go on." I remember how I hovered in the hallway until the woman rounded the corner. I couldn't bear to see the look on her face, or any of their faces. The headshaking. The pity. The horror. In Seattle, the shadow of my past would be under cloud cover.

I take a deep breath and look up when I hear the distant creak of a door hinge. I pause, bracing for confrontation. But the only movement I detect is a kayak gliding slowly across the lake. Its lone passenger nods at me, before disappearing into the moonlight. The dock rocks a little, and I wobble, steadying myself. New York is a long way from Seattle, and I'm still groggy from the transcontinental flight. I stop and wonder, for a moment, what I'm doing here.

I pass two more houseboats. One is gray, with French doors that face north and a weather vane perched on the roof. The next is tan, with window boxes brimming with red geraniums. Various urns and planters line the deck in front of the home, and I stop to admire the blue hydrangeas growing in a terra-cotta pot. Whoever lives here must be a meticulous gardener. I think of the garden I left behind on my balcony in New York, the little garden box planted with chard and basil and the sugar pumpkin for . . . I bite my lip. My heart swells, but the porch light on houseboat number seven anchors me to the moment. I stop to take in the sight of what will be my new home: Situated on the farthest slip on the dock, it floats solemnly, unafraid. Weathered cedar shingles cover its sides, and I smile when I notice an open porthole on the upper floor. It's just as the advertisement depicted. I sigh.

Here I am.

I feel a lump in my throat as I insert the key into the lock. My legs are suddenly weak, and as soon as I open the door, I fall to my knees, bury my head in my hands, and weep.

*Three weeks earlier*

It's nine in the morning, and the New York sun streams through the eighth-floor windows of Dr. Evinson's office with such intensity, I drape my hand over my eyes.

"Sorry," he says, gesturing toward the blinds. "Is the light bothering you?"

"Yes," I say. "Well, no, it's . . ." The truth is, it isn't the light that's burning, but my news.

I sigh and sit up straighter in the overstuffed chair with its brash white and green stripes. A signed, framed photo of Mick Jagger hangs on the wall. I smile inwardly, recalling how I walked into Dr. Evinson's office a year ago, expecting a black leather couch and a clean-shaven man in a suit holding a notebook and nodding reassuringly as I dabbed a tissue to my eyes.

According to my sister-in-law, Joanie, he was Manhattan's most sought-after grief therapist. Past patients included Mick Jagger— hence the wall art—and other big names. After Heath Ledger's death, his ex, Michelle Williams, came to see Dr. Evinson on a weekly basis. I know because I saw her in the lobby once flipping through an issue of *Us Weekly*. But his celebrity client list didn't impress me. Frankly, I'd always been scared of therapists, scared of what they might cause me to say, cause me to *feel*. But Joan encouraged me to go. Actually, *encourage* is the wrong word. One morning, she met me for breakfast in the restaurant on the ground floor of Dr. Evinson's office building, then put me on an elevator destined for the ninth floor. When I reached his foyer, I thought about turning around, but the receptionist said, "You must be Dr. Evinson's nine o'clock."

I walked into the room reluctantly, noticing the green-and-white-striped chair, the one I'd sit in every Friday at nine for a year. "You expected a couch, didn't you?" Dr. Evinson asked with a disarming smile.

I nodded.

He swiveled around in his desk chair and patted his gray beard. "Never trust a therapist who makes his patients lie on a couch."

"Oh," I said, taking a seat. I recall reading an article about the great debate over the couch as a therapeutic mechanism. Freud had subscribed to the method of sitting *behind* his patients, while they reclined on a couch in front of him. Evidently, he despised eye contact. Still, others, including Dr. Evinson, found the whole couch scenario to be unproductive, even stifling. Others agreed, saying it put the therapist in a place of dominance over the patient, squashing any chance for real dialogue and meaningful feedback.

I wasn't sure which side I was on, just that I felt awkward in his office. But I sat in that overstuffed chair anyway, sinking down into its deep cushions. The soft fabric felt like a great big hug, and I proceeded to tell him everything.

I lean my head back into the thick cushion.

"You're still not sleeping well, are you?" he asks.

I shrug. He prescribed sleeping pills, which help . . . a little. But I still wake up at four each morning, eyes wide open, heart hurting no less than it did when I closed my eyes the night before. Nothing has helped. Antidepressants. Sedatives. The Valium they gave me in the hospital the day my world changed forever. None of it takes the pain away, the loneliness, the sense of being forever lost in my own life.

"You're keeping something from me," he says.

I look away.

"Ada, what is it?"

I nod. "You're not going to like it."

His silence, I've learned, is my cue to continue. I take a deep breath. "I'm thinking about leaving New York."

He raises his eyebrows. "And why is that?"

I rub my forehead. "It's the memories of them," I say. "I can't bear it anymore. I can't . . ." Tears well up in my eyes, though I haven't cried here in months. I'd reached a level of healing, a plateau, as Dr. Evinson called it, and had felt a little stronger—until now.

"If I leave," I say with a trembling voice, "if I go away, maybe this pain won't follow me. Maybe I . . ." I bury my face in my hands.

"Good," Dr. Evinson says, always quick to find the positive. "Change can be beneficial." He nods as I look up from my hands, but I can tell his skepticism mirrors my own. The fight-or-flight response has come up in our sessions, but I've never been one to act on the latter.

"Let's talk about this," he continues. "So you'd really want to leave your home, your work? I know how important both are to you."

Last month, I was named deputy editor of *Sunrise* magazine, and at thirty-three, I'm the youngest person to hold the post. Just last week, as a spokesperson for the magazine, I shared travel tips for families with Matt Lauer on the *Today* show. My career is thriving, yes, but my personal life, well, it withered and died two years ago.

Everywhere, from the window seat in the apartment to the little café on Fifty-Sixth Street, memories linger and taunt me. "Remember when life was perfect?" they whisper. "Remember when you were happy?"

I grimace and look Dr. Evinson square in the eye. "I fill my days with work, so much work," I say, shaking my head. "But I don't work because I love it. I mean, I used to love it." The tears well up in my eyes again. "Now none of it matters. I feel like a kid who works so hard on an art project at school, but when she brings it home, no one's there to care." I throw up my hands. "When there's no one there to care, what does any of it matter? Does any of it even matter?" I rub my eyes. "I have to get out of this city, Dr. Evinson. I've known it for a long time. I can't stay here."

He nods thoughtfully. I can tell my words have registered. "Yes," he says.

"So you think it's a good idea?" I ask nervously.

"I think it could have value," he says after a moment of thought. "But only if you're leaving for the right reasons." He looks at me intently, with those knowing eyes that seem to peer right into my psyche. "Are you *running* from your pain, Ada?"

*I knew he'd ask me that.* "Maybe," I say honestly, wiping a tear from my cheek. "Really, all I know is that I don't want to hurt anymore." I shake my head. "I just don't want to hurt anymore."

"Ada," he says, "you must come to terms with the fact that you may hurt for the rest of your life." His words gouge me like a dull knife, but I know I must listen. "Part of what we're doing here is helping you live with your sadness, helping you manage it. I worry that you're compartmentalizing your pain, that you've made yourself believe that the hurt you feel exists only in New York, when it actually lives in here." He points to his heart.

I look away.

"Where will you go?" he asks.

"I don't know," I say. "Somewhere far from here."

He leans back in his chair and scratches his head before clasping his hands together. "My daughter has a friend in Seattle who owns a houseboat, and it's for rent," he says suddenly.

"A houseboat?" I furrow my brow slightly. "Like that movie with Tom Hanks and Meg Ryan?"

"Yes," he says, digging a card out of his desk drawer. "She was here visiting and mentioned that my wife and I should come stay."

"I don't know," I say. "I was kind of thinking of someplace warm. Doesn't it rain a lot there?"

"You know what they say about rain," he says with a smile. "God's tears."

"So I won't be crying alone," I say, half-smiling.

He hands me the card, and I read the name Roxanne Wentworth. "Thanks," I say, tucking it in my pocket as I stand up.

"Remember what I said," Dr. Evinson reminds me, pointing to his chest. I nod, but I pray that he's wrong, because I know I can't bear to feel this way much longer. My heart can't take much more.

The phone rings once, then twice. I consider hanging up. Suddenly this idea of mine seems crazy. Leave my job? Move to Seattle? To a *houseboat*? My finger hovers over the End Call button, but then a cheerful voice answers. "Ms. Wentworth's office, how may I help you?"

"Yes," I say, fumbling to find my voice. "Yes, this is, um, my name is Ada Santorini, and I'm calling to inquire about . . . the houseboat for rent."

"Santorini," the woman says. "What a beautiful name. I knew a family with that last name when I studied abroad in Milan. You must be Italian?"

"No," I say quickly. "I mean, my husband was—I mean, listen, I'm sure you've already rented the houseboat."

"No," the woman says. "It's available the first of the month. It's absolutely charming, though I'm sure you already know as you've seen the photos online."

"Photos?"

"Yes," she says, reading me a Web site address, which I quickly key into my computer. My office door is open and I hope the nosy intern in the cubicle outside isn't listening.

"Wow," I say, scrolling through the images on my screen. "It's . . . really cute."

Maybe Dr. Evinson is wrong. Maybe I *can* escape my pain. I feel my heart beating wildly inside my chest as an e-mail from my editor in chief pops up on my screen. "The *Today* segment was a hit. The producer wants you to share more tips on traveling with children. Be in studio for hair and makeup by five a.m. tomorrow." My head is spinning a little. *No. No, I can't do this. Not anymore.* "I would like to rent it," I say suddenly.

"You would?" the woman asks. "But don't you want to hear more details? We haven't even talked about the rent."

The nosy intern is standing in my doorway now. She's holding the cover image of the August issue. A little girl and her mother are smiling, swinging in a hammock. "No," I say immediately. "It doesn't matter. I'll take it."

# Chapter 2

I open my eyes, and for a moment I have no idea where I am, and the void is blissfully frightening. Then I hear the sound of the lake outside, and the scene comes into focus.

I'm on a couch draped with a stark white slipcover. My sandals are still strapped to my feet, and my large black suitcase is beside the door. I gaze around the houseboat as if seeing it for the first time. The clock says it's quarter till six, nearly nine on the East Coast. This is a fact I find shocking, because I haven't slept this late in years.

I stand up and walk to the little kitchen. Running my hand along the tile countertop, I find a brass key resting on top of a note written on Wentworth Real Estate letterhead. "Welcome to Seattle!" it reads. "Here's an extra key. If you need anything, give us a call." I tuck the key in my pocket and notice a coffeemaker. I pour fresh water into the tank and toss in a packet of pre-ground Starbucks Breakfast Blend, listening as the machine hisses and spurts.

I peek inside a cabinet and open a few drawers, happy to find all fully stocked. A set of well-worn pots and pans hang from hooks over the stove. Many meals have been cooked here. Wineglasses line an open shelf, champagne glasses on the next. I wonder about the people who have pressed their lips against them over the years, and I can almost hear them blowing noisemakers and shouting, "Happy New Year!" before huddling on the dock to sing "Auld Lang Syne." *Were they happy here? Will I be?*

I reach for a mug on the shelf and fill it with coffee. I hold it up to my nose, then take a sip before proceeding down the hall, where a daybed is wedged against the wall facing a white bookshelf. The shelf is stocked with castaways from renters of years past. Maeve Binchy. Stephen King. I smile when I see a copy of *The Ultimate Hitchhiker's Guide to the Galaxy*. It used to be James's favorite.

I close my eyes tightly, then proceed around the corner, where I pass a pint-size stacked washer and dryer set, a linen closet, and a small bathroom. A generous skylight presides over the shower, with a tiny square window that looks out from the stall to the dock and the lake beyond. I can see a young family motoring past in a small boat. There's a little girl in a pink life jacket and an older boy on the stern with his father. I look away.

I walk back down the hall, passing a framed painting of an old sailboat. I squint and see the name *Catalina* painted in blue on her side. My mind turns to the island off the coast of San Diego. *Sunrise* sent me there nine years ago, the year after the wedding. I remember watching seabirds swooping into the cove. James came with me. We had panini at a little café on the beach. I take a deep breath, turning back to the painting. The boat's two sails puff out proudly over its wooden hull. The blue water below is tropical. Perhaps this is the Bahamas, or somewhere else in the Caribbean. Where is she sailing, this ship called *Catalina*? She looks unbounded, full of life, pushing ahead with no anchor, no concerns to hold her back. I reach out and touch my finger to the canvas. I know it's bad etiquette, but I can't help it. It's as if the painting is magnetic. I feel the lines, the texture of the artist's brush.

Behind me are the stairs—well, more like a ship's ladder—that lead to the loft above. I duck my head and climb up until I reach the upper floor, where the fir plank floors creak beneath my feet. There's a double bed—its crisp, white linens look freshly laundered and pressed—and an old dresser with brass door pulls shaped like lion heads. Above the wooden headboard is the porthole. It's been propped open, and I feel the cool morning air on my face. I listen as a pair of Canadian geese fly by, alternating squawks as they skim the water with their feet.

I carefully climb down the ladder to the living room. Outside the French doors, a sailboat bobs on the water. The rental office didn't say anything about a sailboat. Its hull is wooden, stained the color of honey. It looks old but well kept. I unlock the door and walk out to the dock. I notice a yellow Lab snoozing outside a houseboat on the slip to my left. By now in New York, I'd already be sitting at my desk, having my second espresso and editing layouts. I would do that until one, until someone pried me away for lunch, which I would eat, reluctantly, before rushing back. I'd stay past nine, leaving only when the cleaning crew came in. I hated going home.

I sit down on a white Adirondack chair that looks out to the west side of Lake Union, where boats and floating homes nestle against the water's edge. I see a green, grassy hill on my right—Gas Works Park, I think, remembering the Seattle guidebook I thumbed through on the plane—covered with rusted-out industrial relics that look almost sculptural. I watch the boats glide by for the next hour. Violin music lilts through the air, and I can't make out the source. I remember something James always said, that sound is deceiving on the water, that sometimes you can hear a whisper from a half mile away. I listen for a moment, transfixed by the melody, until the music stops. I hear footsteps behind me, and then a voice.

"Henrietta!" It's a man, on the dock. "Henrietta!" He sounds concerned, and for a moment, I wonder if someone is in trouble. Cautiously, I walk to the end of the deck, and I peer down the dock. I see his back first. He's tall and in good shape for his age. Judging by the weathered look in his eyes, I'd peg him at a young sixty. His gray hair is parted at the side and falls over his forehead the way Ernest Hemingway's did in the Key West photos, charming in a sort of boyish, brash way. "Oh," he says, noticing me suddenly. "You must be the new neighbor." He smiles warmly. "I'm sorry about the boat," he continues, pointing to the sailboat moored outside my deck. "I meant to move that over to my slip before you arrived. I've just got to get the contractor out to fix the dock, and, well—"

"It's OK," I reply, taking a few steps closer.

"I'm Jim," he says.

"Ada," I say, taking his hand. "I arrived last night. I'm the new renter."

He smiles. "Well then, let me be the first to welcome you to Boat Street."

I give him a confused look.

"Oh, it's what we call our dock," he says.

I nod. "Oh, I'm sorry. You were looking for someone? Henrietta?"

His grin morphs into a frown, as if he's remembering an upsetting fact. "Oh, yeah," he says, shaking his head. "Haines, where are you, old boy?" I watch, perplexed, as he looks behind him. A moment later a mallard duck peers cautiously around the side of the houseboat ahead. He waddles toward Jim, stopping briefly to look up at me. "You see, Haines here is married to a fine duck named Henrietta. But they fight a lot, and they had quite a donnybrook last night." He speaks without sarcasm, as if the love lives of ducks are quite a serious matter. I'm not sure if I should smile, but it's impossible not to.

"Do you think she's run away?" I ask, giving my best effort to keep a straight face.

"Oh no," Jim says. "She's just off sulking somewhere. Last week I found her in a kayak. She'd been gone for two days, and Haines was beside himself." He kneels down beside the duck, who fluffs his feathers and lets out a little quack. "Mallards mate for life, you know."

"I've heard," I say. "It's really sweet."

"Anyway," he says, standing, "we're all hoping for ducklings this spring."

I smile. "Ducklings?"

He nods. "They've been going together for five years, and you'd think they'd consummate this marriage at some point."

"Maybe this is their year," I say.

"Maybe. Anyway, if you see Henrietta, let me know. I live four houseboats down."

"Oh," I say, remembering the garden I passed the night before. "You must have potted all those flowers—they're so pretty."

"No," he says quickly. "That's my mother's garden. My parents live next door. I grew up here on the dock." He looks thoughtful for a moment. "I stayed away for a long time, but when the house next door came up for sale last year, I decided to buy it." He looks down the dock as if seeing it through the lens of the past, exactly how it appeared fifty years ago. "When I left this dock, I swore I'd never return. But I guess every eighteen-year-old thinks that, right?" He shrugs. "If there's one thing I've learned, it's that time mellows things." He eyes the potted plants in front of his parents' houseboat. "No matter what, home is home. It's where you belong."

I nod hesitantly, thinking of my own home. I haven't been back to Kansas City in years. The reason pains me, and I let my mind extinguish the thought like a flickering ember doused with water. And New York City—no, it isn't home anymore either. I'm not anchored to any place.

"Anyway, I needed to come back," Jim continues. "Mom and Dad aren't in the best health. Mom broke her hip last fall. She's finally up and about, but she's frail. And Dad, well, he's been having memory trouble. Some days are better than others."

"I'm so sorry," I say, thinking of my own parents for a moment. I feel guilty for the great wall of silence I've built between us. I didn't do it intentionally, of course. I just couldn't bear to hear their voices, see their faces—mirrors of the pain I felt. We went out to see them the summer before . . . I close my eyes for a moment, and I can see Ella jumping around in the steamy Midwest night air, reaching for fireflies. "Look, Mama," she squeals, her voice still so fresh in my mind. She runs to me with hands cupped together. "I caught one! What should we call him?"

I smile and take her inside, where I find an old mason jar in a cabinet in my mother's kitchen and show her how to make a proper firefly home, adding some twigs and leaves to the bottom, then piercing the metal lid with a steak knife to provide airflow for the little critter. "There," I say. "Your very own firefly."

She presses her nose to the glass. "Can we take him home to New York?"

I shake my head. "No, honey," I say softly. "He belongs *here*."

I don't have to explain any further. She understands.

Ella understood so much more than most little girls her age. I sigh, thinking of that magical summer trip, thinking of James, and my parents, who'd had a new swing set installed in their backyard that month for Ella, their only grandchild. I shake my head. No, I couldn't face them. So when my parents called, I didn't answer the phone one day, and the next, and the next. Eventually, I sent a letter. I promised I'd call when I was ready. But I didn't know when that would be.

Jim looks down at Haines and smiles. "Anyway, it's nice to be here for them, you know?"

"Yeah," I say vacantly.

"How about you?" he asks. "Where's home for you?"

I look in the distance, as if I can actually see my Manhattan apartment beyond the Seattle skyline, then I turn back to face Jim. "I've lived in a lot of places," I say.

"Right," he says. His eyes sparkle as if he gets it, as if he has secrets of his own. He nods. "Well, you're going to love it here."

"I hope," I say. "By the way, is there a grocery store nearby, someplace to pick up the essentials?"

Jim nods and points to the street above the dock. "Pete's Market," he says. "Just a few blocks from here. It's been around as long as I have. Great wine, too. But then again, if you need anything, just pop over. We're very communal here when it comes to bread, eggs, and milk."

I smile. "Thanks." I turn back to the lake, then again to the street above the dock. "It was dark when I arrived last night, so I'm still trying to get my bearings. Can you walk to much else around here?"

He nods. "Best coffee shop in Seattle is just up the hill on Eastlake, and you don't want to miss the Italian restaurant, Serafina."

"Sounds nice," I say. If James were here, he would have already scouted it and made reservations for dinner tonight.

"You won't find a better little community on the West Coast."

He turns back to Haines, who's been listening to our conversation intently. "Well, I better get back to the search party," he says, digging a hand into his pocket and pulling out a crust of bread. "Her favorite: stale ciabatta."

"I hope you find her," I say. Haines tilts his head as if he understands exactly what I'm saying.

Jim nods. "I'll be back around this afternoon to move the boat back to my slip."

"Oh, please don't worry about it," I reply. "I really don't mind. It's actually kind of quaint."

He scratches his head. "Well, if it's all right with you."

"I insist," I add.

"She has quite a history here, the *Catalina*."

I shake my head. Her name must be painted on the opposite side. And then I remember the painting. "The *Catalina*?"

He grins.

"Inside my houseboat," I say, pointing back toward the French doors, "there's a painting—"

"Yes," he says. I see the sparkle in his eyes again. "Well, I'll be seeing you around."

# Chapter 3

PENNY WENTWORTH

*Seattle, June 8, 1959*

Dexter is gone. Again. I rise and walk out to the deck in front of the houseboat and dip my feet in the cool water. The dock sways as it always does in the mornings when the boats are leaving the south lake and making their way toward the locks. I don't like it when they go. It makes me feel lonely, abandoned.

I look to my right, where the new neighbor on the next dock over, Collin, is crouched over the hull of the boat he's building. He sands a strip of the railing with long, smooth motions. I'm mesmerized, until he suddenly looks up and smiles. My cheeks redden and I turn away quickly. It's still early, and people keep to themselves on the dock in the morning hours. There are unspoken rules. I stare at the lake until my eyes cannot be tamed a moment longer, and without my permission, they wander back to Collin's dock. He's wearing a white V-neck T-shirt that's stained with sweat. I can make out the lines of his chest, the definition of his muscles beneath the thin cotton. He wipes his brow with the back of his hand. I look away before our eyes meet again and kick my feet back and forth in the cold lake water—so dark, like a vial of cobalt blue paint tinged with too much black. I lean forward and try, as I always do, to see below the surface. Instead, I make out only my reflection, blurred and distorted. I hardly recognize myself, and in that moment, I wonder how I ended up here on this houseboat, so utterly and profoundly alone.

❧

It was by complete coincidence that I met Dexter. If he hadn't forgotten his portfolio. If I hadn't stepped out for coffee at precisely nine thirty a.m. If the construction crew on Fifth Avenue hadn't blockaded Madison Street. If the rain hadn't picked up—our paths may have never crossed.

On March 9, 1956, Mr. Dexter Wentworth's cab pulled up into my life. He rolled down the window and said, "Come on in out of the rain. I'll take you wherever you need to go." Nearly twenty years older than I, he was frighteningly handsome, with a square jaw, chiseled face, and thick dark hair. He spoke in a cool, deep voice. Calm and sure, like a movie star.

"But I'm only going around the corner to the café," I demurred, smoothing my hair. *What would Miss Higgins think?* Surely it was breaking every finishing school commandment to speak to a strange man, much less to share a cab with one. But the rain was falling harder now, and he'd opened the cab door and was extending his hand to me.

"All right," I said. "Thank you."

Inside, the cab felt warm and smelled of a mixture of cologne and cigars. "What's a beautiful girl like you doing out in this weather?"

"I'm getting coffee," I said. "For my teacher."

He looked amused. "Your teacher?"

"Yes," I said. "I'm a student at Miss Higgins Academy."

His grin turned into a smile. "Finishing school, huh?"

My cheeks burned. I didn't like the tone of his voice. And if I was completely honest with myself, I didn't like the whole concept of finishing school. But Mama had insisted I go. She'd said the only way a girl from South Seattle would ever meet a decent husband was to attend Miss Higgins Academy. *A husband.* I didn't even want a husband. But Mama wanted things for me that she'd never had. So I went.

"And I suppose today's lesson required you to walk fifty paces with a book on top of your head?"

I frowned as the cab came to a stop in front of Bette's Café. "Thank you for the ride," I said, reaching for the door handle.

"Come, now," he said. "I didn't mean any harm. Listen, let me buy you coffee."

I shook my head. "No, thank you, Mr. . . . ."

"Wentworth," he said. "Dexter Wentworth." *Why does the name sound so familiar?*

I nodded and stepped out of the cab.

"Wait," he said, rolling the window down. "You can't leave without telling me your name."

I hesitated. What would be the harm? I'd never see him again. "It's Penny," I said. "Penny Landry."

"A pleasure to meet you, Miss Landry."

I didn't tell any of the girls about meeting Dexter Wentworth, but they found out when an enormous vase of lilies arrived that afternoon—stargazers, the ones that jump out of a vase and beg to be noticed, admired—with a note that read, "Dinner at the Olympic tonight. I'll pick you up at eight. Dexter."

At first I thought it was very presumptuous, if not appallingly conceited, of him to assume I'd say yes. But then the girls huddled around me, oohing and aahing. Miss Higgins, tall and thin with gray hair set in tight curls against her head and perfectly applied red lipstick, read the card herself. Her skeptical expression quickly melted into approval. "You do know who this man is, don't you, Penny?"

I shook my head.

"Dexter Wentworth," she said. "The *artist*. His paintings are in galleries all over the world. He's the most eligible bachelor in Seattle." She shook her head as if trying to make sense of how *I* had managed to lure such a catch.

"I met him this morning," I said defensively. "He gave me a ride to the café." The girls' mouths gaped open. "It was raining," I added.

"I'm absolutely green with envy," Sylvia squealed. "And to think, if I had gone out for coffee instead of you. Some girls have all the luck."

Miss Higgins patted Sylvia on the back. "Let this be a lesson to you all," she said. "Penny has excelled in her coursework here, and look at how it's paid off." I smirked. Of course Miss Higgins would try to take credit. "Sylvia, you'd do well to practice your cosmetic application this afternoon. You're consistently applying your rouge too high on your cheekbones, and it's making your face appear much too angular."

"Yes, ma'am," she said, scurrying off to the beauty room.

"And, Vivien," Miss Higgins said to the youngest girl, who was seventeen and the heaviest at the academy.

"Yes, Miss Higgins," Vivien replied in a high-pitched voice.

"I see you've been eating pastries again," she said disapprovingly. "I thought we discussed your new diet goals."

"Yes, ma'am," she said.

"You will do an extra hour of calisthenics this afternoon."

"Yes, Miss Higgins," Vivien said, turning to the stairs.

"And you, Penny," Miss Higgins said, clasping her hands together and smiling at me as if I were a star pupil. "We must spend the rest of the day readying you for this very important occasion."

When Dexter asked me to marry him three months later, I said yes. What other answer was there, really? If someone dropped a diamond necklace in your palm and said, "Put it on; it will look lovely on you," of course you'd smile and drape it around your neck, admiring your reflection in the mirror. Yes, I accepted his marriage proposal, maybe even before I knew whether I loved Dexter Wentworth or whether I loved the *idea* of being in love with Dexter Wentworth. But when the whirlwind of our courtship settled, I saw him for who he was: a sensitive, creative, and deeply caring man, who loved me, and whom I loved in return. We'd tell our love story to our children, and they'd giggle and grin. Ours would be punctuated with a "happily ever after," or so I thought.

I almost fainted when Mama laced up the back of my wedding dress. "My water baby swims to shore," she said to me as I stared into the mirror, surveying myself in the enormous white dress. I remember looking away, unable to look into my own eyes.

After the reception, Dexter carried me over the threshold, a floating one. He owned a home on Queen Anne Hill, but he preferred living in his houseboat on Lake Union. He painted better there, he said, and the water helped clear his head. I remember the feeling of swaying when he set me down, though that could have been me as much as the boat. How could a woman ever fit into this very masculine place, I wondered, surveying the mass of canvases and art supplies, the brown davenport, assorted painted oars, and carved wooden fish, gifts from a Native American artist friend. But then he turned to me and whispered, "Don't worry, you can change everything to your taste." He was generous, always generous.

I close my eyes and try to remember the way he used to look at me then, with such love, such desire.

The oven timer beeps from the kitchen, extracting me from my memories. I almost forgot the blueberry muffins. I lift my feet out of the lake and run inside to grab an oven mitt, then pull them out, breathing in their sweet, steamy scent. Last week I confided in Dexter about my dream of opening a bakery, but he only laughed. "You'd hate it after five minutes," he said, dismissing the idea.

"That's not true," I said.

He patted my leg. "Sweetheart, you'd be bored to pieces."

What I didn't say was that I'm bored to pieces *now*. Dexter has his art. I have . . . nothing. Mama says I should be grateful not to have to work; she says women would kill to be in my position. But I want to do *something*. And after the house is cleaned, mending done, clothes ironed, there is nothing more. I *want* something more.

I stare at the pan of muffins and wonder if Dexter is right. What do I know about business? I shake my head as I transfer the muffins from the pan to the cooling rack. I select three and wrap them in a white tea towel. I'll offer some to Collin, as a welcome-to-Boat-Street gesture. I won't eat them all, I rationalize, and Dex, well, who knows when he'll be home, so there's no sense letting them go to waste.

I run to the back door to get my shoes, which is when I hear a sniffling sound coming from the deck.

"Hello?" I say, before peering out the back door. "Is someone there?"

Little Jimmy Clyde is huddled against the houseboat with his knees pressed to his chest and his face buried in them. He's the eight-year-old son of Naomi and Gene Clyde, who live three houseboats down on the dock. On weekends, Jimmy likes to sit with his fishing pole in sight of my front windows. He caught a trout last Saturday, and I helped him clean it. His little legs dangled over the barstool at my kitchen counter while I fried the fish in a cast iron skillet. I served it for lunch with butter and parsley, and Jimmy said it was the best meal he ever ate, which was a compliment, given that his mother is a proficient cook.

"Oh, honey," I say, rushing to him. "What's the matter?"

"Mommy hates me," he says, wiping a tear away.

"No, she doesn't, dear," I say, patting his head. "No one could ever hate you."

"Then why did she tell Daddy that she wants to send me to boarding school?"

I shake my head. "I'm sure that's not what she meant."

He nods. "But she *did* say it. They never think I can hear them from upstairs, but I can."

Jimmy is the only child on the dock. It's clear that he doesn't fit into his parents' carefully curated world of cocktail parties and career achievement. I once saw Naomi trip over one of Jimmy's toys in the kitchen during a dinner party, and the look on her face still shakes me. It was as if she was allergic to her son's presence.

Jimmy looks up suddenly. "I know!" he exclaims.

I cock my head to the right and smile. "What?"

"I could come live with *you*. You could be my mother."

I am certain that I feel my heart break then, just a little. I squeeze his hand. "As happy as I would be having you around all the time, your parents love you too much to give you up. And you know that, dear."

He nods, but his eyes are distant, lonely. Just like mine.

# Chapter 4

ADA

I fish my cell phone out of my bag, relieved to see I have reception, and dial Joanie.

She picks up after one ring. "Ada?"

"I'm sitting here in the houseboat," I say. "And I can't decide whether I love it or if I want to catch the next plane home."

"Don't do *that*," she says. "Give it some time."

A horn sounds in the distance.

"Is that a boat?"

"Yeah," I say, looking out to the lake. It sparkles as if it's covered in diamonds. "It's a tugboat. I think."

"Well, it sure beats traffic noise," Joanie says. I can hear engines racing and horns honking on the New York City streets. And for the first time, I realized I haven't heard a car horn since I arrived. I like that.

"Yeah," I reply, walking out to the deck and sinking into the Adirondack chair. "I actually slept in this morning. I haven't done that since . . ."

"Good girl," she says. "Maybe you can ditch those awful sleep-ing pills. I read something in the *New York Times* last week linking them to a higher death risk."

"Great," I say. "So if insomnia doesn't kill me, the sleeping pills will."

"Well, it sounds like Seattle may be your antidote," she says. "Maybe there's something medicinal about living on a boat. I imag-ine it would lull you to sleep. Sounds relaxing, actually."

I nod to myself. "A floating home," I say, correcting her. "But yes, this place definitely has a different feel to it. So different from New York. It's a slower pace."

"Good," she says. "You need that. So have you met any of the neighbors?"

"Just a guy," I say.

"A *guy*?"

"Stop," I say. "It's nothing like that. He's as old as my dad."

"Oh."

I change the subject. "I thought I'd go for a canoe ride today."

"You should," she says. "Remember how James loved kayaking?"

Panic floods my senses. My palms are sweating and my mouth feels dry.

"You OK, honey?"

"Yeah," I say. "It's just that I—"

"I know. I shouldn't have brought it up. Did you see Lauren Cain on *Today* this morning?"

"They put *her* on?" Lauren is an assistant editor at *Sunrise* who desperately wants my job and has always rubbed me the wrong way.

"She wasn't as good as you are on TV," Joanie says. "She said 'um' a lot."

Somehow this makes me feel a little better, though I am still second-guessing my choice to leave the only thing I did well, the only thing that kept me going. Part of me wants to grab my suitcase and head back to New York to reclaim my place at the magazine, to go back to the way things were. Was life really that bad? Was I really that miserable?

I say good-bye to Joanie and let my mind wander east, back to the life I left behind. I hear Dr. Evinson's voice. "Don't edit your thoughts," he'd say. "Let them come." So I do, even when it hurts.

*One year prior*

I'm sitting in a swivel chair in front of a mirror while a woman named Whitney dabs concealer under my eyes. The lights in the *Today* show dressing room are harsh and hot, and I wriggle in my chair a little. I know she can see my dark circles. Insomnia hasn't been kind to my complexion.

"You should drink more green tea," she tells me. "It's good for your skin."

I nod. I'm scheduled to be on-air in thirty minutes, where I'll be talking about the top five travel destinations for family vacations. I don't want to be here. To be fair, no one forced me. My editor in chief offered to send the executive editor if I wasn't ready. *Ready.* What does that even mean? One thing's certain: I'll never feel OK about anything ever again. So why not just jump back into the numbness of work, the hamster wheel of TV segments and heels and chunky necklaces?

Whitney swivels my chair around so I'm facing the mirror. "There's the gorgeous girl we know and love," she says. I hardly recognize myself. It's like she's used her magic wand to banish my dark circles and erase puffiness. Any traces of last night's tears are expertly hidden under a pint of foundation. I recall my old deputy editor at *Real Living* giving me advice during my years as an editorial assistant: "Fake it until you make it." At the time, I rejected this sentiment. It just seemed wrong to me. But now, gazing at my improved reflection in the mirror, I find myself clinging to those words like a codependent lover. I study my face in the mirror, a woman with flawless skin. No hint of the pain that hides deep inside. Yes, I can fake it until I figure out how to live again.

Stacey, the stylist, spends the next ten minutes blowing out my limp hair into sleek locks that hang in perfect submission over my shoulders. A cloud of hair spray completes my transformation.

"You're on in five," the producer calls into the room. I barely hear her, but I nod and stand up, walking robotically in my heels to the green room. I scan the note cards that my assistant gave me earlier. The Horseshoe Ranch at Yosemite, with horseback riding for families. The Canyon Lodge in Wyoming, where every child gets her own private ski lesson. And . . . I feel a lump in my throat when I see the words on the next card. *How could they?* "Just a short jaunt to the coast of Maine, the Waterbrook Inn is nestled beside one of the most magnificent yet lesser known waterfalls in the world."

The room feels like it's spinning when the producer waves me into the studio. Matt Lauer is wearing a red tie and sitting on a high stool. "I'm so sorry to hear about your family," he says. "It's good to have you back."

I nod automatically, the way I've done a hundred, a thousand times since the accident, then take my seat on the stool beside him.

I hear music in the distance, the scuffling of producers and cameramen, and then the lights brighten, and Matt Lauer sits up higher on his stool. "Welcome back to the *Today* show," he says. "We're joined now by *Sunrise* magazine's Ada Santorini, who's here to share her picks for the top five family vacation destinations this year."

Pain pulsates in my chest, but I try to ignore it. I answer Matt's questions and even tell him about the trail that leads up to the waterfall at the Waterbrook Inn. I smile and nod. I get through the interview. I fake it. And then when the segment ends and my mic comes off, I run backstage, down the long hallway to the restrooms in the distance. I can hardly breathe. And when I look into the mirror, I despise the woman who stares back at me.

I wipe away the tears on my cheeks and look out at the overcast Seattle morning. I take a deep breath. I can't fall apart. Because if I do, I fear I won't be able to put myself back together. But how do I keep going without a reason to wake up every morning? And then it hits me: I need to give myself an assignment. I think of the memoir I began writing months ago and remember why I came here. I stopped at twenty-five pages because the process was too painful. But now, after Joanie has uttered James's name—*James*—I feel the urge to click open the folder again and pull up the document. I feel like writing.

I reach for my laptop and lift it out of my bag and onto my lap. I pull open the untitled memoir. A large boat must have traveled through the lake while I was on the phone, because its wake rocks the little houseboat gently; I feel like a duck bobbing on the water. I stare at the blank cover page, and I type.

### Floating

*A Memoir by Ada Santorini*

# Chapter 5

PENNY

S tay here as long as you like, honey," I say to Jimmy. I want to be sure to offer Collin the muffins when they're still warm. They're much better that way. "I have to run over to a neighbor's house for a sec." He nods and dips his feet into the lake.

I step back inside and self-consciously check my reflection in the mirror beside the door before stepping out front. The muffins, wrapped in the tea towel, are still warm in my hands. I straighten my pale blue dress and fasten the top button of my blue cardigan before walking ahead. I look up when I hear heels clacking toward me on the dock.

"Look at you," Naomi croons. "Dressed so pretty for a Tuesday morning." She gives me a once-over. "Where are you off to? It's too early for lunch."

She speaks to me as if I'm a child, the way most of Dex's friends do. It's true, I'm twenty-two, and she's at least ten years my senior and a practicing psychiatrist with an MD, when I didn't even officially graduate from Miss Higgins Academy.

I glance down at the muffins and feel a pang of guilt. "I was just going to offer—"

"For me?" She reaches out and takes the muffins from my hands. "How kind. You know I don't have time to bake with my crazy schedule." She's wearing white pants and a blue sweater with a belt cinched tight to show off her narrow waist. She's beautiful in a sophisticated, literary sort of way. Her long, manicured fingers are rarely without a cigarette, stuffed into a long, jewel-studded holder. She opens up the tea towel and smiles, amused. "Oh look, *muffins.*"

I think of Collin, then nod. "Dex never eats them. I don't know why I bake."

Naomi rewraps the muffins. "Well, he does like French pastries," she says. "You ought to take a class at the culinary school. I bet he'd love that."

I want to ask her how she knows that my husband likes French pastries. I want to tell her that muffins are just as nice as any fussy croissant, but I don't. I smile, and I thank her for the suggestion. Naomi is the only psychiatrist I've ever known, and she frightens me a little with that sharp gaze and that perfect dark hair cut to a blunt bob and angled down across her face, every strand obedient. I once tried to emulate her hairstyle, spending two hours hovering over an ironing board, burning my thumb in the process. But it looked wrong on me. Dex came home that night and said, "What happened to your hair?"

"I haven't seen Dex home in a while," Naomi says. I hear the curiosity in her voice. "I suppose he's staying at his studio these days?"

I don't like that she calls him Dex. That's what *I* call him. But I smile and nod, thinking of my husband in his studio in Pioneer Square. He rented it shortly after New Year's, and it seemed like a good idea at the time, especially since his canvases and easels were threatening to take over the living room. But I didn't anticipate how much time he'd be spending away and how lonely I'd feel. "Yes," I say, feigning confidence, "he's getting so much work done there. I hate to disturb him, you know."

Naomi makes a face and points to the potted flowers near the front door of her houseboat. "Just look at that," she says, as if something upsetting has happened.

She reaches into one of the pots and pulls out a green vine, a few feet long, with several bell-shaped white flowers. "There," she says with a vindicated look in her eye, as if this vine has wronged her in some way.

"What is it?" I ask.

She flashes a patronizing smile. "An invasive weed," she says, tossing the vine into the lake. I watch the little white flowers flutter in the water. I want to kneel down and rescue them from drowning. "Morning glory," Naomi continues, shaking her head. "It'll take over if you let it."

I watch as the vine drifts away on the lake. The little flowers bob up and down as if gasping for air. I consider that the vine might find its way to shore and wash up on a patch of soil, where it will start a new existence, maybe sink its roots and thrive. Maybe Naomi has set it free.

I think of the bluebells that grew in my mother's garden when I was a child. Weeds, really. But I'd pick them by the handful, and when bunched together they looked stunning.

"Weeds can be so pretty sometimes," I say.

"Pretty?" Naomi snorts. She blows a strand of her dark hair out of her eyes and smirks. "Weeds aren't pretty, my dear."

"Right," I say as Naomi's husband, Gene, peers out the door. They're an unlikely match. He's quiet; she's outspoken. He's warm; she's not. And yet, it's clear by the way he looks at her that he is deeply in love with this woman, for reasons I may never be able to understand. "Sweetheart," he says, "I was just making an omelet. Care for one?" He notices me and waves. "Oh, hello, Penny. I can put one on for you if you like."

Naomi's cold gaze isn't exactly welcoming, so I shake my head. "Thank you, Gene; I already ate." He's easy to like, with his receding hairline and unpretentious ways. He teaches English literature at the University of Washington and often leaves novels on my doorstep.

"Did you read the last one?" he asks. Naomi acts disinterested, the way she always does when she's not directing the conversation.

I nod. "Yes, Hemingway. It was good. I'd like to go to Paris someday. I'll bring it back later this afternoon—"

"It's yours to keep," Gene says with a smile. "Everyone needs Hemingway on their bookshelf. In fact, I have another of his I think you'll also like. I'll drop it by sometime."

"Thanks," I say.

Naomi walks toward him and straightens his tie. "Gene, you mustn't wear plaid shirts. They look so *hodgepodge*."

He kisses her on the forehead and smiles obediently. "Yes, dear." Then he asks, "Did you find Jimmy?"

"No," she says, rolling her eyes. "That *child*."

Gene frowns. "I worry we're being too hard on him."

Naomi rolls her eyes. "You realize he's *flunking* the second grade, don't you?"

"Well, I'd better be going," I say, feeling awkward to be overhearing a parental disagreement.

Gene waves and turns back to the house.

"Wait," Naomi says, following me. "I must speak to you about Jimmy."

I think of him huddled in a ball behind my home. I should tell her he's there, but I don't. I decide to give him a little more time.

"We're going to be keeping him in on the weekends," she says with a stern expression that reminds me of my fifth-grade teacher, the one who spanked my bottom so severely, I developed a bruise the size of a saucer. "Gene and I think it's best that he spends less time with . . . well, less time near your houseboat."

"Oh," I say, a little wounded. "I'm sorry, I didn't—"

Naomi's smile returns, but it looks stiff and plastered on. "It's nothing you've done, dear," she says. "It's just that we think he needs more supervision. We've hired a tutor, and he'll be seeing a new psychiatrist to address some of his *issues*."

We both look up when we notice Collin, hard at work on his boat in the distance. He's using a hand tool to hone the wood on the hull. I can almost see the boat in its finished form, with its glistening teak and mast with puffy white sails. How I'd love to sail away. To feel the wind on my face. To be free. But Dex would never leave his beloved Seattle; I know that. The city is his muse.

I watch Collin work. His muscles flex and ripple as his arms move up and down the hull with expert precision. He's taken off his shirt now, and his tan skin glistens in the morning sun. For a moment I forget that Naomi is standing beside me, but then I feel her eyes on me.

"So I take it you've met our new neighbor," she says.

"No," I say quickly. My cheeks are flushed; I know it. "But I've been admiring the boat he's working on. I'd love to own one just like that someday."

"Wouldn't we all," Naomi says, her voice trailing off. "Well, I should be going. My first patient arrives in a half hour, and I need to get Jimmy to school, then somehow make it to my office downtown. That is, *if* I can find him."

"Good-bye," I say, returning my gaze to Collin. He looks up, and our eyes meet momentarily. He smiles, and I smile back.

"I'm sorry I've been such an absent husband these days, Penn," Dex says over dinner that night. He came home at seven, after I'd already put away the pot roast. After being rewarmed in the oven, it's tough, but Dex doesn't complain, and I'm grateful. "I've been working on a big commission."

I nod. "I know," I say, weaving my fingers through his. "I just wish you'd come home more, that's all."

There are dark shadows under his eyes, and the lines across his forehead look deeper. The twenty-year age difference between us seems more apparent than ever.

"You haven't been sleeping, have you?" When Dex is working on a painting, he doesn't sleep.

"Not much," he says, rubbing his brow.

I move my chair beside his and kiss him, but he turns away.

"What is it, Dex?"

"It's nothing," he says. "I already told you, dear, I'm tired."

I feel a lump in the back of my throat. "Are you unhappy? Have I made you terribly unhappy?"

He turns to face me. "No," he says quickly. "Penny, of course not." He looks down at the table. "It's just that . . . listen, I asked Naomi for a referral to see a psychiatrist. The thing is . . . I've been suffering from depression."

"A psychiatrist? Depression?" I shake my head. "Dex, I don't understand."

"I don't expect you to understand," he says, before forcing a smile. "Listen, I told you only because, well—let's not dwell on this, OK? What we both could use is a little fun." He kisses my hand lightly. "Why don't we invite the neighbors over, throw a cocktail party, the way we used to do?"

I nod mechanically. "If it would make you happy."

Happy. Dexter and I used to be happy. I close my eyes, and try to think back to the last time I felt he was mine, wholly mine, without secrets, sadness, or this heavy fog of depression that I cannot understand and that I can only blame myself for. My mind sorts through disheveled memories of distant expressions and broken promises, until it stops and homes in on the night of the Seattle Charitable Foundation's annual ball last summer. I remember how people buzzed around Dexter, especially women. And yet, he saw only me that night. I remember the way he took my hand in his and kissed my wrist lightly before we walked out to the dance floor together. He held me tight as the band played, and his eyes sparkled as bright as the crystal chandelier overhead. "You're the most beautiful woman here," he said proudly. "And you're mine."

I loved how he took pride in *me*. And why? I had no artistic abilities, no special skills or training. I tried my best to fit into his world, to match the intelligent remarks of his contemporaries with witty banter, but I felt as if they saw right through me.

I looked up at Dex that night on the dance floor, with his arms draped lovingly around me. I'd often wondered about the place I occupied in his heart, and that night, I asked him, "Why? Why me?" And he told me.

"Because you're lovely," he said. "Lovelier than any woman I've ever met." He kissed my forehead, then continued. "It's every boy's fantasy to grow up and find a wife like you."

I thought about Dex's childhood, what little I knew of it. His mother was strict and rigid, so unlike mine. There was no warmth in her embrace. Dex had been raised by nannies and kept at arm's length. I looked up at him then, and saw that he longed for the type of maternal love he'd never had, and I realized that he had found it in me. It was an honor and a challenge. Could I be the woman he needed me to be? That night I felt I could. I vowed to show Dexter so much love, enough love to fill the deep and painful void in his heart. But now? Now, I stood in the face of the stark, brutal realization that I was not enough. Dexter's demons were bigger than me, perhaps even unsolvable by me.

The houseboat sways, and I look out to the lake and the sparkling lights of the city above. He tucks his hand in mine, briefly, before reaching for the newspaper. We are right next to each other, and yet, I have the overwhelming sensation that my husband is slipping away from me.

# Chapter 6

ADA

By two, I'm starved, so I decide to visit the little market Jim told me about. Pete's, I think. I walk up the dock, which is when I notice a pretty houseboat on the left, with white siding and window boxes that look as if they once held beautiful flowers. The place is clearly empty, because mail spills out of the weathered copper mailbox near the door. I kneel down to retrieve a letter that's fallen to the ground and eye the address label: Esther Johnson. I tuck it back into the mailbox, and wonder who Esther is and whether she's coming back to collect her mail.

The short walk to the market affords me a look at the docks that comprise the floating enclave, and I look curiously down the wooden moorings. Each seems to have its own personality. Some are quirky and artsy, with houses painted bright colors and wind chimes clanging in the light breeze; others are lined with expensive-looking modern homes, where Sub-Zero refrigerators and Viking ranges undoubtedly appear inside the gourmet kitchens. Regardless, however, the houseboat community, as a whole, feels like an ecosystem all its own. Rich, and brimming with a variety of life.

I cross the street when I see Pete's Market ahead. Inside the little store, I grab a cart and wander from one aisle to the next. A half hour later, a clerk with a gray beard bags up a carton of milk, apples, bananas, bread, a block of cheddar cheese, eggs, carrots, five frozen meals, two chicken breasts, a container of basil, a head of garlic, a box of pasta, and a bottle of white wine. I notice he's grinning at me as I swipe my credit card.

"New here?" he asks.

"Yes," I say, wondering if I have a sign on my back that reads, i'm from out of town, *obviously*!

"Staying on a houseboat?"

I nod.

"Which dock?"

"Boat Street," I say.

"Ah, Boat Street," he continues, raising an eyebrow. "One of my favorites. It has quite a history, you know."

"Oh?" I say, taking the receipt.

He leans in as if he's about to divulge a secret. "A lady went missing there a long time ago. Just disappeared one night. Cops never did figure out what happened to her. And if you ask me, the residents of Boat Street weren't terribly helpful either."

A woman with a full shopping cart clears her throat behind us. "Well," I say. "Thank you, I—"

"Which houseboat did you say you're living on?" he asks as I take two paper sacks into my hands.

"The last one on the slip," I say.

His eyes widen. "That one was hers."

❧

It's nine, and I should be tired, but I'm not; I'm restless. Insomnia strikes again. I slip into a pair of leggings and a nightshirt and walk

out to the deck. It's been a warm day, a rarity for June in Seattle, I
hear. But now the sun is setting and there are dark clouds hovering
overhead, waiting for the sun to dip behind the horizon so they can
roll in and have their way with the city. I remember seeing a can of
cocoa in the cabinet, so I head back to the kitchen and boil some
milk in a pan on the stove, then mix in a generous scoop of the
chocolate powder. I close my eyes and I can see her, my baby.

"Mama!" Ella says, barreling through the door with James following close behind. Her bunny hat, with the two pink ears, dangles
from her neck. She's missing one of her front teeth, and her cheeks
are rosy and full of life. "Look what I made for you at school!" She
hands me a painting and I smile. It's the three of us—me, James,
and Ella—standing in front of what looks like a gingerbread house.
"It's the North Pole," she says. "Look," she adds, pointing to a sleigh
in the sky, "there's Santa and Rudolph."

I scoop her into my arms. She's little for seven, still light enough
for me to cradle her. "Oh, honey, I adore it." Her cheeks feel cold.
"Let's get you warmed up," I say. "Hot chocolate?"

She claps her hands. "Yeah!"

"It's supposed to snow tonight," James adds, planting a kiss on
my cheek. His lips are cold. "It's already in the twenties out there."

I frown. "Do you still think Santa will be able to come?"

"Of course," he says. "Santa has four-wheel drive."

I smile. Even though James has lived in New York for the past
fifteen years, he grew up in Montana and spent his formative years
helping his parents on their ranch. They still don't understand how
he can be happy going from wide-open spaces to a cramped city, but
they're proud of him, exceedingly proud. James excelled in college,

graduating from Harvard with honors and landing an internship at the *Washington Post*, which led to an editorial assistant position at the *New York Times*, where he eventually became a travel writer. But when Ella came along, he decided to give it all up and stay home with her. It wasn't easy coming to that decision, but I'd just been named features editor at *Sunrise*, and my paycheck was almost double what James was making at the newspaper. It just made sense.

I run my hand through his dark wavy hair, and whisper, "Did you get the presents on her list?"

He nods. "Already wrapped and tucked away in the closet."

"You're Superdad, you know?"

He grins. "I know."

"Mama," Ella says from the barstool at the island, "Lindsey and Jane get presents on lots of days in December. Can we be Jewish too?"

I smile. "No, honey, we're Italian, remember? Well, you and Daddy are Italian. But I can join along."

"And Daddy was born in Italy?"

"Daddy was born in Montana, but your nonna and papa were born in Italy."

"Can we go there sometime?" She looks just like her grandmother with those striking hazel eyes, and olive skin and wavy hair just like James's.

"Yes," I say. "Daddy and I are taking you there next year. You have many cousins who'd like to meet you."

I hand her a cup of hot chocolate, with a handful of mini marshmallows on top. "Careful," I say, "it's a little hot."

I take Ella's bunny hat off and untie her braid. James drapes his arm around me as I smooth her hair.

I want to stay here forever, in this vision of my past, but I hear a knock at the back door. I try to ignore it, as if resisting being roused from a good dream. *Just five more minutes,* I think. *Let me sleep a bit longer!* But there it is again. *Knock, knock, knock.*

"Hello? Is anyone home?"

I snap out of my memories and turn around to see a man I don't recognize peering inside the houseboat from the back door. He's wearing a long-sleeve plaid shirt with a navy fleece vest and jeans. His short sandy blond hair looks mussed, and I have absolutely no idea if it's on purpose or because he doesn't care.

"Yes," I say, a little taken aback. I force myself to smile even though I don't feel especially chatty. And I would prefer to be wearing something other than a nightshirt when meeting neighbors, especially handsome male ones.

"I'm sorry," he says, "but I just thought I'd check to make sure everything's all right."

Suddenly I smell smoke, but I don't know where it's coming from.

"I smelled something burning."

For the moment, I'm less concerned about who this strange man is and more worried about burning the houseboat down. "I don't know what happened," I say, looking down at the stove. "I just turned on the burner to warm up some milk for hot chocolate and . . ." I see smoke coming from the oven vent; I open the oven and the smoke billows out.

I jump back, and the neighbor guy, whom I haven't properly introduced myself to yet, runs in and opens the front door to let the smoke out. He then presses a button below the range hood and the fan turns on. He looks inside the oven, then nods. "No fire," he says. "Something must have burned in there."

"That's so strange," I say. "I must be tired. I thought I was turning on a burner. I guess I somehow turned on the oven instead."

The man extends his hand. He looks younger up close, the way most people do in their thirties or early forties, when the subtleties of age show in the lilt of a smile or the curve of the eyes. He's no more than thirty-eight, I'd guess. "I'm Alex," he says.

"Ada," I say. "I just moved in yesterday."

"Welcome to the dock," he says, smiling. "Technically, I live on the next dock, but Jim and the others have made me an honorary neighbor." He leans in and cups his mouth as if he's about to let me in on a little secret. "If you want to know the truth," he says with a wink, "my dock's a bit of a buzzkill."

"Oh yeah?" I say, grinning. We walk out to the deck, and he points to the houseboat across from mine. It's a little smaller, more masculine, somehow, with its straight lines and modern roofline. "I moved here five years ago. Got the place for a steal because it was this close to sinking."

"Oh, wow," I say. "So you remodeled it?"

"Yes," he replies. "Anyway, sorry to barge in like that. But after the houseboat fire in 2003, I'm a little skittish about smoke on the lake."

"Fire?"

"Yeah," he says. "I'd just moved in the month before. Five houses burned on a nearby dock. It was awful."

"Wow," I say. "Was anyone hurt?"

"No, thank God," he replies. "And it's an amazing thing, too, because when a houseboat catches fire, the next goes very quickly. You can't be too careful out here."

"Sorry for the scare," I say.

"It's OK." He grins. "Actually, if I'm being completely honest, it was a very creative excuse to meet the new neighbor."

I feel momentarily embarrassed when I remember that I'm wearing my old ratty black leggings and a green flannel nightshirt. But I recall something Joanie said about Seattle being allergic to fashion, and I feel a little better. And why do I care what I look like, anyway?

"Well," I say, "it's very nice to meet you."

"Will you be staying long?" Alex asks. He pulls his left hand from his pocket and I notice, without trying, that his ring finger is bare. I've long been suspicious of mature, good-looking men who are single. I once briefly dated a thirty-year-old financial planner who seemed perfect. I even met his family at his sister's wedding, and was secretly dreaming about ours when I found out that he was gay and that our entire relationship had been concocted to convince his family that he was straight.

"I'm not sure how long I'll be here," I say honestly. "I signed a lease through the end of summer, but it's somewhat open-ended."

He nods. "What do you do, in . . . ?"

"New York. I'm from New York." I'm surprised I've told him this, but he's easy to talk to, and his presence makes the burden I carry feel a little lighter. "I'm a writer," I say. "Well, an editor, at *Sunrise.*"

"The magazine?"

"Yes," I say. "How about you?"

"I'm a photographer," he replies. "I do food photography, mostly. But don't let that fool you into thinking I can cook, because I can't. Not even scrambled eggs."

I grin. "You can't cook and you take pictures of food?"

"I know, it's nuts," he says. "But if you make it, I'll shoot it."

"I take it you like to *eat* the food?"

"Yeah," he says. "Best part." He peers around the corner of the kitchen. "I gave Roxanne a few of my books to keep here, for the renters."

"The owner, right?"

"Yeah," he says. "Last I heard she lived in Alaska."

I nod, remembering what the clerk at the grocery store said about the missing woman, but I don't mention it.

"Anyway, I'm sure the cookbooks are still around here some-where."

"I'll look for them," I promise.

He smiles. "Well, I'd better be going. Nice to meet you, Ada."

"Alex, right? I'm terrible with names."

"Me, too," he says, heading out the door. I watch through the window as he steps into his canoe and glides across the little channel back to his houseboat.

I climb the ladder to the bedroom and attempt to sleep, but after twenty minutes, I'm still not drowsy. I remember reading a magazine article advising that if you're not sleepy, get up and do something for twenty minutes, then try again. I prefer this to Ambien, anyway.

I look through my suitcase—I haven't unpacked my things yet—until I find a novel, but after two pages, I lose interest. I remember Alex's books, and I'm suddenly overcome with curiosity. I walk to the bookcase I glanced at when I first arrived and scan the spines. Lots of novels; some well-loved paperbacks that look like they're held together by love and a single drop of glue; a guidebook about the Northwest, and one about dog-friendly hiking in Seattle; and then I see a stack of larger books high on the shelf. I stretch to reach the one that looks like a cookbook and pull it down. I see the name Alex Milstead on the cover and smile. It's a cookbook about barbecue, written with a woman named Kellie Adams. I thumb through the pages. *Wow. He's really good.* The images are crisp and bright, as good as anything I've seen in the pages of *Sunrise*. I look at the front cover again, and see it has won a James Beard award. Impressive. Curious, I turn to the last page, where I find the author bios. From her photo, I can tell that Kellie Adams is quite beautiful. And prolific—according to her bio, she's penned fourteen award-winning cookbooks, and I recognize one of her titles, *Sunday Brunch*, because we featured it in *Sunrise* a few years back. I immediately wonder if she and Alex were ever involved. I turn to his bio: "Award-winning photographer Alex Milstead spent years photographing the conflict in Sudan for *Time*, before trading in his bulletproof vest for an apron. Though he's a self-proclaimed novice in the kitchen, his photos have appeared in *Gourmet*; *O, The Oprah Magazine*; the *New York Times*, and many other publications. He lives on a houseboat in Seattle."

*Wow, he's accomplished.* I set the cookbook on the shelf and rub my eyes, then yawn. Finally, drowsiness is setting in. I walk back to the living room and notice the water glass I left on the coffee table. Well, it's not so much a coffee table as an old wooden chest-turned-coffee-table. It's very old, held together with tarnished brass hinges. I set the water glass on the counter in the kitchen, then turn back to the old chest. There's a little lock attached to one of the hinges, and when I attempt to tug it open, it doesn't budge. What could be inside?

I walk up the ladder and crawl into bed. Even after two years, it still feels strange to sleep alone. Strange and lonely. The porthole is open, and I can hear the rain falling outside. It's soft at first—just a fine mist hitting the lake. Then I hear a thunderclap and the pitter-patter amplifies.

God's tears.

I pull the goose-down comforter up to my neck and listen to the pelting rain outside. The steady sound consoles me, and as I close my eyes, I decide that Seattle may be the perfect place for someone with a broken heart.

# Chapter 7

PENNY

Dex walks out of the bathroom with a towel wrapped around his waist. He's put on cologne and slicked his hair back the way I like.

He kisses me lightly and I breathe in the smell of his skin, piney and sweet. I wonder if he'll notice my dress—red and white checked, a bit lower cut than my usual style—but instead he walks to the counter and pops a few green olives into his mouth. "Did you remember to pick up vermouth?"

I nod. "I also got the little toothpicks you like," I say, pointing at the box. We've had many parties here before, and yet I feel that tonight must go off without a hitch. I feel that Dex is counting on me to be perfect. The oven timer beeps and I jump.

"What are you making?" he asks.

"Your favorite artichoke dip."

"Oh," he says.

"What? I thought you liked it."

"I do. I just thought you'd make the bean dip."

I feel like crying. I feel like dropping the Pyrex casserole dish on the tile floor and calling in the ducks to clean it up. At least they'd appreciate my cooking.

Dex puts his hand on my arm. "I'm sorry," he says. "I don't know what's wrong with me. The artichoke dip is wonderful." He pulls me closer to him. "*You* are wonderful."

I force a smile, but the wound still stings.

Dex dips a slice of French bread into the artichoke dip, then turns to me before I can slap his hand away. "Did you invite the new guy?"

"The boat builder, you mean?"

He nods.

"Should I?"

He looks at his watch. "Why not? He seems like a nice enough fellow." He scratches his head. "I wish I could remember his name."

*Collin. His name is Collin.* But I don't say anything. I'm embarrassed to admit that I know.

"Well, I have to get dressed," he says. "Do you want to go extend our welcome?"

"I don't know," I say, turning back to the stove. "I still have a lot of prepping to do."

"Don't be antisocial, Penn," Dex says. "He'll think we're a couple of hermits."

"OK," I say, untying the strings of my apron. Dex walks down the hall to get dressed, and I pinch my cheeks in the hallway mirror before stepping outside to the deck. Collin's houseboat is on the next dock, so instead of walking all the way around, I decide to paddle over in the canoe. I slip off my heels and climb into the boat, brushing away a seagull feather on one of the oars. I push off from the dock and a moment later, the tip of the canoe hits Collin's dock. I find a cleat, and I tie the canoe to it before climbing out of the boat.

Timidly, I look around the deck. Collin's tools are laid out neatly next to a green metal toolbox with a rusted handle. The wooden sailboat looks more beautiful up close than I could have imagined, and I find myself in awe of it. I see he's been working on the railing, and I run my hand along the teak, which has been sanded smooth as silk. I stand up and walk to Collin's back door. I knock, but there's no answer, so I cup my hands around my eyes and lean in to have a look.

Inside, the houseboat is tidy and sparsely furnished with a small sofa and coffee table. I notice what looks like an army medal lying on the coffee table and a few photographs splayed out. I squint but can't make out anything in particular. On the floor is a record player, with the sleeve of a Frank Sinatra record beside it. I love Frank Sinatra.

I turn around when I hear footsteps behind me. Collin sets a grocery sack down and smiles awkwardly.

"Hi," I say quickly. "I—I just—I just paddled over to invite you to our cocktail party tonight."

"Oh," he says, smiling.

The silence between us feels thick and stifling. I don't know what more to say, so I shuffle back toward the canoe.

"Did you enjoy having a look?"

I shake my head. "Having a look at what?"

"My house," he says. "I saw you peeking inside."

My cheeks burn and I feel foolish, like a little girl who's been caught sneaking into her mother's makeup bag.

"I wasn't *peeking*," I say. "I was only trying to see if you were home."

"Of course," he says. He's still smiling, and his head is cocked to the right as if he finds my embarrassment highly amusing.

"Listen," I say, stepping back into the boat. "Forget it." I untie the canoe and give myself a shove backward. "I was only trying to be hospitable."

I secure the canoe to our dock just as Naomi and Gene appear in front of our deck. "Good evening, Penny," Gene says.

I step out of the canoe, feeling Collin's eyes on my back, but I don't turn around.

Naomi takes a step toward me and straightens a wayward lock of my hair with her hand. "You look shaken, dear," she says, casting a glance in the direction of Collin's houseboat. "Is everything all right?"

"Everything's perfect," I say in my most confident voice.

She hands me a sad-looking yellow chrysanthemum in a terra-cotta pot. "They're such cheerful flowers, aren't they?"

I nod, but I do not tell her that I hate chrysanthemums and that their skunky, peppery scent gives me a headache.

"Let's go inside," I say, setting the plant down by the front door. "I'll make you a drink while we wait for the others."

I watch from the kitchen as Naomi slips out of her sweater, re-vealing her bare arms. They're long and beautiful, and I inwardly wish I could wear sleeveless tops with an ounce of the confidence that she does. Dex kisses her cheek, then shakes Gene's hand. Naomi tugs at her diamond necklace rhythmically as Dex says something funny that I can't detect over the sound of the cocktail shaker. Everyone laughs. I keep shaking, vigorously. Dex likes a layer of ice across the top of his martinis.

I select three glasses, pierce a few olives with toothpicks, then fill each to the top with a shaky hand. While entertaining makes me anxious and nervous, Dex is a born host.

Tom and Lenora arrive as I set the drinks on the tray. They're closer to Dex's age than mine. I feel like a schoolgirl, but I remember I am Dex's wife. Mrs. Dexter Wentworth. I smile at Ellen and Lou March and Joe and Leanne Hofstra. Dex dated Leanne a long time ago, when he first moved to Boat Street. Long before me. Leanne is beautiful and refined, a practicing attorney before she met Joe. I lift the tray in my hand and steady myself, as I overhear snippets of a conversation between Naomi and Leanne. They're standing in front of the doorway and speaking in hushed voices.

"The problem with marriages these days is that there are so many men who choose wives who are not on their same intellectual plane," Naomi says, before taking a long sip of her martini.

Leanne nods.

"I call it the Mommy syndrome," Naomi continues. "Men think they want a mother, but what they need is a woman. A partner, not someone to tuck them in at night with a mug of warm milk."

Leanne says something in response, but I can't make out her words.

Naomi rolls her eyes. "Exactly," she says.

My heart beats faster. I try not to dwell on Naomi's words. Of course, she wasn't talking about *me*. And yet I can't help but wonder if that's what she, and everyone else, thinks of Dex's and my marriage. *Why does my left hand feel numb?* I take a deep breath and make my way to the living room, where everyone is hovering around Dex. He's so close, but there may as well be miles between us. I don't know what he's saying. It's all a blur. Just his voice and then roars of laughter. He is a star. I walk ahead, eager to take my place beside him. Mrs. Dexter Wentworth. But my heel catches on the carpet, and I lunge forward. I lose my grasp on the tray, and it slips from my hands. I hear the sounds of women gasping and glass shattering.

"Darling, are you all right?" Dex croons, leaning over me. His dark eyes are filled with concern. Then Lenora and Tom. Lou and Ellen and Joe. Leanne. Gene, and then Naomi. Her arms are folded as if I've spoiled her evening.

I find Dex's face again, and I shake my head apologetically. "I'm sorry. I'm so clumsy."

"You just tripped, dear," he says. "It's this damn carpeting. I should have had it replaced a year ago." I love that Dex can smooth anything over.

Everyone's staring at me, and my cheeks feel hot. "I think I'll go get some air," I say.

"Let me sit with you," Dex says, helping me up.

I see the look in his eyes, the sadness that hovers behind the animated, happy face our guests see. His sadness has been palpable lately, and just last night, I pretended to be sleeping when I heard him weeping quietly in bed beside me. His body, curled up in a ball, shook with grief. I so desperately wanted to comfort him, but I knew it would just make him feel worse. Lately, my attempts to help were only met with resistance, embarrassment, and more pain. Whatever fog he is wandering through, he's made it clear that he must find his way on his own. It pains me to know that I can't offer him my assistance, that I can't even light a lamp to brighten his path.

But tonight, I can step back. I can quiet my fears and let him shine. His depression is more important than my anxiety.

"No," I say. "You stay inside. I'll be fine." I know how much this party means to him. I know how he *craves* it, and I don't want to put a damper on his evening. "I could use some air. I'll just be a moment."

I step out to the deck, sink into the Adirondack chair, and stare at the lake. The party resumes in my absence. I hear a cocktail

shaker. Someone flips on the record player. They're probably dancing. A heavy feeling grips my chest. I cannot go back inside. I stand
up and walk to the front of the deck, where I left the canoe. I'll go
paddling. No one will miss me.

I reach for the oar, then hear a voice behind me. "I hope I'm not
too late."

It's Collin. He looks different, maybe because he's changed out
of his work clothes and shaved. He's wearing jeans and a freshly
pressed pin-striped shirt with the top two buttons open. In his right
hand is a bottle of wine; in his left are two tumblers.

I don't say anything.

"I saw you sitting out here all by yourself," he says, uncorking
the bottle and pouring red wine into a glass. He hands it to me and
I take it. "I figured you could use some company."

I take a sip. The wine feels warm and comforting, medicinal
somehow, as I swallow. Collin sits down on the dock and leans
against the side of the houseboat, and I decide to do the same. I
spread the skirt of my gingham dress over my legs.

"Why didn't you bring me muffins the other day?" he asks.
Upon seeing my confused expression, he immediately explains. "I
could smell them baking, and I got my hopes up." He shrugs. "Were
they good?"

"They were," I say.

"You do know that there's a wind current that blows directly
from your kitchen to my deck," he continues.

I smile. "I didn't know. But now that you mention it, I ought to
bake brownies more."

He places his hand on his forehead in a dramatic fashion. "That
would be sensory torture."

I grin mischievously.

"So what is it about baking? Is it your *thing*?"

Before answering, I stop to think about the way I feel when I'm kneading bread or baking a cake, and it warms me. "I guess it takes my mind off everything else."

Collin nods. "That's how I feel when I'm working on a boat. Nothing in the world matters but the plank of wood in my hands." He takes a sip of wine. "Can I ask you something?"

I nod.

"Do you like it here, in Seattle?"

"Why, yes," I say honestly. "Well, I mostly do. And you?"

He shrugs. "It's all right. But I'm not going to be here forever."

"Oh?"

He looks away, as if his eyes might give away his past, or maybe his future. "After I finish my current project, I'm moving on."

I indicate the little boat in progress. "So you'll sail somewhere?"

"Not in that," he says. "That boat's special. It's a customer's." He looks at my houseboat briefly, and I wonder if the client is one of Dex's patrons, a wealthy family in Seattle, perhaps.

I nod. I feel a little sad to think that a stranger will one day own this beautiful creation, and I wonder if it'll be hard for Collin to give it up. "When it's done, what next?"

Collin shrugs. "I'll get my payment and then it's on to the next adventure."

I fold my hands in my lap once, then twice. "I'd like to sail somewhere, someday," I finally say shyly.

"Why don't you?" Collin says. I like his casual way of speaking, as if at any moment one might pick up and leave. If only it were that easy.

"Because my husband doesn't like sailing," I say. "He gets seasick."

"And he lives on a *houseboat*?"

"Protected water doesn't bother him, but the big swells out on the open sea do."

Collin nods. "Well, let's just say you could take a trip, that you could sail anywhere you wanted. Where would you go?"

I think for a moment, then smile. "Catalina Island."

Collin appears amused at my choice. "Why?"

I take my last sip of wine and he refills the glass. "Because it sounds romantic. There's a song about it, you know."

" 'Twenty-six Miles Across the Sea,' right?"

"That's right," I reply with a grin. "Anyway, I wanted to go there on my honeymoon, but Dex preferred Mexico."

"Well, Mexico's pretty great too," Collin says. "I've seen most of the Pacific Coast. I'd like to sail the Baja."

"Oh?" I ask, intrigued. "How did you end up traveling the coast?"

Collin's smile fades, and I worry I've stumbled into forbidden territory, but then he shrugs and simply says, "I don't like to stay in one place too long."

I want to ask him more about his past, but my attention is pulled back to the houseboat when I hear a round of uproarious laughter.

"Sounds like they're having a good time in there," he says, indicating the back deck.

I nod. "Will you sail your boat? I mean, when it's finished, before your customer picks it up." I feel my cheeks getting warm, and my speech hastens, the way it always does when I'm nervous. "You see, I've always dreamed of sailing the world, leaving from here and going from port to port, letting my skin get dark from the sun."

Collin searches my eyes for a moment. The sun has set, and the light is dim now, so I can't make out his expression exactly, just his eyes, and they're bright and big, and maybe somewhat entertained. "Are you asking me to take you sailing?"

I'm embarrassed. I wasn't making an obvious hint, but if I'm honest with myself, it might have been a tiny one. I'd love nothing more than to step onto that beautiful craft and feel the wind in my hair beneath its puffy sails. "Well, no. I just—"

"I'm only teasing," Collin says. "I'd love to take you sailing."

I smile and turn away, concerned that I'm blushing.

"You're rare, you know," he says.

I worry he's just trying to flatter me, so I shake my head. "Go on."

"No, really," he says. "Not many women would dream of a life on the seas the way you just described."

"I don't see why not."

He shakes his head. "No, so many women want the safe, comfortable life."

I think of my life with Dexter. Safe. Comfortable. I suppose that describes me to a T.

Before I can say anything else, Collin speaks again. "I've lived and died by a quote I read when I was a boy. It goes something like this: 'Twenty years from now, you will be more disappointed by the things you didn't do than by the ones you did do. So throw off the bowlines, sail away from the safe harbor. Catch the trade winds in your sails. Explore. Dream. Discover.'"

"That's . . . beautiful," I say, a little breathless. "It makes me want to set sail."

Collin grins, then reaches into his pocket and pulls out a ticket stub. I can see that it's from a movie theater ticket to *An Affair to*

*Remember.* I wanted to see the film last month, but Dex complained of a headache, so we stayed in.

"I don't understand," I say.

"Your ticket. For the maiden voyage."

"Right," I say, unable to contain my smile.

I look up when I notice Dex walking toward us. "There you are!" he says.

I stand up quickly, and tuck the ticket into the small pocket of my dress. "Hi, honey," I say.

"Feeling better?"

"Yes, much."

Dex smiles at Collin, and extends his hand. "I'm glad you could come. I'm Dexter Wentworth. And I see you've met my wife, Penny. Come, have a drink with us. They've just started dancing."

Collin nods and follows Dex and me back to the house. Naomi is drunk. I can tell by the way she's standing, a little off-kilter, and smiling, like a Cheshire cat. I wonder where Jimmy is tonight. I imagine him home by himself, lonely, reading comic books or watching the television set. Gene stands up and collects Naomi's martini glass, and she stumbles toward us. "Oh, look, it's the handsome boatman," she says.

The smoky sound of Stan Getz's saxophone wafts through the speakers. "Oh, goody," Naomi says in a childlike voice. "Someone's finally put on some decent dancing music." She takes Collin's hand and clumsily attaches it to my waist. "You two are the youngest people here; you must dance."

Collin flashes me an apologetic smile. "It's a party," I whisper. "Let's dance."

He pulls me a little closer, as if my words have put him at ease. I feel everyone's eyes on me. Leanne smiles at me, but I look away quickly. I search the room. I don't see Dex. Or Naomi or Gene. Collin dances well. I hardly have to think about my feet, so I don't. I don't think about anything. And when his eyes catch mine, they lock for a moment, and I feel a flicker inside me that I cannot ignore.

# Chapter 8

## Ada

I'm having coffee on the deck when Jim peers around the corner. "Sorry, am I disturbing you?" He's a friendly man, but there's something a little off about him. Sad, maybe. He's one of those people whose smiles can't hide everything beneath the surface. Maybe that's why I like him so much.

"No," I say. "Of course not."

He hands me a card that looks like it's been printed on an inkjet printer. The edges run with blue ink. "Mother insists on doing these invitations every year," he says.

I look it over:

SAVE THE DATE

The Annual Boat Street Bach on the Dock Party

July 30th at 6 p.m.

BYOB

"'Bach on the Dock'? That's cute."

Jim shrugs. "It's been going on as long as I can remember. We used to have a full quartet. But one by one, they died or moved away. Dad's the only musician left. He plays the violin."

"Oh," I say. "I *thought* I heard violin music the other day. It must have been your father."

"Yeah," Jim continues. "I'm so thankful that he has his music. His eyesight has deteriorated, so he doesn't have his books anymore. Of course, he can't see the sheet music anymore either. But he's stored it all up." He points to his head. "He plays from memory."

"That's amazing," I say.

"Dementia's an awful disease. He seems fine one moment, and the next he's addressing me as if I'm a colleague from the English department. It's hard on Mother. He's brought up things she'd just as well forget." He shrugs. "His mind is completely unpredictable."

"Sorry," I say. "It must be so hard for all of you."

He shrugs again. "Anyway, Mother wanted to be sure you knew you were invited."

"Thank you," I reply, smiling. "Have you found her?"

He gives me a confused look.

"Henrietta," I remind him.

"Oh, no. She hasn't come home yet."

"I'm sorry to hear that. How's Haines?"

"Terrible," he replies. "He won't eat."

"I'll keep an eye out for her," I say, turning to my back door. "Well, please thank your mother for the invitation."

Jim smiles as if struck with sudden inspiration. "Why don't you come over and meet her? It will do her a world of good. Dad's having a bad day, and, well, when he's having a bad day, she's having a bad day."

"Are you sure?" I ask. "I haven't showered. I'm not exactly—"

"Mom has cataracts," he says. "To her you'll look like Angelina Jolie."

I smile and follow him up the dock. I notice a green vine that has wrapped itself around the edge of the dock, its white flowers craning up toward the morning sun. "That vine," I say, turning to Jim. "What is it? I've never seen anything like it in New York."

"Morning glory," he replies. "Kind of pretty, isn't it?"

"Yes," I say, kneeling down to touch one of its delicate white flowers.

"Mother doesn't think so. In the old days she'd never let the morning glory grow like this. She'd be out here pulling them out by the root. It was her thing."

I think for a moment about why people pick a person, place, or thing to have a vendetta against. For my dad it was gas stations. He always said they were cheating him. He'd eye the pump suspiciously, sure that the meter was lying to him. Joanie has a thing about baristas. She was convinced that a college kid behind the counter on Tuesday mornings was spiking her venti nonfat latte with decaf and whole milk just to spite her, which made her suspicious of all baristas and is ultimately the reason why I refuse to visit cafés with her. I stifle a laugh as I remember the time we had a tense exchange with a manager at a Midtown Manhattan Starbucks. *Oh, Joanie.*

But why? Why does the human psyche seek out things to become bitter about? What has the morning glory ever done to Jim Clyde's mother other than be beautiful?

We stop in front of the home with the beautiful potted plants. "Here we are," Jim says. He opens the door, and I follow him inside. The avocado green walls and brown shag carpeting make me feel as if I've stepped into a day in the life of 1963, and perhaps I have. I recall that this is where Jim grew up. "Mom, are you decent?"

An old man appears in the hallway. He's tall and thin and

hunches over in a way that makes me wonder if he has osteoporosis. His trousers look three sizes too big, and his white cotton shirt is wrinkled and inside out. "Hi, Dad," Jim says.

"Son?" He has a kind face.

"Yes, it's me, Dad," he says. "I'd like you to meet someone. This is Ada, our new neighbor."

"Who?"

"Ada," he says again.

He extends his hand automatically, but his face still looks very confused. "Gene Clyde. Pleased to meet you."

"C'mon, Pop, let's sit down," Jim says.

In the living room, Gene asks me what novels I'm reading, and I tell him that I've picked up something at the airport, but can't remember the title.

"Dad's a former English professor," Jim says with a wink.

"Now, Penny," he says, "did you have a chance to start the novel I left on your porch yesterday?"

"Dad," Jim says, a bit startled, "this is *Ada*."

"I don't mind," I say, hoping Gene isn't worried that I've been offended. I wonder what it must be like to live with dementia, and I also wonder who Penny is.

"Jim, dear!"

Behind me is Jim's mother. She's wearing a blue velour leisure suit. Her delicate skin is wrinkled and hangs over her high cheekbones. By the way she looks at me, I can tell that though her exterior may have aged, she's still as sharp as a tack. "Who's this young lady?" she asks, walking toward us with a bit of a limp. I remember her broken hip, and I'm surprised to see her out of bed.

"Mother," Jim says with a tsk-tsk in his voice. "Should you be up walking?"

She kisses his cheek as her gray hair, cut into a blunt bob, swishes against her cheek. "I'm fine, dear," she says. "Your father, on the other hand . . ." She lowers her voice to a whisper. ". . . is *not* having a good day."

Jim nods. While his mother seems a little annoyed, he just looks saddened by his father's state. "I know."

"So who is this beauty?" she asks, looking at me. "Tells us about yourself, Miss . . . ?"

"Santorini," I say.

"Oh, you're an Italian? You don't look Italian." She's blunt and bold, and I might take offense if she were thirty-five rather than pushing eighty.

"Yes," I reply. "I mean, well, I was married to an Italian."

"Ah, divorced," she says. "Everyone is these days."

"No," I say a little more defensively than I intended. "My husband died."

"I'm so sorry, dear," she says, shaking her head. "What a pity." She offers me her hand. "I'm Naomi."

"So nice to meet you. You have a lovely home." I don't know why I said it. The home isn't lovely. It's actually dark, and the air smells like medicine and sadness. But I have a habit of talking too much when I'm nervous, and I'm nervous now.

"You're tense," she says. "Come sit down."

"Mother worked as a psychiatrist for forty years," Jim says in an apologetic tone. "She can't help herself."

"I'm fine," I say, forcing a smile.

"No, you're not, dear," Naomi says. "Where's your grief coming from? The death of your husband?"

She is not like Dr. Evinson. Her eyes pierce the wounds I've tried to keep hidden, the ones that, after two years, still feel raw. She can sense my pain, and I feel as if her prodding isn't the least bit therapeutic.

I glance at my watch. "It's been lovely meeting you," I say quickly, "but I really must go."

Naomi smiles curiously at me, and her eyes follow me as I walk to the door.

Jim's expression says, "Sorry," and I nod to him, then look to the couch, where his father has fallen asleep.

❦

No matter how much time passes, I know I won't be able to stop cooking for two and a half. And as I warm the cast iron skillet and drizzle in a bit of olive oil, I can almost feel James's arms around my waist, his lips against my neck. How many times did I push him away because I was too busy? How many times did I say, "Not to-night"? I drop the chicken breasts in the pan and listen to them sizzle. How I wish he were here now. How I wish I could have those moments back. All of the moments.

I slice the bread, prepare a quick vinaigrette to drizzle over the chopped romaine, then squeeze a lemon wedge over the chicken in the pan and sprinkle it with chopped garlic, the way James used to. Finally, I uncork the wine and pour a splash into the pan, breathing in the intoxicating scent.

"Hi, my love," I hear him say. No one ever called me that before him. It was the Italian in him. The romantic. My Romeo.

"I miss you," I say. My words reverberate in the lonely space in the kitchen.

"I want you to be happy," he says.

"But I can't," I say. "Not without you."

He shakes his head. "You have to try."

"I don't know if I can, James," I say.

"Do it for me?"

I wipe away a tear and carry my plate of chicken, salad, and a slice of crusty bread out to the deck. It's after six, and though the breeze is light, there are still a few sailboats inching along the lake with sails puffed out. I take a bite and notice Alex paddle up to his dock in a green kayak. "Hi," he says, climbing out onto the deck as his eyes meet mine. He's wearing jeans, a blue T-shirt, and a gray baseball cap.

"Hi," I reply.

"I take it you haven't burned the place down yet," he says with a grin.

I hold up my plate and smile. "Success."

He nods. "Whatever it is, it smells amazing."

I shrug. "Just chicken. Nothing fancy."

"Well, it sounds better than takeout."

I think of the extra chicken breast in the pan, the bread on the cutting board, and the bowl full of salad I'll never eat. "Why don't you come over?" I say suddenly, hardly recognizing my own voice.

He sets his oar in the kayak and his smile widens. "Really?"

"Sure," I say. "But full disclaimer: It's nothing cookbook-worthy."

"That's the best kind," he says. "I'll just get my camera, then."

He returns from the houseboat with his camera strapped around his shoulder, then climbs into the kayak again to paddle toward my dock. "Hi," he says a moment later. I watch as he climbs out onto the deck and ties the kayak to a cleat, then he takes his hat off, holds it to his chest, and bows. "Thank you."

I can't help but laugh at the dramatic gesture. "For what?"

"For saving me from Thai food."

"*Oh*, but I *love* Thai food."

"So do I," he says. "But after fifty-six consecutive nights of green curry and spring rolls, well, you know."

"Come on," I say, standing up. "Let me make you a plate."

He follows me inside to the kitchen, and I dish up his dinner. I set it on the bar, and he immediately whips out his camera. "Do you have a cloth or a piece of fabric? Something for a background?"

"I really don't think this dinner is photo-worthy."

"Yes," he says. "It is. Look at the gloss on the chicken." I don't tell him it's one of the few things I know how to cook.

I pull out a striped dishcloth from a drawer near the sink. "Will this work?"

"Yeah," he says, looking into the viewfinder. The flash goes off once, then twice. He slips off his shoes and climbs onto the counter. I can't help but notice how his biceps move as he lifts the camera and then positions it over the plate. One more flash, then another. "There," he says, jumping down beside me. His arm brushes mine as he keys through the images stored on his camera. "See?" he continues, pointing to the image, which looks one hundred times more appetizing than the dish I made.

"Wow," I say, astonished.

"Not bad, huh?" he says, grinning. "And I didn't even have a food stylist." He leans in and whispers mockingly, "They're a fussy lot."

He leans over the bar, slices into the chicken, and takes a bite. "Good," he says, covering his mouth.

I smile. "Well, anything would taste good after a thousand days of takeout."

"No," he says, with sincerity in his eyes, "you're a great cook."

I nod and find another wineglass in the cupboard. "Can I pour you some white?"

"No thanks," he says. "I don't drink."

We make small talk as he finishes his dinner, then I refill my wineglass and we sit on the sofa overlooking the lake.

"I found your book," I say. "The barbecue one."

He nods. "What did you think?"

"It looks great. James Beard award—very impressive."

He shrugs. "I gained fifteen pounds shooting that book."

"I can see why." I want to ask about his coauthor, but I don't. Instead, I inquire about his former career. "Do you miss traveling? The work you did in Sudan?"

"Yeah," he says. "Sometimes." He looks out to the lake, as if willing a stiff wind to carry him away. "I didn't ever think I'd give up foreign correspondence work. It was my calling."

"So why did you?"

His eyes look distant for a moment, faraway, before he looks at me again. "Because I thought I had a more important job to do at home."

"And did that 'job' work out?"

"I wanted it to," he says, "but it never could. It never would." He rubs his brow. "How about you? Did your work bring you out here?"

"No," I say. "I left all that behind in New York. Time for a new chapter."

Our eyes lock. "It's awfully quiet in here," I say a bit nervously. "There must be a stereo."

Alex points to a cabinet on the wall and walks toward it.

"I see you know my house better than I do," I say.

He grins. "The guy that rented it before you was a fisherman. Friendly guy, but he had a thing for whiskey. Lots of whiskey. I had to help him home more than a few times."

"Oh," I say. "That explains the fishhook in the laundry room."

He smiles and turns back to the stereo. He fiddles with the antenna, but all that comes out of the nearby speakers is static. "No reception. Let me see what old Joe left in the CD player."

"Old Joe?"

He nods. "The fisherman." A familiar melody suddenly drifts through the little living room. It makes me freeze, and I don't know why. And then I hear the silky, sweet sound of Karen Carpenter's voice.

"'Rainy Days and Mondays,'" Alex says.

I can't find my voice. I just stare ahead, fighting back the tears.

Alex sits down beside me. I know he senses that something's wrong. "I'm sorry," he says quickly. "If you don't like it, I'll turn it off."

"No," I say. "No. Please don't." I wipe a tear from my eye, just as another spills onto my cheek. "My husband loved this song." I smile. "Which made him the only straight man on earth to love the Carpenters."

Alex grins. "The only two straight men on earth."

I smile again. For some reason, I feel as if someone has lifted a great weight from my shoulders, just for a moment. "James died on a Monday," I say.

We sit there for a moment listening to the song together, each alone in our own thoughts, until Alex reaches over and takes my hand in his. I don't let go.

# Chapter 9

PENNY

I've just cleared the breakfast dishes and have put a loaf of bread in the oven for lunch, honey whole wheat, when I nestle on the couch next to Dex. "Did you have a good time last night?"

He doesn't take his eyes off the newspaper. "Yes, it was a good party." He has a headache, I know. I saw him reach for the aspirin after he woke up.

I smile when I think of the way he carried me up the stairs to our bed and held me like he used to. But a mere eight hours later, the spell has lifted. He seems distracted and sullen.

He sets the paper down on the coffee table and turns to me. "I'm going to be spending the next week in my studio," he says matter-of-factly.

I bite my lip. "I don't understand."

"What don't you understand?" he snaps. "I have to work. And that's that."

I stand up and walk to the kitchen. My eyes sting.

"Penny," Dex says, his face momentarily softened.

I nod, then open the oven door and peer in at my bread, which is rising nicely and taking on a perfect shade of golden brown. I hover long enough to let a lone tear fall from my eye. It lands on the oven door and evaporates as if it never existed.

"Darling," Dex continues, walking to the kitchen. "Please, don't take my work so personally."

Dex is right, of course. He's an artist. And being married to one requires the patience of a Tibetan monk. Hasn't Dex always said that he divorced his first wife because she required constant maintenance? No, I don't want to be high maintenance, and yet I do want to be *loved*. Is it too much to ask for him to come home each night?

"I'm sorry," I say, finally facing him. "I just hate it when you're gone so long. I get lonely here."

"My psychiatrist thinks alone time is good for me," he says.

I want to say, "Does your *psychiatrist* ever consider what's good for *me*, your wife?" But I let a few moments pass, and then I nod. "Dex, you know I only want you to be happy."

He pulls me close to him and kisses my cheek. "That's why I love you so much."

❦

Dex left before noon, opting for the café downtown over a home-made Reuben sandwich on fresh-baked bread. I try not to take it personally and wrap the extra sandwich I made in waxed paper before putting it in the fridge, which is when I hear a quiet knock at the back door.

I look up and see Jimmy standing on the deck outside, with his nose pressed up against the glass.

"Morning, honey," I say.

"Can I come in?" he asks, wide-eyed.

"Does your mother know where you are?"

He shrugs. "She's working today. Besides, she doesn't care where I am as long as I'm not bothering her."

"I'm sure that's not the case, Jimmy," I say.

He walks into the living room and plops onto the couch. "It always smells nice in your house," he says. "Like a bakery."

"Thanks," I reply. "Are you hungry?"

He nods.

I hand him Dex's sandwich and he unwraps it hastily. "I got an A on my book report," he says between bites.

"Good job, honey," I say. "I bet your mother was proud."

He shakes his head. "She doesn't like bugs."

"Bugs?"

"The book was about bugs."

"Oh."

"She wanted me to do a report on a book about a guy named Fried."

"Do you mean Freud?"

"Yeah, I think so."

I smile. "I'll be honest," I say, "I like bugs better."

Jimmy looks vindicated. "Will you take me out in the canoe?"

"I don't know," I say, remembering Naomi's warnings about Jimmy. "Your parents will be looking for you soon."

He shakes his head, and something about his eyes, pleading, lonely, makes me say OK. "But we can't be out long."

He stands up and wraps his arms around my waist. "Thank you, Penny."

The lake is glorious today, sparkling and smooth as glass. The canoe glides through the water effortlessly, like a knife through butter.

After we paddle out to the center of the lake, we stop and bob on the water for a while. It's peaceful here. Jimmy sets his oar down in the well of the canoe and turns around in his seat up front to face me.

"I wish I was good at something," he says suddenly.

"Oh, Jimmy, you're good at lots of things."

He shakes his head. "I'm not smart in school."

"That's not true," I say. "You just haven't found your thing yet—you know, your special skill. Everyone has one. It just takes a while to figure out what it is."

He's wide-eyed. "What's yours?"

"Well, I do like to bake."

"You make good cookies," he says.

"Someday I'd like to open a bakery."

He looks thoughtful for a moment, then smiles to himself. "I'd like to be a comic strip writer."

"Jimmy!" I exclaim. "That's a wonderful goal!"

He pulls a piece of paper from his pocket and hands it to me. It's folded several times into a small square, and I unfold it carefully.

"It's not very good," he says quickly.

I shake my head, astonished by the way he drew the people and dog in the little comic strip, then smile at the punch line. "It's excellent," I say. "You should show this to your parents."

Jimmy shakes his head and quickly retrieves his creation, folding it again before tucking it in his pocket. "No. They don't understand comics."

"Well, they understand talent, and they'll be very proud of you."

He shrugs and turns back to the water, and I look to the shore, where our dock looks like a tiny speck in the distance.

"Penny?" he asks, turning to me again. "Will you ever have a baby?"

I smile nervously, a bit startled by his question. I think of the last time I spoke to Dex about the subject. He patted my knee and said, "Become a father at my age?" And yet, I long for a child. I can't help but think that if I had a baby, I wouldn't feel so alone. That it might complete the missing piece of me, fill the hairline crack in my heart that I knew Dex can never fully occupy. But after almost three years of marriage, it has become clear that something is wrong. And maybe that something is *me*.

"Jimmy," I say, choosing my words carefully, "I'd love to have a baby, more than anything in the world. But sometimes things don't work out the way you want them to."

"It's not fair," he says, frowning. "You want a child and don't have one, and Mother has me, but she never wanted one."

"Oh, dear," I say quickly. "Don't say that. You know that's not true. Your mother loves you very much."

He doesn't say anything else as we paddle back to the dock, but then his eyes light up when he sees Collin on his boat. He's fastening a thin piece of wood in place at the stern. "Can we go say hello to him?"

I don't see the harm in paddling over, so I nod and change course, parking the canoe in front of Collin's deck.

"Well, hello there," he says, tipping his cap at us.

Without asking permission, Jimmy leaps out of the canoe onto the deck. "May I see your boat?"

"Jimmy, I—"

"It's all right," Collin says kindly. "I could use another pair of hands this afternoon."

"Really?" Jimmy beams. "I'm good at helping."

I smile. "As long as you don't mind."

I watch the two of them attach the piece of wood to the boat.

Jimmy presses his fingers against the edge as if he's been given the most important job of his life and he's determined to succeed.

"There," Collin says. "Now, we'll varnish it to match the rest of the wood here." He hands Jimmy a small can and a brush and watches as the child paints the strip with great care.

"That's the way," Collin says encouragingly. "You'd make a fine shipbuilder."

He'd make a good father; that much is clear. I wince when I think about the way Dex is with children, anxious and awkward. It's not his fault, though. He never knew love as a child. He was never taught how to be around children. Or is it something that needs teaching? Is it something you're born with? Still, I don't blame Dex; I just admire Collin's gentle ways with Jimmy and smile to myself.

"There," Collin says. "It's perfect. I couldn't have finished this part without you."

Jimmy casts a glance at me, still in the canoe, then back at Collin. "Can I help you again, some other time?"

"You mean, you're willing to be my assistant? Because I've been looking for a good assistant. Someone with strong, steady hands like yours."

"I'd like to be your assistant," the boy says earnestly.

"Good, then. You can—"

We all turn when we hear the click-clack of heels on the dock. The tread of an irritated woman.

Naomi. She glances at me and grimaces before turning to her son. I sense Jimmy's nervousness.

"Jimmy Allan Clyde," she says. "Get over here at once."

Jimmy nods quickly and steps out of the sailboat. "Yes, Mother."

She sighs. "You're filthy. I won't have you wearing your shoes in my living room again." She snaps her fingers. "Penny, bring him home."

Collin watches in silence as Jimmy climbs back into the canoe. He casts me an apologetic smile, and I nod without saying anything.

I paddle Jimmy to his back deck and steady the canoe so he can climb out. "Mama," he says exuberantly. "I helped Collin build his boat!"

"That's the last time you'll be doing that," she snaps. "Get inside."

"But Mama," he pleads.

She closes her eyes tightly and points to the back door. He obeys.

"How dare you," she says to me. Tears tinged with black mascara stain her face.

"I only, I . . ." I don't know what to say.

"Leave my son alone," she says. "He doesn't need your pity."

"But I wasn't—"

"You think I'm a bad mother, don't you?"

"No, I—"

"Well, save your self-righteousness. He is my son, and you can get your hooks out of him right now."

"Yes," I say, her words stinging as I paddle away.

I look behind me once, and Naomi's seated on the ground, on her knees with her head hanging down over her hands. She's crying—sobbing, really. I feel a pang of emotion then. I'm surprised by it. I don't expect to feel anything for Naomi, this woman who's been cold to me since the day I arrived on Boat Street. And yet I see her now, aching like I ache. I see her with new eyes. For once I detect the hidden wrinkles in her carefully starched and pressed world.

Poor Jimmy. I wish I could fix his problems. I wish I could make life happier for him somehow. I grab the rope on the edge of the canoe and wrap it around the cleat in front of my houseboat.

The wind has picked up, and I shiver. Upstairs, I select a yellow cashmere cardigan from the closet, remembering how Dex brought it home in March with matching yellow earrings. I slip my arm into the sweater. It feels like warm butter on my skin, luxurious. Dex always buys the best. I notice my dress from last night lying on the chair. I think of Collin and retrieve the ticket I tucked in the pocket. I hold it in my hands for a moment, staring at its wrinkles, studying the words. May 15, 1959. He went to see the movie just last month. *With who?* The thought makes me feel guilty. Wasn't that part of my brain supposed to have been lobotomized when I took my marriage vows? I walk to the porthole above the bed, and glance toward Collin's houseboat, but he isn't there. I think about how wonderful he was with Jimmy. It makes something flicker inside me. I stare at the sailboat. I'd like to sail away on it, but I know I never will. I never could.

I crouch down beside the dresser and reach for the little brass key I keep in a slat below the bottom drawer. I've never liked the dresser, with those awful drawer pulls that look like roaring lions, but a friend of Dex's who makes furniture gave it to him as a birthday present, and it didn't seem right to ask him to replace it.

Downstairs, I kneel beside the only piece of furniture I brought to the houseboat—Grandma Rose's old chest. When I was a little girl, I used to think it was a treasure chest, and maybe it was. Grandma said she'd fallen in love with a seaman before she met Grandpa. She said he'd given it to her as a gift and that she'd kept it, even after she and Grandpa got married. I never knew anything more about her mysterious seaman, but I saw the way Grandma talked about him. I know she still loved him, but I will never know why they parted. And I'll never know what treasure the chest, lined with its red silk fabric, once held.

For me, Grandma stocked it with the sort of treasure that appeals to little girls: porcelain dolls of varying sizes, a silver brush and comb set, four teacups painted with roses, and an old cigar box filled with costume jewelry. Over the years, I've tucked in other things—the bracelet Mama gave me on my sixteenth birthday, a book of poems about the sea, the acceptance letter from Miss Higgins Academy, my blue notebook filled with recipes.

At first it felt wrong to keep these things, this part of myself, from Dexter. But he kept things from me, too. Big things. I found a photo of his first wife in his desk drawer, and letters. He didn't mention a word of his past before we were married. When I finally worked up the courage to ask him about his ex-wife, he did two things: acknowledge that, yes, he was married before, and tell me never to bring up the subject again.

Yes, Dexter has secrets, and so can I. I slip my key into the little lock and lift the lid, breathing in the familiar scent of my past—musty, floral, and damp like a rainy night. I survey the treasures inside. Like old friends, they're all there, just as I left them. I tuck Collin's ticket inside, beside a box of old photos, then close the lid and secure the lock again.

# Chapter 10

ADA

I feel as if I could talk with Alex all night, and I think he feels that way too. But it's late. "Well, I should probably be going," he says, looking up at the clock on the wall. "Thank you for dinner."

"Of course," I reply. "Let's do this again."

Alex grins. "I'd love that."

After he's gone, I walk upstairs, thinking of our unexpected date. Was it even a date? I rub my forehead, aware of how sorely out of practice I am in matters of men. No, it wasn't a date, I tell myself. I feel silly for even considering the idea. But if I'm honest with myself, I can't deny that when I'm around Alex, I feel something flicker deep inside, something I haven't felt since . . . James.

I climb the stairs to the loft and decide to finally unpack my suitcase and move in properly. I tuck my clothes into the drawers of the old dresser, until the suitcase is finally emptied. James had a knack for packing. Before a trip, I'd just pick the clothes I wanted to pack and toss them on the bed. Like magic, he'd fold them in tidy stacks—always rolling the pants to prevent wrinkles—and tuck them into our suitcase with expert precision. I close my eyes, and I remember the time we went to Paris together. He surprised me the week after Ella's fourth birthday. I came home from work, and my parents were there playing a game of Uno on the floor with Ella.

"Mommy, Mommy!" Ella cries as I walk through the door. "Daddy has a surprise for you! You're going on an airplane."

I groan inwardly. I just returned from Portland yesterday for a shoot for the magazine, and the last thing I want is to set foot on another airplane. I glance at James and he smiles, pointing to the suitcase in the hall by the door. "Everything's taken care of," he says. "I'm taking you to Paris."

"But," I protest, glancing toward Ella. While I've traveled alone many times for work, I've taken James and Ella with me as often as possible. But now? It would be the first time we'd travel together without our little girl, and I'm not sure if I can do it.

Sensing my concern, my mom stands up and walks toward me. "Don't worry about a thing, honey," she says. "You go and have fun. Your father and I will take care of everything."

I nod robotically and walk to the kitchen for a glass of water, which is when I realize that I forgot to stop at the grocery store on the way home. "James, we're out of her favorite applesauce," I say, shaking my head, as if an applesauce shortage is reason enough to stay home from Europe. Somehow, for me, it is.

"Picked up a new pack this morning," he says with a grin. He wraps his arms around me in the kitchen, and whispers in my ear. "Look, it's our anniversary tomorrow, and I know you've always wanted to go to Paris. Let me take you there. Let's see it together."

I turn around to face him. I can tell this trip means a lot to him. Day after day he cares for Ella while I work. It occurs to me that he needs this trip a lot more than I do. "Yes," I say, looking into his eyes.

"Good," he says with a smile. "The car will be here in an hour to pick us up."

How I wish I could return to that moment, to feel his arms around me just once more, to hear Ella's giggles in the living room.

I bend over to shut the bottom drawer and hear the ping of my earring hitting the wood floor. *Darn.* I kneel down to look for it, patting around under the bed, then toward the dresser. I lie on the floor to see if I can get a better look from that angle, which is when I notice the glint of metal beneath the dresser. I reach my hand under the drawer and discover a little brass key wedged beneath the frame. I hold it up to the light. It's one of those old-fashioned keys— long with a hole at the top. I wonder what it's doing here, what it could possibly unlock, and then it hits me. The chest in the living room.

Downstairs, I hesitate for a moment before giving in to my curiosity. I slip the key into the old lock and jiggle it a little. It releases immediately, and I feel butterflies in my stomach.

I lift the lid of the chest. Inside, the air is musty and stale, held hostage for years in its three-foot-by-four-foot tomb. I lean in to survey the contents cautiously, then pull out a stack of old photos tied with twine. On top is a photo of a couple on their wedding day. She's a young bride, wearing one of those 1950s netted veils. He looks older, distinguished—sort of like Cary Grant or Gregory Peck in the old black-and-white movies I used to watch with my grandmother. I set the stack down and turn back to the chest, where I find a notebook, filled with handwritten recipes. The page for Cinnamon Rolls is labeled "Dex's Favorite." *Dex.* I wonder if he's the man in the photo.

There are two ticket stubs from 1959, one to a Frank Sinatra concert, another to the movie *An Affair to Remember*. A single shriveled rosebud rests on a white handkerchief. A corsage? When I lift it into my hand, it disintegrates; the petals crinkle into tiny pieces that fall onto the living room carpet. At the bottom of the chest is what looks like a wedding dress. It's yellowed and moth-eaten, but I imagine it was once stark white and beautiful. As I lift it, I can hear the lace swishing as if to say, "Ahh." Whoever wore it was very petite. The waist circumference is tiny. A pair of long white gloves falls to the floor. They must have been tucked inside the dress. I refold the finery and set the ensemble back inside.

Whose things are these? And why have they been left here? I thumb through the recipe book. All cookies, cakes, desserts. She must have loved to bake. I tuck the book back inside the chest, along with the photographs after I've retied the twine, which is when I notice a book tucked into the corner. It's an old paperback copy of Ernest Hemingway's *The Sun Also Rises*. I've read a little of Hemingway over the years—*A Moveable Feast* and some of his later work—but not this one. I flip through the book and notice that one page is dog-eared. I open to it and see a line that has been underscored. "You can't get away from yourself by moving from one place to another."

I look out to the lake, letting the words sink in. *Is that what I'm trying to do? Get away from myself?* I stare at the line in the book again and wonder if it resonated with the woman who underlined it so many years ago. Did she have her own secret pain? *Was she trying to escape it just like me?*

I close the lid of the chest, then notice something I've missed on the floor. A bracelet—well, a hospital bracelet. It's made of plastic, and the print on the front is worn and barely legible. I turn on the lamp and hold it closer. "Wentworth, Penny," it reads.

I tuck it in the pocket of my jeans and vow to learn more about this woman. Could she be the one the grocery store clerk alluded to? The woman who disappeared? "Penny," I say aloud. *Who were you?*

Alex is my first thought when I open my eyes the next morning. Yes, we did have a good time together last night, but I'm in no place to take it any further. I came here to heal, not to get mixed up in a relationship I'm not ready for.

I hold fast to my resolution as I walk down the ladder to the living room, which is when I notice his navy fleece vest on the chair. I pick it up and press my nose to it instinctively. The fabric smells woodsy and clean, like a mix of soap and pine trees. I feel a little flutter in my stomach as I set it down.

I decide I'll go kayaking this morning, then swing by Alex's houseboat and drop it off. Besides, he invited me to come by. It wouldn't be weird. Or would it? I close my eyes and shake my head. Stop. Enough overanalyzing. I'm just returning a stupid vest.

Still, I find myself lingering over the mirror a moment longer than usual. I brush my hair and part it three different ways before throwing on some lip gloss.

"Morning," Jim says from the dock as I zip up my life vest. "Going out for a row?"

"Yeah. It looks like a nice morning to be on the water."

"Is it ever," he says. "I'm taking the boat out later." He nods toward the sailboat moored on my back deck.

"Have a good time," I say.

"You could join me," he offers a moment later, smiling.

I shake my head. "Thank you, but maybe some other time. I've been dying to see the lake from a duck's point of view."

His smile widens. "No better way."

I climb into the kayak, tucking Alex's vest behind my back for comfort, then inch my way out to the lake. The wake from a boat rolls in, and at first I feel like I'll tip at any moment. I grasp the edges of the kayak and hold my breath, bracing myself for going under. But I don't tip, so I venture out farther. I dip my paddle into the water and propel myself toward the center of the lake. I remember going canoeing in high school with a boy named Corey. I was sure we'd tip over, and when he leaned in to kiss me, we nearly did. I smile to myself. The farther I row, the farther I want to go, so I don't stop. And I let my mind wander as I do. I let it travel freely, so of course, it goes to visit James and Ella. I see them sitting together, dangling their feet over the dock at the boat launch in Key Largo. *Sunrise* sent me to the Florida Keys to research a travel piece, and I brought James and Ella. I loved it when they traveled with me on my assignments. It made me feel less guilty. We could be together instead of the two of them in New York and me in a lonely hotel room worrying about everything from whether Ella ate her vegetables to the window in the living room. Did James remember to lock it? She was only three then, her cheeks still round, and her tiny hands still with their little fat pads on top. I loved the baby fat years.

"Mommy," she says, "Daddy and I are looking at our sand castles." She points to two creations in the distance. One is tall and smooth. Symmetrical. The other looks like it may have been hit by a tornado.

"They're both beautiful," I say, but I point to hers. "That one is *especially* nice."

"That one's mine," she says proudly.

"We thought we'd drive into town and grab some lunch," James says. "Want to join us, or do you have work to do?"

"I wish I could," I say, "but I have that interview at noon."

Ella tugs at my skirt. "Mommy, *please!*"

"Oh, honey, you know I'd go if I could."

"Ella, remember Mommy's working on this trip," James says. "We just came along to keep her company." I sigh then, remember how much I love him, how much I appreciate the way he respects my work, respects me.

"OK," Ella says.

"Have fun!" I watch them walk to the car a few feet away, he in his T-shirt and shorts, and she in her white linen sundress and pink Salt Water sandals.

I have an interview in the hotel lobby with the mayor of Key Largo, so, not wanting to be late, I walk straight there. When I reach the foyer, I hear the sound of sirens in the distance. An ambulance? A fire truck? The sirens are coming from the main highway, which is not far away. James and Ella would've taken that route to get lunch in town. Suddenly, I panic. What if there was an accident? I try to quell my worries, but I can't stop the fear rising up in my chest. It's mixed with guilt and the agonizing thought of losing the two most important people in my life. What if the ambulance is coming for them? I run to the desk. "If the mayor shows up, tell him there's been an emergency," I say. "Tell him I'll be back as soon as I make sure my family's all right."

I don't know what I'm doing, just that I have to run to the road. If James and Ella have been hurt, well, I can't think about what I'd do. I just want to be there. I run to the sidewalk and look out to the roadway. I don't see anything. I call James's number. No answer. I call again. He doesn't pick up. Another ambulance speeds by, rounding a corner ahead, where a palm tree's branches hang low over the road. The siren stops just beyond the corner. What if they're hurt? I swallow hard. What would I do? How would I go on? I walk fast and then pick up my pace to a sprint. What seemed like a few blocks turns out to be a mile, maybe more. I'm not a runner, so I feel winded and develop a side ache that slows me down to a walk. I double over in pain, then stand again, keeping on. I can make out the flashing lights now. I see police cars and two ambulances. It must be a bad wreck. I look overhead and see a medical helicopter circling. I haven't always been a praying sort of person, but I believe in God. I believe he listens, and I need him to listen now. *Dear Lord*, I pray aloud, *let them be safe. Let them be all right.*

I'm close enough to see the officers standing in front of the accident scene. I remember that our rental car is a blue sedan. So far, I just see a black Jeep. It's crunched, accordion-style. My God. I peer farther ahead and see a stretcher. A dark-haired child, a little girl, is being wheeled into an ambulance. I can't make out her face, but I see a fleck of pink. "Ella!" I scream. "Ella! Mommy's here!"

Another police car pulls up along the roadside, and an officer leaps out of his car and restrains me. "Ma'am," he says, "you'll have to stay back."

"But my daughter!" I cry. "She's my . . ." And then I see the minivan with a huge dent in the side. I see blood on the roadway. A man with a torn shirt is hovering over a woman who is screaming into the ambulance. "My baby!" she cries. "My baby!"

I step away. I feel scared and horrified but also relieved. My heart aches for this mother whose baby is fighting for life, and yet, mine is safely buckled in her car seat with her dad somewhere on the road ahead.

I hear my phone ringing in my bag. It's James. "Hi," I say, sighing.

"Where are you? I hear a lot of noise in the background."

"There was an accident," I say. "I thought it might be you, so I walked up to make sure. Oh, James, I was so scared."

"Honey, don't worry about us. We just got to the restaurant. Ella ordered mac and cheese."

"Mac and cheese," I say, the words instantly soothing me. "James, I thought—"

"Hey," he says. "Everything's fine, honey. Please, don't worry." I hear Ella making adorable noises in the background. I want to be there, sitting beside her. "I was thinking that after we're back from this trip, maybe you could take some time off, or at least talk to your editor about not taking on so many assignments." He pauses for a moment. "I mean, if you want. It's your decision, and I don't want to pressure you. It's just that, well, we miss you."

I take a deep breath, then exhale. I hear Ella giggling about something. "You're right," I say. And he is. Something has to change.

An hour has passed, maybe more. I've paddled across the lake and back, narrowly avoiding an incoming seaplane, and am now staring ahead to my houseboat and the adjoining dock. It's not one of the fancier docks, comparatively speaking. Most of the houseboats on the neighboring docks are newer, two stories, and generally less cobbled together than the ones on my dock. But there's something a little stiff and cold about the newer ones, with their elaborate architecture and pristine finishes.

I see Alex ahead. He's waving at me from his deck. I smile and paddle toward him.

"Hi," I say, handing him his vest. "Sorry if it's a little wet."

"I'm glad it served as a nice seat cushion," he says, grinning.

"Want to come in for a bit? I could offer you three-day-old takeout. I think there's some pad Thai somewhere in the fridge. We could scrape off the layer of mold."

"Sounds appetizing," I say, smiling again.

He helps me tie the kayak to the cleat, then offers his hand to help me out. I take it, just as I begin to lose my footing. He reaches for my waist and catches me before I fall backward into the lake.

"Sorry," I say as I steady myself on the deck. I unzip my life vest and survey my jeans. They're a little wet, but not soaked.

"Did you enjoy your three-hour tour?" he asks.

"Yeah. There are some ritzy houseboats out there. I was shocked. I saw one that looked like an Italian villa."

Alex nods. "The newer docks don't have the same character. They're McMansions on barges." He shrugs. "It just doesn't fit. This community was built by poor artists, bohemians. Fifty years ago, you could buy a houseboat for five hundred dollars. Nowadays, on most docks, you have to be a millionaire to move into the neighborhood. I don't know, somehow that just doesn't seem right."

I nod, admiring his idealism. I've read a bit about the history of the houseboat community myself and was surprised to learn that the neighborhood sprung up from such humble beginnings. In the late 1800s, for instance, Lake Union's "houseboats" were simply crudely built shacks on barges, inhabited by poor laborers, mostly loggers, and their families. There was even a saloon and adjoining brothel perched at the end of one of the docks. "How about you?" I say, suddenly curious about Alex's own history. "Have you always lived in Seattle?"

"No," he replies. "I grew up in Oregon, on a farm. My parents moved there when I was four."

"Wow. What did you grow?"

"Hops," he says. "For beer making."

I grin. "So your parents were fun loving, I take it?"

"Well, I guess you could say that." I imagine him in overalls, running through fields with vine-covered trellises. "How about you?"

"I grew up in Kansas City," I say, "in a quiet little neighborhood. Church every Sunday, you know."

"Do you still attend?"

"Church?"

Before the accident, we began going to church as a family, but now, well, I couldn't imagine a God who would take two beautiful lives in one fell swoop. "I used to pray," I continue, "but I'm not so sure what I believe anymore."

"I go to Saint Mark's," he says. "It's up on the hill. They have a wonderful choir. Sometimes I don't even listen to the sermon. I just sit in the pews and think. I guess it just feels good to *belong*, you know?"

"Yes." His words hit me on a deep level, maybe because I've been unattached for so long, floating aimlessly. I miss belonging.

"Anyway, if you'd ever want to," he says, "you're welcome to join me."

"Thanks, but I'm still ambivalent about church, God, about all of it." I nod toward his houseboat, changing the subject. "So what was it like when you bought it?"

"Pretty bad," he says. "It had been a rental for decades, and the last round of college students who lived here nearly destroyed it. Jim said they packed in one hundred people one night and it actually took on a foot of water."

"Wow," I say. "So you gutted it?"

"Pretty much." He gestures toward the door. "Come in. I'll give you the grand tour."

I follow him into a tidy living room. There's a beige sofa and coffee table facing a flat-screen TV and two matching armchairs. The air smells of fresh laundry. James used to do all of my laundry—fold it, too, making him the rarest man in America. I notice a laundry basket by the couch and a pair of boxer briefs on top and smile to myself.

"I redid every detail," he says. "The walls, the kitchen, the bathroom."

"The kitchen is gorgeous," I say, walking over to admire the solid wood cabinets and slab granite counters. They're nearly bare, but then I remember that Alex doesn't cook.

He shrugs. "I don't know why I bothered. I've never even used the stove."

"You're kidding."

"I'm not," he says.

I run my hand along the gas range and admire the elaborate range hood. I wonder if Kellie, his coauthor, ever cooked on this stove. I envision her standing in front of the stove on a lazy Saturday morning. She's wearing a red lace negligee, and one of the spaghetti straps falls down her shoulder as she drizzles syrup over buttermilk pancakes.

"Can I offer you something to drink? OJ, Pellegrino?" Alex asks, jarring me from the daydream.

"Water's fine."

He fills a glass and hands it to me. I like that he doesn't ask me too many questions about why I'm here. He's giving me space in a way that no one did in New York. And it makes me want to open up.

He gestures toward the couch, and we both sit down. He begins to speak at the same time I do, and we laugh.

"You go first," he says.

I nod. "Well, I was at Pete's the other day, and someone told me that there was a woman who lived in my houseboat years ago, and that she disappeared under mysterious circumstances. And then I—"

"Penny," Alex says, nodding.

I remember the hospital bracelet I found in the chest. "How do you know her name?"

"It's one of those unspoken agreements on Boat Street," he says. "Everyone knows, and yet no one ever discusses it."

"Why is that?"

He shrugs. "When I bought this place, the real estate agent mentioned the story, that some woman disappeared here in the 1950s. She said the bad memory has haunted the dock since, and that residents don't like to talk about that night."

"I wonder why."

"I don't know," he says. "But I've learned that it's best not to bring it up around the old-timers—Jim, too. It was a painful time for them, I think."

I nod. "Alex, I found something, in the houseboat."

His eyes widen.

"A chest," I continue. "I think it belonged to Penny."

"Really? How do you know?"

I tell him about the contents—the wedding dress, the dried flower, the memorabilia from a love story long past—and he nods. "I just keep thinking that there's a clue inside. If she disappeared, it had to be for a reason. Or, do you think she was . . . ?"

"I've wondered the same thing," he says. "Hey, we're a couple of journalists. If anyone could dig up the truth, it's us, right?"

I grin. "Except that I write about resort vacations and you photograph food."

Alex returns my smile. "Yes, there's that."

His phone rings in the kitchen. "Sorry," he says. "I'll be right back."

"Hello," he says, picking up the cordless on the wall. A moment later, he frowns, then presses the phone to his chest. "I'll just be a minute," he says.

I smile and pick up a book on the coffee table about sailboats. "No problem."

I flip through the pages of the book, but I can't help but overhear snippets of Alex's conversation in the back bedroom. "Are you serious? . . . Unless you've changed your mind. . . . Yes, you know that. . . . No! . . . Kellie, honestly, I'm not going to have this conversation for the one thousandth time. . . ."

*Kellie.* So my hunch was right. But why is she calling? Why does he sound so angry? I hardly recognize his voice, so bitter and defensive.

"Sorry," he says a moment later, setting the phone back on the wall. He sighs and takes a big drink of water. "Where were we?"

"Listen," I say, thinking of his past with the mysterious Kellie, a past that might not be resolved, and suddenly I feel tired. "That kayak trip exhausted me. I think I'll head back and take a nap this afternoon."

Alex looks momentarily wounded, but his smile returns. "OK. But promise you'll have dinner with me one night soon."

"I promise."

I secure the kayak to the cleat, then walk around to the front door. I reach into my pocket for the house key but instead find the hospital bracelet I displaced from the chest.

Darn. I've locked myself out. I think of paddling back over to Alex's, but then I notice Jim ahead. He's whistling a familiar tune and holding a bucket of paint. He appears to be touching up the trim on his parents' houseboat.

"Hi," I say, walking toward him.

"Morning," he replies. "I'm finally getting around to painting the house. Mom's been on my case."

"It looks nice," I say. "Hey, I seem to have locked myself out. You don't happen to have an extra key, do you?"

"No," he says, setting the bucket and brush down. He wipes a smudge of beige paint on his T-shirt. "But I know how you can get back in."

"You do? How?"

He winks. "Remember, I grew up on this dock."

I smile and we walk down the dock to my houseboat. Jim turns over an empty flowerpot and uses it as a stepstool to pull himself up to the roof. He climbs to the rooftop deck, reaches his hand through the open porthole window, then unlatches the door to the deck.

"There you go," he says. "I'll open the front door downstairs and meet you there."

I'm not sure how I feel about the ease with which he has just broken into my bedroom, but I'm also grateful not to have to call a locksmith. "Thanks," I say once I'm in the living room. "I take it you've done that a time or two?"

He grins, but seems distracted. "Wow," he says. "It always amazes me how little this place has changed over the years."

I'm not surprised, actually. The houseboat is charming in its simplicity. Fir floors. Whitewashed, wainscot walls. Sturdy, classic cabinets and finishes. "What was it like when you were a boy?"

"Well," he says, looking around, "the sofa was here, just as it is now. But there was art everywhere, really abstract pieces that looked strange to a boy of eight." He walks to the kitchen counter and eyes one of the barstools. "I used to sit here and watch her in the kitchen."

I reach into my pocket and feel the plastic bracelet between my fingers. "Penny?"

He looks as if he hasn't heard this name uttered in a very long time. It has power over him; I can tell.

"Can you tell me about her?" I ask gently.

He rubs his jaw, and it's obvious that what he's about to share may be hard for him. "I was just a boy when Penny came to live here," he says. "She was the young bride of Dexter Wentworth. The artist."

I point to the painting. "So he was the one who painted the ship?"

"Yes," he says. "He didn't deserve her."

"What do you mean?"

"Listen, from what I understand, he wasn't the best husband. She loved him, though. I used to like to sit out there in front of her deck and fish or just look at the boats. She was always baking. You'd walk in, and this place smelled just like vanilla cake. She'd always have a cookie or a muffin to offer. She was kind that way. Once I overheard her crying. I think she had a fight with Dexter. It made me so mad. Even then, I wanted to go in and punch that man in the face."

"He didn't love her?"

"Everyone loved Penny," he says. "Well, either they loved her or they were jealous of her." He shakes his head and his eyes narrow. "Mom was jealous of her. Penny was so beautiful. She didn't need makeup or a fancy hairstyle; she had a natural sort of beauty. But it was her kindness that I remember most." He smiles to himself. "I used to fantasize about her being my mother."

"Did she have children?"

"No," he says. "But she wanted them. Dexter had children from a previous marriage. They were estranged. I don't think he ever wanted to be a father again. Besides, he had his art. He was really in demand back then, had his paintings in galleries all over town, even in some Hollywood homes. I think Penny tried so hard to fit into Dexter's world, but she never could. She should have married someone like Collin, someone who would have worshipped her."

"Collin?"

He points to Alex's houseboat. "He lived there during the summer of fifty-nine."

"Jim, do you know what happened to Penny?"

His eyes fix straight ahead to the stove, as if he can see her there, inserting a toothpick into a cake. "I wish I knew," he says, standing up a little hurriedly. "Well, I'd better get back before the paint dries."

I sit down on the sofa and pull out my laptop. It's beginning to drizzle outside. Perfect writing weather. I think about what Jim said about Penny, about Dexter and the man named Collin. I wonder about them all. But mostly, I wonder if Penny was happy and if she felt loved. I key down to my cursor and recount the day I met James.

*Eleven years prior*

"You do know who that is, don't you?" My friend Jessica nudges me in the side. We're both editorial assistants at *Condé Nast Traveler*, and we've been sent to a briefing at the Waldorf sponsored by the Caribbean Tourism Board.

Jessica is the daughter of a Rockefeller, so she fell into the position, not that she didn't deserve it. She's whip-smart. Me, on the other hand? Just as smart, I guess, but I practically had to kill for an interview and only moved on to the second round because of my portfolio. The article in the *New York Times Magazine* helped—so did fetching coffee for the editor in chief of *Town & Country* for one torturous year. So when I look at Jessica, it's hard for me not to roll my eyes. "I don't know who you're talking about," I say, trying to take notes. Someone from the island of Saint Lucia is speaking. My goal is to take notes, get a few quotes, then head back to the office. I have a date with Ryan tonight. He's visiting from Duke, where he's getting his graduate degree in finance, and he's taking me to Jean Georges. I don't want to read into his intentions, but we've gotten serious this past year, and I can't help but think that a proposal is in the works. I feel giddy for a moment, to think that I could be Mrs. Ryan Wellington. His family has homes all over the country, and his parents travel by private jet. Theirs is an exciting, if not a little intimidating, lifestyle, but Ryan could be the son of a gas station attendant for all I care. It only matters that he loves me.

"James Santorini," Jessica whispers.

I give her an *I care because?* look, and she frowns. "He's a travel writer for the *New York Times*. He's a total catch."

I glance over at the dark-haired man Jessica is speaking of, just as he looks in our direction and smiles.

"See?" Jessica says a little too loudly. "He wants you to come over and say hello."

"Why don't you go over and say hello, seeing how I'm doing all the work here?"

She shrugs. "He's looking at you, not me."

❦

I'm able to leave work early enough to run home and change. I pick out a skirt and blouse, then toss them on my bed. This could be the night I'm proposed to. I will remember this moment for the rest of my life. I don't want to look at the photos and think, "Why did I wear *that*?" I have to look the part of Mrs. Ryan Wellington. I select a black shift dress and put it on, then fasten my grandmother's pearls around my neck before gazing at my reflection in the full-length mirror. Yes, just right.

I decide to burn through my last twenty and take a cab to the restaurant. It's raining lightly when I arrive, but I don't care. I'm beaming. This is the first night of the rest of my life. I feel it. I smooth a wisp of hair, then give my name to the hostess. I look around the dining room. Ryan isn't here yet. That's OK. I'll wait for him at the table.

"I'm sorry, miss," the tight-lipped hostess says. "There's no reservation under Wellington."

"That's strange," I say. "There must be some mistake. My boyfriend and I are having dinner here tonight. His name is Ryan Wellington."

She stares at me, emotionless.

"Maybe he made the reservation in my name. Ada Miller."

She scans her clipboard, then shakes her head. "Nothing for Miller either."

"Oh," I say, glancing back at the door. Ryan will show up soon and sort this all out. He always does.

"What would you like to do, miss?" the woman asks. She sounds a little impatient. "I can put you on the list, but we're booked until nine thirty." I glance at my watch. It's only six. "Or I can seat you at the bar. I think there are a couple of spots left at the counter."

I'm disappointed. It isn't exactly how I've envisioned my marriage proposal happening. But what does it matter? It will be just as joyous a moment at the bar as it would at a table with a pressed white tablecloth. "Yes," I finally say. "That'll be fine."

She escorts me to the bar, and I sit on an uncomfortable stool. I feel like my dress is too short, so I tug at the hemline to pull it lower on my legs. I order a glass of white wine and look down to the end of the bar, where I suddenly see the guy Jessica was making a fuss over at the briefing today. James, I think his name was, from the *New York Times*. He must recognize me, because he smiles and lifts his glass at me. I nod and quickly turn back to my wine. I sip slowly, but a half hour passes, and then an hour. When the bartender asks if I'd like a refill, I nod and check my cell phone for the ninth time to see if I've missed a call from Ryan. I haven't. I decide to call him, but the phone just rings five times and clicks over to voice mail. "Hi," I say flatly. "I've been sitting here for an hour. Where are you? I miss you. I thought we were having dinner tonight. Anyway, I'm at Jean Georges. I love you."

I hang up the phone just as Ryan appears at the entrance to the restaurant. He's wearing a heavy overcoat. I watch as the hostess points to his jacket, offering to check it, but he shakes his head. I wave to him from the bar, and he walks over to me.

"Hi," I say, kissing him. His face is unshaven and he's wearing jeans. I would have expected him to dress up a little, but all that matters is that he's here. I pat the barstool next to me. "Somehow they didn't have our reservation," I say. "But that's OK. It's actually kind of cozy up here."

Ryan doesn't sit down; instead he rubs his forehead nervously.

He looks awful. Something's happened; I can see it in his eyes. There's been a tragedy in his family, maybe. His father's plane— did it go down? "What is it? What's wrong?"

"Look, Ada," he says. "Shoot, I don't know how to say this."

That pesky guy from the *New York Times* is looking at me again. I try to ignore him. "What is it?" I say. "Honey, you can tell me anything."

"That's what I love about you, you know?" he says. "You're such a good person. It's just that I—"

I lean back. *No, this is not happening. Is this really happening?*

"I just see our lives going in two different directions," he says.

"Oh." I feel like I've been hit with a Taser. I am stunned, in every way possible. "You're breaking up with me." I have to say the words to make sure that this is real and that I'm not imagining it.

"You don't hate me, do you?"

"No," I say robotically. "No, Ryan. I could never hate you."

"Good," he says, the smile returning to his face. He picks up my wineglass and takes a big gulp. "I have to go."

I nod. "Yes."

"Keep in touch?"

I fake a smile. "Always."

And then he is gone. I bury my face in my hands. I don't know how much time passes, but at some point, the bartender taps me on the shoulder. "Miss," he says, "the gentleman at the end of the bar sent over this bottle for you." It's white, something French. I don't know what to say, so I glance down toward the end of the bar, but he's gone.

"Looking for me?" a man says from behind me.

I turn around, and there he is, holding two empty wineglasses. He points to the barstool next to me. "May I?"

I think back to that night, and I write exactly what happened. How James made me laugh until my sides hurt. How we stayed out until two talking at a greasy spoon diner. How I came to realize that some of life's most beautiful things grow out of the darkest moments.

# Chapter 11

PENNY

Dex is coming home today, and my heart skips with anticipation. I've dusted the living room and changed the bed linens. On the walk home from Pete's Market, I stopped and picked sweet peas on the roadside, and now they wait attentively in a crystal vase we received as a wedding present from one of Dex's society friends. I reapply my lipstick before checking the cinnamon rolls in the oven. He told me once how much he loves them, that his beloved nanny used to make them for him when he was a boy. I wish he would talk about his past more, but when I ask questions, it only makes him cagey and uncomfortable. I know little of his formative years, only that his father, a wealthy shipping magnate, ruled the home like a dictator, and his mother died when he was young. He experienced so little joy as a child, and I want so desperately to make him happy now.

I slip my hands into a pair of oven mitts and pull the cinnamon rolls out of the oven. I let them cool for fifteen minutes before inching each out onto a platter. I drizzle them with icing, then turn to

my notebook of recipes and open a new page. I've made these from
memory so often, I've decided it's time to write the recipe down:

## Cinnamon Rolls (Dex's Favorite)

*Makes 1 dozen*

### Ingredients

¾ cup milk
¼ cup butter, softened
3 ¼ cups all-purpose flour
¼ cup white sugar
1 package yeast
½ teaspoon salt
1 egg
¼ cup water

### For filling

1 cup brown sugar, packed
1 tablespoon ground cinnamon
½ cup butter, softened

### Preparation

1. Heat the milk in a small saucepan until it bubbles, then
remove from stove. Mix in butter; stir until melted. Let cool slightly.

2. In a large mixing bowl, combine 2 ¼ cups flour, sugar, yeast,
and the salt; mix well. Add egg, water, and the milk-butter mixture;
beat well. Add the remaining flour, ½ cup at a time. Knead dough
until smooth. About five minutes.

3. Let dough rise for about an hour or more. Meanwhile, in a small bowl, mix together brown sugar, cinnamon, and softened butter for filling.

4. Preheat oven to 375 degrees. Punch down dough, then roll out into a 12×9-inch rectangle. Spread filling mixture on dough. Roll up and pinch seam to seal. Cut into 12 equal-size pieces and place in a greased 9×12 glass dish. Cover and let rise until doubled, about an hour.

5. Bake for 20 minutes, or until golden brown. Let cool, then drizzle with royal icing if desired.

❦

I make a little heart beside the recipe, then close the book, just as I hear Dex's key in the door. He tosses his gray hat on the davenport, and I run to him. "Oh, honey, I've missed you so much!" I cry.

He kisses me and then carries me upstairs the way he used to, and I think for the first time in a long while that everything is going to be all right.

❦

Dex reaches for my hand, but I stand up and dress. "I have a surprise for you," I say.

"Another?" he says, grinning.

"Come downstairs," I say, fastening the buttons on my dress.

He sits up and reaches for his pants on the chair, then follows me down the stairs to the kitchen. I put a cinnamon roll on a plate and hand it to him, smiling.

He shakes his head. "I already had breakfast."

"Oh," I say, wounded. "I thought you liked my cinnamon rolls."

"I do. It's just that I already had a huge omelet at Gill's."

My heart sinks. He used to take me to Gill's. Now he goes alone. I nod and walk out to the deck.

"Penn," he calls after me. "What is it?"

It's so many things. His absence. His distance. The way my heart longs for a baby. But I don't say anything. Instead, I try to smile like the wife I know he wants me to be.

"I feel awful," he says, leaning against the doorway. He's so incredibly handsome with that dark hair, those eyes. "But I have to go back to the studio today."

"Why?" I protest. "But you just came home."

"I know." He looks guilty, conflicted. "But I'm so close to completing the painting. It's being installed next Tuesday. I can't afford to be late this time. It's for the Duboises."

I know who they are. I know that they are very rich and that Mrs. Dubois has taken a liking to Dex, the way all of his female patrons seem to do. I saw the way she smiled at him at the theater last spring. It was intermission, and she wore a peach dress with a sweetheart neckline. She batted her eyelashes at Dex between sips of champagne.

"Yes," I say, emotionless, looking ahead.

"Don't be like that, Penn," Dex says. He reaches into the pocket of his pants and pulls out a small white envelope. "Take it," he says. "It's a surprise. For you."

I bite my lip as I turn the envelope over in my hand, lifting the flap reluctantly. I pull out two pieces of cardstock. Tickets. I squint, and see the words *Frank Sinatra* printed on the front. I smile. "Really, Dex?"

"I know how you've always wanted to see him in concert," he says, kneeling beside me. "I thought we could go together. He's coming next week, to the Fifth Avenue Theatre."

I'm crying now, and he's smiling because he thinks they're tears of happiness. But they're not. These tickets are not a gift. I know that. They're a consolation prize.

He kisses my forehead and walks back inside to gather his things before closing the door softly behind him and heading back to his private world away from me.

The cinnamon rolls sit untouched on the counter.

# Chapter 12

ADA

So," Joanie says, the next day on the phone. "How's life on the lake?"

I think of Jim and what he told me about Penny yesterday. He didn't give me any particulars, but I sensed the sadness associated with the subject. I decide that I won't ask him what happened. Her memory is very personal to him; I can tell.

"I'm making my way," I say. "But there's something I'm trying to figure out."

"Oh?"

Joanie works in human resources for the NYPD, and she can find anything out about anyone, a skill that has come in handy over the years. On behalf of a reporter friend, I once asked for her help digging up some dirt about the shady owner of an art gallery in Brooklyn, and her sleuthing led to the discovery of a stolen Picasso in the basement a month later. Joanie and I took Ella to see the painting hanging in the Met the next month, and we both felt a wonderful sense of justice seeing the result of our teamwork.

"Well," I say, "I found something in the houseboat."

"What?"

"There's this old chest. It was locked, but I found a key, and I—"

"Discovered a chest full of gold coins?"

"Not quite," I say, smiling. "But it's kind of fascinating in and of itself." I tell her about the hospital bracelet, the photos, the book, the wedding dress and other relics.

"Kind of creepy," she says.

"There's more," I continue. "This woman, who I assume the items belong to, well, she disappeared years ago. No one here will talk about what happened to her. And I can't figure out if it's because they don't know, or they don't want to tell."

"So you want me to do a little digging. What was her name?"

"Penny. Penny Wentworth."

"OK," Joanie says. "I'll see what I can do. Check your e-mail a little later. I'll send what I can find on my lunch hour."

I set the phone down and step outside when I hear commotion on the dock. A splash in the water. Footsteps. Someone shouting. Jim's standing at the edge of the dock, rubbing his forehead.

"Is everything all right?" I ask.

He shakes his head. "She came home, and then she left again. Just like that."

I see Haines by his side, and I realize he's talking about the duck.

"Henrietta?"

Jim nods gravely.

"Oh no."

"These two," he says, looking down at the stoic mallard. "They need a marriage counselor."

I grin, just as Alex appears on his deck. I wave.

"Hi," he says.

"Hey, happy birthday," Jim says.

"Thanks."

"Happy birthday," I say quickly. "What are you doing to celebrate?"

"Absolutely nothing," he replies, looking to the north lake. "I may paddle up to Gas Works later."

"Oh, the park?" I've been fascinated by the green grassy hill since the morning after I arrived. Its rusted-out industrial remains of old Seattle look almost sculptural in the distance.

"Yeah," he says, adjusting his sunglasses. "You could join me—I mean, if you're not doing anything."

I sense Jim's eyes on me. I know he's smiling, but I don't make eye contact.

"That would be nice," I say.

"Jim," Alex says politely, "care to join?"

"Nah. You two go ahead." He's still smiling.

"I'll go grab my sweater," I say.

❦

Alex paddles over in front of my houseboat a moment later, and I climb into the back of the kayak. "Here," he says, handing me a paddle. "I brought some sandwiches." He gestures toward the middle section of the kayak.

My cheeks flush suddenly when I think of where I am. In Seattle. Off to a picnic with a man I've just met days ago.

"So, how old are you today?" I ask.

"Thirty-seven."

"An old man."

"I know." Our paddles touch for a moment. It's the nautical equivalent of stepping on someone's foot on the dance floor. "Sorry," we both say in unison.

I realize how rusty I am at all of this, and maybe he is too. I think of his ex. Kellie. And I think of James. Their memories hover in the kayak with us, like ghosts.

We make it across the lake and tie the kayak to a dock that leads into the park. Alex steps out first and offers me his hand. He collects the bag of food and a blanket, and we climb up the grassy hill dotted with tiny white flowers. It's sunny, and there's a light breeze. Four children are flying kites along the hillside.

"How's this?" he asks when we reach a place where the roundness levels. I can see the dock in the distance, my little houseboat perched at the tip.

"Perfect," I say, peeling off my sweater. Despite the breeze, the sun is warm, and I've worked up a sweat.

Alex lays out the blanket, and we both sit down. He offers me a turkey sandwich and opens a plastic container of sliced apples and strawberries.

"I haven't been on a picnic in a really long time," I say. "Not since—"

"Since before the accident?" Alex isn't intimidated by my past; I can tell. It's rare, actually. The few times I've talked to men about what happened, they've clammed up, changed the subject.

I nod.

"Well," he says, "I'm glad I could reintroduce you to the joys of picnicking."

I smile and take a bite of my sandwich. "You actually made these?"

"No," he says. "Picked them up this morning at Pete's."

I grin, looking out at the Space Needle in the distance.

He follows my gaze. "I'd love to take you there," he says. "You haven't lived until you've had an ice cream sundae on top of the Needle."

"Oh, is that right?"

He finishes his sandwich, then rolls to his side, propping himself up on his elbow. "They call it the Lunar Orbiter," he says. "Ice cream on top of a bed of dry ice, drizzled with loads of chocolate sauce."

"OK," I say. "You had me at chocolate sauce."

"It's the only item on the original Space Needle menu from the 1962 World's Fair."

"I've always wanted to see the Space Needle," I say. "My dad went to the World's Fair as a kid. He still talks about the Space Needle like it's the Eiffel Tower.

"Hey," I say, setting my sandwich down. "I asked my sister-in-law to see what she can dig up about our little unsolved mystery."

Alex looks up. "You did?"

"She works for the NYPD. She can find out anything about anyone."

He nods. "They're all good people in their own ways, truly. But I've long suspected that the residents of Boat Street are practiced in the art of concealment." He takes a drink from his water bottle, then turns back to me. "After you left yesterday, I remembered something."

"What?"

"Tom, who lived on Boat Street and knew Penny, took me into his confidence the month before he died. He said they'd all been in on a 'pact.'"

"A pact?"

He nods. "I didn't think much of it at the time," he continues. "Tom wasn't in good health at the end but spoke as if he wanted to get something off his chest. Before I could ask him anything further, his nurse interrupted us. I never did get a chance to learn what he meant by that. I can only assume it had something to do with Penny."

I think of the others on the dock. Most are relative newcomers, having arrived during the past fifteen years. And at least two houseboats have been empty for some time, only rented out occasionally. Then I think of Jim's parents. "What about Naomi and Gene?"

"It's a touchy subject," he says. "Jim's awfully protective of them. None of them like to discuss the past, so I don't."

"Well," I say, "we'll see what Joanie comes back with."

Alex shrugs. "If there was any foul play, it would have come out."

"But it was the fifties, don't forget," I add. "They didn't have DNA testing or computers or any sophisticated crime analysis."

Alex nods. "I've thought a lot about Penny over the years, and I have to say, your discovery of the chest makes this all a little more eerie."

The air feels suddenly cooler, and then I notice that the sun has dipped behind a cloud. A little boy on the hill has fallen and scraped his knee. His mother runs to him and pulls out a bandage from her purse. I think of Alex's past. A war photographer. I wonder about the atrocities he must have seen.

"What was it like?" I ask him suddenly. "In Sudan?"

He doesn't respond right away, and at first I worry that I've offended him. What if this is a taboo subject? He clasps his hands together, and I think about apologizing, asking a different question, but then he finally opens his mouth to speak. "It was raw," he says. "My brain was imprinted with images I'll never be able to get out of my head. Mothers being separated from their babies. Death. Destruction. Humans being slaughtered. I saw just how ugly the human spirit can get and also how beautiful it can be." We watch as the little boy with the skinned knee embraces his mother. "There weren't a lot of happy endings over there. And it still kills me that I couldn't save those people. I couldn't do anything but capture them on my camera. The only thing that kept me going was knowing that no matter what happened after I left, they wouldn't be forgotten. I vowed to preserve the memory of their plight."

I remember seeing the framed covers of *Time* and *Newsweek* on his wall. "You were so good at what you did," I say.

He takes a deep breath. "No one can do that kind of work forever. But a piece of my heart"—he pats his chest—"will always be with those people."

"Was it hard adjusting back to American life after being in a war zone?"

He nods vacantly but doesn't elaborate. I wonder what he must have endured.

I feel a raindrop on my cheek. "What? Rain?"

"That's Seattle for you," he says, the smile returning to his face. "Rain always sneaks up on you." He stands up and I follow. "Better get back before we're drenched."

Dark clouds are rolling in all around, and the rain's intensity increases as we paddle back across the lake, which looks like wrinkled gray velvet. By the time we reach my dock, we're soaked, but somehow, I don't mind.

"Door-to-door service," Alex quips, as he parks the kayak in front of my deck. I feel a little disappointed that our excursion is over. I think about inviting him in. But just as I open my mouth, I notice a figure standing on Alex's deck. A woman. She's huddled under an umbrella and she's holding two blue balloons. Of course, his birthday. She looks familiar for some reason, and then I realize where I've seen her. The cookbook. His coauthor. His ex. *Kellie.*

He notices her presence just as I do, and an uncomfortable silence falls over us.

"I'd better—"

"Well—"

We both talk over each other, then smile. "Thank you," I finally say. "For letting me share your birthday with you. I had a wonderful time."

"Me, too," he says before glancing back to his deck. She stares at us but doesn't smile.

"Well," I say, climbing out of the kayak, "I'd better let you go. You have a guest."

"I, well," Alex fumbles. "Yes. I'll see you around."

"I'll see you around."

❧

Inside, I peel off my wet clothes and take a warm shower, then put on a sweater and leggings and reach for my phone.

"Joanie?"

"Hi, honey—everything OK?"

"Yes, yes, fine," I say. "I, well . . ."

"What is it? You're nervous about something."

"I've been keeping something from you," I say. "I met someone."

"Ada, really?"

"Yes, and he's wonderful. His name is Alex, and he lives in a houseboat across the dock."

"Is he cute?"

"Um, yes!"

She squeals across the line, and I have to pull the phone away from my ear momentarily.

"What does he do?"

"He's a photographer," I say. "He was a war photographer for years, but now he specializes in food photos, for cookbooks."

"He was a *war* photographer?"

"Yeah, in Sudan."

"Oh," she says.

"What's wrong?"

"Nothing. I'm sure it's no big deal."

"You're sure *what's* no big deal?"

"Oh, I'm thinking of a specific situation, one probably not relevant to you, but, OK, I'll share: A girl in our department dated a foreign correspondent for *U.S. News & World Report*. He was in Somalia. Anyway, he came home with a terrible case of post-traumatic stress disorder and almost killed her."

"You are adorable for your concern, but Alex does not have post-traumatic stress disorder. Besides, he's been home for years now." I feel the familiar worry tugging at the back of my mind, partly because Alex seems too perfect, and also because I don't know the full extent of his story. His grief. Kellie. All of it. But I extinguish my uneasiness.

"Well," she says, "just be careful, you. Take it slow. This is your first relationship after James."

Her words sting a little, and I suddenly fear I'm betraying James's memory, betraying our love.

"I know," I say. "But Joanie, I haven't felt this way about a man since I met James. That has to be a good sign, doesn't it?"

"Yes," she says. "It is. And I'm happy for you. I just want everything to go perfectly. I don't want you to experience any more hurt."

What I want to tell her is that my heart has already been pushed to the most painful place possible, the brink of no return, and I've survived. There's strength in that. But I can't find the words to explain how I feel, so I simply agree with her. "I know," I say. "And I love you."

"I love you too."

I hang up and reach for my laptop. I type "Penny Wentworth" into Google and wait expectantly.

# Chapter 13

PENNY

"Hello?" I say into the phone, trying my best to mask my sadness.

"Penny?" It's Mama, and she sounds concerned.

"Hi, Mama," I say as cheerfully as I can.

"You've been crying, haven't you?"

I dab a handkerchief to my eyes and shake my head. "Of course not; I'm just a little stuffed up today," I lie. "I must be coming down with a cold."

"Well," she continues, "I do hope you're taking care of yourself. You know, Caroline's daughter Mary took sick in her first trimester and lost the baby."

"Mama, I'm not pregnant," I say.

"But you may be, soon."

Her words reverberate in my ear. They taunt me like the schoolchildren who used to make fun of my pigtails on the playground. "Mama, I've been married for three years—don't you think it would happen by now, if it was going to happen?"

"Honey, we can plan and wish and hope all we like, but sometimes these things just take paths all their own," she says. "Remember how I got you?"

Mama had me when she was seventeen. I never knew my father, just that he was a navy sailor who was deployed shortly after they met, and he died at sea not long after. She's never said if they were married, and I've never asked. And yet, it doesn't matter. Mama loved him so much that no other man can replace him. I imagine I would have loved him too. I've concocted quite a picture of the father I never knew—his warm smile, broad shoulders, and strong hands. And I can never look out at open water without wondering about him.

You'd think I would hate the sea because its waters took my father from me, but I don't. It intrigues me, even calls to me, somehow. Every day after school, I'd take the long way home just so I could look out from the top of the hillside to the Puget Sound. I'd watch the seagulls fly overhead, swooping down and calling to me, as if daring me to follow them. Sometimes I'd find a spot on the hill a mile from my house and gaze at the frothy waves crashing onto the shore and imagine what it might feel like to sail away, beyond the horizon. Mama said I was her water baby, though she never uttered those words in the presence of others. She didn't trust the water, for either of us. She refused to teach me to swim, and yet she accepted my love of the shore, as long as I kept it at an arm's length.

"You're right," I say as a passing boat sounds its horn outside.

"You're not still going out in the canoe alone, are you?" Mama asks.

Although she loves Dex down to the very last fiber of his being, she doesn't like that he lives on a houseboat. She would never admit that her fear of water is the sole reason that I can't swim. When we were married, she pleaded with Dex to move back to his house on Queen Anne Hill. But he'd rented it out, and besides, when Dex makes up his mind, there's no changing it.

"I wear a life vest whenever I go out in the boat, Mama," I say. "You don't need to worry about me, you know."

"It's a mother's job to worry about her child."

I pull back the curtain beside the living room window and see Jimmy outside, sitting on the back deck reading a comic book, his chin propped in his hand. I wonder if Naomi worries about him. I wonder if her love for her child is just as strong as Mama's. I close the curtain quickly, before Jimmy can see me.

I wrap four cinnamon rolls in waxed paper and tuck them in a sack before walking out to the canoe. I paddle across the little channel between Collin's dock and mine. He's working on the boat, and his back is turned to me, but he looks up when he hears the canoe slide against the dock.

"Oh, hi," he says, grinning. He wipes a bead of sweat from his brow.

"Hello," I reply, holding up the sack of cinnamon rolls. "Just making good on my promise."

He walks toward me and takes the bag in his hands, then unwraps one. "Cinnamon rolls?"

"Yeah," I say, smiling as I reach for an oar. "Well, I'd better be getting back. I hope you enjoy them."

"Wait," he says. "You won't stay? Just for a bit?"

I look over my shoulder self-consciously. I don't know why. Dex isn't there. And what do I care what Naomi thinks, or anyone else on the dock, for that matter? "Yes," I finally say. "I guess I could stay for a moment."

I tie the canoe to a cleat, and Collin takes my hand to help me out. He points to the sailboat. "Come sit on the boat with me."

My eyes widen. "Really?"

He nods. "I'd love to show it to you."

I climb into the boat after Collin and sit beside him on a wooden bench seat. "She has a long way to go," he says. "But I think she's coming along quite well."

"You've done a beautiful job," I say, running my hand along the smoothly sanded railing.

He takes a bite of the cinnamon roll in his hand, and I wonder how long it takes to complete a boat. Another month? Another year?

"She should be all ready by the end of summer," he says as if reading my mind.

I realize how lonely the dock will feel without Collin there, without the sailboat bobbing on the water. "I suppose you'll be leaving then," I say, without looking at him.

"Yes," he says. "I'll sail her to San Francisco. My client will take her from there."

"Does it make you sad?" I ask, admiring the woodworking on the bow, where planks are forged together so they look almost seamless. "It must be like giving a baby up for adoption."

He looks at me for a long moment, and I see a familiar glint in his eyes. Sadness? Regret? I'm not sure. "It is," he finally says. "But I try not to get too attached. It's always hard, but it's better that way, knowing that there's an end."

I nod and look away.

"Hey," he says. "I was thinking of taking her out today. "Would you like to join me?"

I shake my head. "No, I couldn't."

"Why not?"

"Well," I say, "I—"

"See? You have no excuses." He stands up and begins to untie the sails. "We're going sailing."

He adjusts the rigging and then motors the boat toward the lake. At their full height, the sails look majestic, and I watch in awe as he maneuvers the boat with such precision.

When we're at the center of the lake, he turns to me and says, "Want to take the reins?"

I shake my head quickly. "No. I don't know what I'm doing."

"I'll teach you," he says, grinning. "It's really easy."

"OK," I say, stepping toward him timidly.

He takes my hand and places it on a long wooden shaft. "This is the tiller," he says, keeping his hand firmly over mine. "It steers the boat."

He steps back and smiles at me. "It's the best feeling in the world, isn't it?"

"Yes," I say. The wind is having its way with my hair, but I don't care. I don't have a care in the world right now. I feel exhilarated and unhinged.

"Where should we go?" Collin asks me. There's a sparkle in his eyes, and I think there's a sparkle in my eyes too. I feel it. I feel *alive*.

"Let's sail to the Caribbean," I say suddenly.

Collin nods playfully. "The lady wants to sail to the Caribbean, so to the Caribbean we shall sail."

"What if we get shipwrecked?" I ask.

"And wash up on a deserted island?" Collin adds.

I nod. "I can't swim."

"I can," he says, taking the tiller in his hand again. "We'll be fine. Besides, we have these cinnamon rolls to sustain us."

I sit down on the bench beside him.

"What does your husband do for a living?" he asks suddenly.

"He's an artist," I say, feeling tense at the mention of Dex. "A painter."

"Oh," he replies.

"Does that *surprise* you?"

"Well," he says, rubbing his chin, "I just assumed he was in business. Seemed like the only reason to explain why he's gone so often."

"Dex is an important artist," I say, a little more defensively than I intended. "He has a studio downtown. He works very hard."

"Listen," he says, smiling. "I'm sorry. I didn't mean to sound critical, it's just—"

I cross my arms. "It's just *what*?" Mentally, I run through my list of deepest fears: That we're not well suited? That he's so much more sophisticated than I?

Collin shrugs. "What I mean . . ." His voice trails off. "How can I say this best?" He pauses for a moment. "OK, I'll just say it." He takes a deep breath. "If I had a wife like you, I wouldn't ever want to leave."

I feel my cheeks redden. "Oh. Well, thank you, I guess." I retie my scarf, then turn back to him. "You know what this boat needs?" I ask, changing the subject.

"What?"

"Cushions."

"It does," he agrees. "Next time we go out, I'll bring some pillows from the sofa."

"No," I say. "I was thinking that I could make them. There are some foam blocks in the closet, some fabric, too. I'm not sure what the materials are for, but they've been there forever. If the stash is not completely moth-eaten, I can sew some cushions."

Collin shakes his head. "I couldn't ask you to do that."

I want to tell him that I fear I may go crazy in that little house-boat all by myself day after day without a purpose, without a project. "I want to," I say.

"Well, if you can sew as well as you can bake," he replies, "then I can't refuse."

I smile, and walk toward the front of the boat. I feel Collin's eyes on me as I duck under the sails to the starboard side, but I misjudge the distance between the deck and the sail, and my head hits the heavy wooden section at the bottom of the sail. At first my vision blurs. All I feel is a dull ache, and then I lose my balance and everything goes dark.

# Chapter 14

ADA

Alex meets me in front of my houseboat at five. "I'm taking you to dinner," he says.

I look down at my outfit: leggings and a thin sweater, hardly dinner attire—certainly nothing I'd wear to a restaurant in New York. "Let me go change."

"No," he says, smiling. "You look perfect just as you are. After all, this is Seattle. People wear jeans and fleece to the fanciest places."

I grin. "All right, let me get my purse." I run into the house, pull my hair into a ponytail, and swipe on some lip gloss, then grab my purse before returning to the dock.

Alex offers me his arm, and we walk up the dock to the street above the lake. "Serafina is just up the hill," he says. "If you don't mind a little hike."

"Fine with me," I say. "I walked everywhere in New York. I'm used to it."

The little restaurant is nestled alongside Eastlake Avenue, and Alex holds the door open for me as soft jazz drifts out to the street.

A three-piece band sits on a tiny stage in the dining room, and the saxophonist winks at me as the hostess makes her way over to greet us.

"Two for dinner," Alex says.

The hostess smiles and shows us to a table by the window. I look around the dining room, and I can see that Alex is right. A couple leans over a tiny table across the room. He's wearing cargo shorts and sandals, and her denim skirt is frayed at the edge. It's not New York, but I can see how I could come to appreciate this lack of pretense.

"The gnocchi is amazing here," he says. "Same with the eggplant, and the pumpkin ravioli. Basically the whole menu."

I smile. "I love rustic Italian. My husband came from a big Italian food family." I watch Alex's face carefully for any signs that he may be put off by the subject, but instead he leans in closer with interest.

"I bet he had one of those amazing Italian grandmothers whose kitchen always smells like garlic and basil and tomatoes simmering."

"Yeah," I say. "His nonna." The waitress deposits a glass of Chianti before me, and I take a sip, marveling that I don't feel the least bit uncomfortable talking about James with Alex.

"How about you?" I ask. "Did you grow up in a food family?"

"No—that is, if you don't mean Twinkies and bologna sandwiches."

"Me, too," I say. "Children of the eighties. It's no wonder we all haven't come down with cancer by now." I grin at him from across the table. "So what do your parents think of your new career photographing food?"

His expression changes then. It's less engaged and more closed off. "It's a long story," he says, before taking a sip of his sparkling water. "I—"

"It's OK," I say. I respect his privacy, just as he respects mine. We'll share our pasts when we're ready. And now may not be the time.

The waitress brings over an antipasto plate, and I pop a kalamata olive in my mouth. Its deep, sharp flavor lures me back to Sunday morning brunch in Nonna Santorini's warm New York City kitchen.

*Ten years prior*

Nonna Santorini places a bowl of steaming hot pasta in front of me. The noodles are handmade; so is the sauce. She uses only San Marzano tomatoes, grown in the terra-cotta pots on her balcony. She cans them each fall to have enough for sauces through the rest of the year. "You like Parmigiano-Reggiano?" she asks, wielding a block of white cheese and a grater.

"Yes, please," I say.

James winks at me and refills my wineglass.

"We must fatten her up if she make you baby," Nonna says to James.

My cheeks redden.

"You hear that, Ada?" James says, elbowing me lightly. "Nonna wants great-grandchildren."

I smile and take a bite. It's my first time meeting James's grandmother, and I instantly love her. She's short and stout and beautiful. Her silky gray hair is pulled back into a bun, and she wears a white apron around her waist. Everything about her is warm. Her kitchen. Her smile. Her embrace. Her heart. I decide that when I'm seventy-five years old, I want to be exactly like her.

"Do you like the food?" she asks, pushing the pasta bowl closer to me. "Have more!"

"Thank you," I say. "I will."

"James, dear," she says. "Go out to the fire escape and get a log to add to the fire."

He sets his napkin on the table and stands up obediently.

"You want babies?" Nonna asks after James has left the room.

"Yes," I say, a little startled. "At least I think so."

"Good," she says, pleased. "You make happy babies."

My cheeks redden, and I can't tell if it's just from the wine or the fact that I'm talking to my boyfriend's grandmother about, well, sex.

"He loves you," Nonna continues, smiling to herself. "The way he looks at you. There is much love in his eyes." She kisses the gold locket around her neck. "So much love."

"You OK?" Alex asks.

"Yes," I say, nodding quickly. "Sorry. I was just thinking . . . it's just that this restaurant reminds me of . . ."

"Memories," he says.

I nod.

The band begins playing a soft melody. It's something by Stan Getz, but I can't remember the name of the song. I look at Alex sitting across the table, so kind, so gentle. I want to tell him, now. I want to tell him everything.

But just as I open my mouth, he does too.

"I have to tell you something," he says. "About me."

And instead of speaking, I listen.

# Chapter 15

PENNY

I hear a beeping sound as I open my eyes. Where am I? I look up and see white walls. Everything's white. A woman in a white dress, a nurse, hovers over me. "Morning, sugar," she says, taking my wrist to check my pulse. "My, your husband will be happy to see you. We were worried there for a sec. I'll just go get him."

Is Dex here? I imagine how frightened he must have been to see me in this hospital bed. My eyes fill with tears. What happened? My head hurts; I reach my hand up to my temple and there's a bandage.

The door opens and the nurse walks through the door again, this time with *Collin*.

"Darling!" he says, rushing to my side.

"I don't understand," I say. "I thought—"

"I thought I lost you," he says, kissing my forehead. His face says "Play along," so I do.

"Doctor Hanson is on his way in to see you," the nurse chirps. "So sit tight with your husband now."

I nod as she walks through the door. "What happened? Why does she think you're my husband?"

"When I brought you here last night, they just assumed," he says. "And then I realized that they don't let anyone but family into this wing, so I had to lie."

"Where's Dexter?" I ask.

"I don't know." He looks uncomfortable, and it's obvious he's keeping information from me.

"What do you mean, you don't know?"

"Well, I went to find him. In Pioneer Square." He rubs his forehead. "He wasn't there, Penny."

"I don't understand," I say. "Maybe he just stepped out. He's probably with a client, or maybe he came home. Did you check the houseboat? Surely he's there."

Collin sees that I'm getting upset. He squeezes my hand. "I'm sure I just missed him," he says. "I'm sure once he finds out what happened, he'll be here as soon as possible."

I nod. "Am I going to be OK?"

"Yes," he says quickly. "You hit your head pretty bad, though. You almost drowned. They wanted to keep you for observation."

"And you saved me?"

"Well, that was the easy part," he says with a slow smile.

I hear the door open again, and this time a man in a white jacket appears. "Mrs. Wentworth, I'm Doctor Hanson," he says. "You got a pretty bad bump on the head."

"I hope nothing permanent," I say.

"Well, no," he replies. "But you may have some memory problems in the next week or so." He looks down at a clipboard and scribbles something down before handing Collin a piece of paper. "I've prescribed pain pills. She'll need them for the next few days."

He nods, and tucks the paper in his pocket.

The doctor smiles. "Mr. Wentworth, I must say, when I saw your wife's name on the list of patients, I hoped to have the chance to meet you. My wife's such a fan. We have one of your paintings hanging in our living room."

"Oh, I—" Collin fumbles.

"This is not Dexter," I finally say.

Dr. Hanson shakes his head in confusion. "I don't understand. The nurse said he—"

"His name is Collin," I say. "He's a *friend*."

"Oh, right," Dr. Hanson replies. "I see."

The door closes before I can say anything else. "He's judging me," I say. "He thinks—"

"Who cares what he thinks?" Collin says with a smile.

There's a knock at the door, and I smile when I see Mama standing there. "Darling!" she cries. "I came as soon as I could."

"Oh, Mama," I cry. "Please don't worry. I'm fine."

She dabs a handkerchief to her eye, then looks up at Collin. "Who's this?"

"This is my friend, Collin. He saved my life."

Mama kisses his cheek. "Thank you, dear," she says, before turning back to me. "Where's Dex?"

"I don't know. Collin tried to find him. He wasn't in his studio."

Collin clears his throat and walks closer to my bed. He adjusts the cord of my IV, which has gotten caught on the bed rail. "She's had a concussion," he explains to Mama. "I think the best thing for her is rest. Are you able to stay with her today?"

Mama looks panicked. "Oh dear, it nearly took an act of Congress for my boss to let me sneak away today," she says. "I could be here tonight, after my shift—"

"Don't worry," Collin says, smiling calmly. "I will stay with her."

Mama looks at Collin. She doesn't say anything, and I can tell she's wondering who he is, wondering how he's come to be a part of my life.

"Well," Collin says, breaking the silence. "I'm going to step out for a cup of coffee. I'll let you two catch up."

When the door closes, Mama sits in the chair beside the bed. "Be careful with that one, my water baby," she says.

I shake my head. "I'm sorry, I don't know what you mean."

She sighs. "That boy loves you, Penny. And if I'm not mistaken, I think you love him, too."

"Mama, that's nonsense. He's just a friend."

She reaches for her bag and pulls out a ball of yarn. We sit together without saying anything else. The only sound in the room is her turquoise knitting needles clicking together, and the beating of my heart, when I think about what she's just said.

# Chapter 16

ADA

The waitress brings out our entrées, but I hardly notice, absorbed as I am in Alex's story. When he begins to speak, all I can do is listen intently to the words that cross his lips.

"I was married shortly before I began my work in Sudan," he says. "To a wonderful woman who loved me. But she didn't happen to love my line of work. And for good reason. I was gone eight months out of the year in war zones. I'd go months without calling her. She always said I wasn't married to her but to my work. And she was right. I was. You have to be when your work is so intense. I guess I expected her to get that. But she couldn't." He shakes his head. "She never could."

"So what happened?" I ask cautiously.

"I gave it up for her," he says. "I quit and came home. But I resented her for it. That first year stateside was a dark time for me, partly because we worked together—the business arrangement wasn't a healthy one—and partly because I was going through some of my own issues. I didn't know it at the time, but I was suffering from some serious post-traumatic stress from my time in Sudan. I thought I could just jump back into regular life, but it doesn't work that way. The brain needs time to work through what it's seen. And I saw some ugly things."

"Understandably so," I say. "Surely she understood the difficulty of the transition."

"No," he says. "She expected more of me. I started drinking again, and with my family's history of alcoholism, that was dangerous behavior. Don't get me wrong, there were moments of happiness. I tried. She tried. I got sober. I even saw a therapist for a while. But in the end, I couldn't shake my demons. So on the morning of Thanksgiving nine years ago, I woke up and she was gone. She left a note on the kitchen counter, changed her cell phone number, started a whole new life. A month later I was served with divorce papers, and I signed them. If she wanted out, I wasn't going to stop her. I'd already made her life miserable." He rubs his brow and looks up at me cautiously. "But she kept something from me," he says. "Something I could never forgive her for. But I've come to—" His phone suddenly rings from inside his vest pocket, and he pulls it out and looks at the screen. I see something flash in his eyes, and he looks at me. "I'm so sorry, Ada. I have to take this."

"I'll wait here," I say, still reeling from all he's told me.

He steps away from the table to the nearby lobby, and I think about Kellie now in a whole new light. I actually feel sorry for her. He had the perfect marriage—an adoring, beautiful wife—and he threw it all away because he couldn't get his act together. It's a harsh way of looking at it, but it's true. James would have fought for me. James would have figured out a way to make it work. But Alex is not James.

I try not to listen to Alex's conversation. He's only a few feet away, so I can make out bits and pieces of what he's saying. I take a bite of my gnocchi, and my ears can't help but listen in. "Kellie, please don't," he says. "You know I didn't mean that. . . . Why must you put this on me?" He listens for a long moment, and then his frown turns to a smile. "Oh, honey, I'm here. I love you."

My eyes shoot wide open. It's so sorely obvious that he's still in love with her. How foolish I've been to think that he could care for me when his heart belongs to Kellie. I pull two crisp twenty-dollar bills from my wallet and set them on the table beside my napkin, and before he gets off the phone, I weave my way through the dining room to the back door.

Tears sting my eyes as I run down the hill to Boat Street. I race down the dock, just as rain begins to fall overhead. I jam my key into the lock and close the door behind me. The raindrops hit the lake outside in steady succession, like my tears. And when I hear Alex knocking softly on my door ten minutes later, I don't open it. This was a mistake. All of this was a mistake.

# *Chapter 17*

PENNY

"C areful," Collin says as we step down to the dock. He reaches for my hand and I let him take it.

My head hurts a little, but other than that I feel all right. "I'll bet Dex is home now," I say.

He walks me down the dock, and I'm glad that Naomi and Gene aren't home and relieved that Jimmy isn't milling about. I wouldn't want to worry him, nor would I want to explain myself to his mother.

I know Dex isn't inside the houseboat even before we step up to the front door. He always leaves his shoes on the doormat, right beside the shriveled geraniums in the flowerpot. But his shoes aren't there. I'm relieved, but I'm also a little sad.

"I don't know where he is," I say to Collin tearfully. I didn't expect my voice to quiver like it does.

"There, now," he says, patting my arm. "Let's get you inside."

He walks me to the davenport, where I lean back against the cushions and prop my feet up against the armrest where Dex's head has lain on so many quiet Saturday mornings.

Collin brings me a glass of water and a pill, and I doze off.

The light is bright when I open my eyes. My head pounds. I sit up, disoriented. "Dex!" I cry.

Instead, Collin appears. He's coming from the kitchen, with a plate of cheese and sliced fruit. "Morning," he says cheerfully. "How'd you sleep?"

"What time is it?"

"Eight," he says with a smile. "You slept through the evening, right on to morning. You must have been exhausted."

I rub my eyes and nod my head. "Thank you," I say, "for staying."

He passes me the cheese and fruit plate, and grins. "You talk in your sleep, you know."

I take a bite of sliced apple. "Oh no, what did I say?"

"There was something about a boat," he says, "which isn't surprising, and a whole lot of other gibberish. But you said my name."

"I did?"

"Yes," he says proudly. "I admit, I tried to eavesdrop, but I didn't get very far." He walks back to the kitchen and returns with two mugs. "Coffee?"

"Yes, thank you," I say, sitting up.

"I hope you don't mind that I stayed. I just didn't feel right about leaving you here alone."

I take a long sip before I speak again. "I keep thinking, what if I'd died out there on the lake? I would have been dead for two days now. Dex wouldn't even know. Whenever he'd get around to coming home, whenever he could break away from his precious art, he'd come home and I wouldn't be here."

Collin looks at his feet, as though the very thought of Dex unnerves him, but he doesn't share what he's thinking. "Well, you're

OK, and that's all that matters," he finally says. "Now that you're up, I'm going to go home and shower. I'll be back this afternoon to check on you."

In truth, I don't need anyone to check on me. I bumped my head; I'll recover. But I touch my hand to the bandage on my forehead and nod. I like that he wants to check on me. I like that *someone* wants to check on me. "Thank you," I say softly. He beams back at me.

Three days pass, then four. Dex remains unreachable. If he's at his studio, he's not answering the phone, because when I call, it just rings endlessly. I decide that maybe he's gone on a trip. Maybe he's finally gone to that gallery in Paris where he was invited to exhibit his work. But would he really go to Paris without me? Without even telling me?

When Saturday comes, I am crestfallen. It's the night of the Frank Sinatra concert. I call his studio four times. I don't know why I keep trying; he never answers. But this time, someone picks up.

"Hello?" It's a woman. She sounds young, younger than I am, perhaps.

"Oh," I say quickly. "I must have the wrong number. I was trying to reach Dexter Wentworth."

"Just a sec," she says, setting the phone down.

Maybe she's a model, I tell myself. Dex hires them from time to time to pose for him while he paints. I imagine she has long black wavy hair that hangs in front of her bare breasts. Her hips are round and her skin porcelain. Dex has her on the couch, the way he used to have me pose for him. I close my eyes, then set the phone back on the receiver.

It's four thirty, and I haven't even dressed yet. I should be ironing
my red dress, the one with the deep V-shaped neckline and stitch-
ing around the waist. It flatters me in all the right places, and I've
imagined wearing it to see Frank Sinatra. I've planned it for days
now. Dex would come home, see me in the dress, and wrap his
arms around my waist like he always has. He'd whisper in my ear,
"You look stunning."

I wonder if I'm hallucinating when Dex walks in the door an
hour later and sets his hat on the counter. He looks terrible. He hasn't
shaved in days; his cheeks are gaunt. Dark shadows linger beneath
his eyes.

"Hi," he says, sitting in the chair by the windows. He doesn't look
at me. He doesn't ask why I'm propped up on the couch with pillows.
He just stares at the lake.

"I called your studio today," I say. My words are tense, tinged
with hurt. My voice reverberates in the air, but Dex doesn't seem to
notice or care.

He shakes his head. I can smell the stale, sweet smell of alcohol
on his breath, even from across the room. "I don't understand it,"
he says.

"What?" I ask, sitting up.

He still doesn't look at me. "It was perfect," he says. "It was my
masterpiece, and they . . ." He buries his head in his hands.

"Oh, Dex," I say soothingly, rushing to his side. I wonder why
it's so easy to assume this role with him, so easy for him to keep taking and for me to keep giving. "Tell me what happened." I remember the series of paintings he's been working on for months. "Was
the installation today?"

"The curator hated them," he says, staring ahead.

I sit on the arm of the chair and rub my hand along his rough cheek, then kiss his head. His hair is unwashed, and I breathe in the scent of his scalp. I don't ask him about the woman on the phone at the studio. It doesn't matter anymore. Dex is here. He came home to *me*. "Tonight's the concert," I say cheerfully. "We'll go out and take your mind off things."

He shakes his head quickly. "I can't. I have to go back to the studio. I have to work on the replacement. I only came home to get a few clean shirts."

"Oh," I say, stiffening.

He walks to the hallway and selects four or five shirts that I ironed last week. He wads them up and tucks them under his arm.

"Penn, I'm sorry," he says. "I know how much you wanted to go to that concert." He walks toward me as if seeing me for the first time, as if he's just noticed that I have feelings too.

He touches my waist, but I push his hand away.

"You could still go," he says.

"By myself?"

"Why don't you ask your mother?"

I shake my head. "She hates Frank Sinatra."

He scratches his head. "How about the boat maker, what's-his-name . . ."

"Collin," I say. "His name is Collin." I don't tell him that he saved my life. That he is kind and thoughtful, so much more than a boat maker.

"Yeah," he says. "Why don't you see if he wants to go?" He shrugs. "I paid a fortune for those tickets. You ought to use them."

"Right," I say. "You'd better go." My voice is flat and mechanical.

"Penn," he says, pulling me toward him. "You're not mad at me, are you? Because I couldn't handle that. Not after this day."

I force a smile. I know he needs me to be strong.

"That's my girl," he says, kissing my forehead. "I'll call you soon."

I nod as the door clicks closed, then walk to the chair Dex was sitting in. The air still smells like him, sweet and musky. I sit there until it dissipates, then disappears entirely. Sometime later, I hear a knock at the door. "Come in," I say. I don't have the energy to get up.

It's Collin. "Hi," he says, looking at his watch. "You'd better get dressed. Aren't you going to the Sinatra concert tonight?"

I shake my head. "I'm not going."

"Not going? Why not?"

I turn to face him, and the tears finally come. They spill out over my eyelids and stream down my cheeks, and I don't even try to stop them now. I can't. Collin rushes to my side and kneels down by me. He takes my hands in his. They're large and warm, and encircle my small fingers. "What can I do?" he asks, handing me a handkerchief from his shirt pocket.

I shake my head. "Nothing."

"What happened?"

I look away, then let my eyes meet his again. "Dex isn't going with me to the concert."

"Why not?"

"He has to work."

Collin nods to himself. "Then I'll take you."

In spite of Dex's offhand suggestion, I'd never think of asking Collin. It seems forward, somehow. But now that he's mentioned it, now that he's kneeling here in front of me holding my hands, I want nothing else. "Would you?"

He nods, then stands up. "Now, let's get you dressed." He walks to the hallway closet and sees the red dress I left on the hook. "This one?"

I nod.

"It's perfect," he says, pulling the ironing board out and plugging the cord into the wall. I didn't know men could iron. Dex always acts as if he's allergic to housework. I watch with fascination as Collin spreads the red fabric over the ironing board and smooths the pleats beneath his fingers. His motions are gentle but determined, the way he sands the planks of the sailboat. I think of his hands touching my dress and my cheeks flush.

"There," he says a moment later, holding up the dress on a hanger.

"How did you learn to iron?" I ask.

He grins as if I've just asked him how he learned to read. "My mother raised me to know these things."

I vow to myself right then that if I ever have a son, I'll raise him to be thoughtful like Collin. I'll teach him to iron a dress and to make icing for cookies and to mend a hole in a pair of trousers. "Well," I say. "Your mother did a good job." I take the dress from Collin and eye it on the hanger. Somehow it seems more daring now. I wonder if I ought to have chosen something more conservative. "I'll just go get changed."

"Do you want me to come back?" Collin asks, rubbing his head nervously.

"Stay here," I say, smiling. "It's OK. I'll just run upstairs."

I climb the ladder to the loft bedroom and peel off my dress, then sit on the bed in my slip. The night air is warm and sultry on my skin. Downstairs, just a few feet below me, Collin is fiddling with the record player.

"I saw a Sinatra record on the table," he says. "I hope you don't mind. I thought it could get us in the mood for the concert."

"I could use a lift," I say, letting my slip fall to the floor. It glides over my budy effortlessly. I hear the crackle of the record player, and then the deep, smooth sound of Sinatra's voice. I sway to the melody as I unclasp my bra. I select another, white lace, from the drawer and put it on, then reach for a fresh pair of lace panties. The music is sweet and beckoning. *I could just say his name.* "Collin. Could you come up here, please? Could you help me with the window? The hinge is stuck." My heart beats faster when I imagine what would happen next, when I imagine his strong hands holding me. I hear his footsteps downstairs. I open my mouth to say his name, and then close it quickly. I think of Dex. I can't.

I put on my stockings, then slip into my dress and heels. I fasten my hair back with a clip and swipe red lipstick over my lips. I fiddle with the zipper, tugging it halfway up my back, but it sticks. I try again, but I'm worried I'll tear the dress. Timidly, I climb down the stairs, where Collin is waiting. He's beaming at me as if he's seeing me for the first time. "Wow," he says. "You look great."

"Thanks," I say. "I'm sorry, but do you think I could talk you into zipping me up?" I turn around, and without saying anything, he walks toward me. I feel his warm hands on my back as he rights the path of the zipper. It relents instantly, and a tingly sensation erupts on my skin as he pulls it up to the nape of my neck.

"There," he says, placing his hands on my shoulders to turn me around. "Perfect."

We arrive at the theater and take our seats near the stage. A waitress appears to take our cocktail orders, then returns with two martinis. After taking a sip, I eat the olives from the toothpick in my glass.

"Here," Collin says, handing me an olive from his glass.

"Thanks," I say, popping it in my mouth. Dex never gives me his olives.

The waitress returns with another round of martinis, and by the time the lights dim, the crowd is applauding and I feel light and happy, like I could float away. Frank Sinatra takes the stage, and everyone stands, cheering. He's handsome, with mature, chiseled features like Dex's. The band begins to play and I hear the opening melody to "How Deep Is the Ocean," and I sway beside Collin until the band preludes into a soft ballad. A couple in front of us begins to dance, and then another. Collin looks at me, and I don't hesitate. I lean into his arms and press my cheek against the lapel of his jacket.

The cab drops us off on Fairview Avenue. I know I've had too much to drink, because my legs aren't cooperating and my face feels numb. "Take my hand," Collin says softly, helping me out of the cab. I stumble a little, but he steadies me. "Let me carry you."

He doesn't wait for my reply before lifting me into his arms effortlessly. I feel as light as a feather. He steps onto the dock, and we pass the neighbors' houseboats. The old lady near the stairs must be asleep, because her house is dark. I realize I have no idea what time it is. Or what day it is. I see the potted flowers in front of Naomi and Gene's house and detect the ruffle of a curtain in the window, but I don't care. Let them all see me. Let them all think what they want.

Collin stops suddenly, and I look up. I recognize the front door of my houseboat. He sets me down, and I lean back against the door. His eyes sparkle under the house lights, and I feel dizzy looking into them. I think about going back inside my houseboat, alone. "I don't want this night to end," I whisper.

"Me either," he says. His arms are at his sides, but I wish he'd wrap them around me, press me against the door, and kiss me. I wish he'd carry me over the threshold like Dex did on the day of our wedding.

Without thinking, I lean toward him so that my lips are close to his. I feel the warmth of his skin as I close my eyes. I can hear music, the sound of waves lapping against the houseboat. I hear my future. Laughter. Children's voices. Music. Happiness. But Collin pulls away suddenly and lets go of my hands.

I look down. "Oh," I say. "I'm sorry, I . . ." I search his eyes. "Why can't you kiss me? Do you not want to?"

"I do," he says, rubbing his forehead. "More than you could ever know." He shakes his head. "Listen, it's late. I should say good night."

He turns to the dock, and in a moment he's gone.

Inside the house, I sink into the couch. My dress falls all around me like a heap of red velvet frosting, and I lean back against the cushion. My heart is beating wildly. There's a half-drunk bottle of wine on the counter. I uncork it and pour some into a glass. I stare at the phone and think of Dex. I dial the number to his studio and take another sip of wine as the phone rings.

"Hello?" It's the same voice. The same young woman. I look at the clock—after midnight—then slam the phone down.

I slip off my heels and run outside to the deck, then climb into the canoe, forgetting my life vest. It doesn't matter now. Nothing does. I paddle across the little channel and tie the rope to the cleat hurriedly. I don't care if it floats away. I don't care about anything but falling into Collin's arms.

There's a light on inside, and I run to his back door and knock quietly but persistently. There are tears in my eyes and anticipation in my heart. Collin appears a moment later. He's changed into Levi's and his shirt is unbuttoned. I don't say anything; neither does he. We speak a language all our own. He lifts me up to him, and I wrap my legs and arms around his body. I look into his eyes and feel his breath on my skin. Our lips are close now, and this time, he kisses me.

# Chapter 18

ADA

I don't see Alex the next day, or the day after. I feel bad about rushing out of the restaurant the way I did, and yet, after what I heard him say on the phone, how could I not? How could I trust him with my fragile heart when his is already in the possession of someone else? And then, on a quiet Saturday morning on the dock while I water the flowers outside my deck, our eyes meet.

"Hi," he says.

"Hi," I reply timidly.

"Can I come over?"

I nod.

He jumps in his kayak and crosses the little channel before attaching the craft to the cleat beside my deck. It's a warm day, and he's wearing a navy T-shirt and cargo shorts.

"Do you want to sit?" I ask.

"That would be nice."

At first, we don't say anything. We just watch the sailboats stream by, and then Alex turns to me.

"What did I say? What did I do to make you leave the other night? Did I say too much? Did I frighten you? I'm so sorry if I did." There's a tinge of desperation.

"You don't have to apologize, Alex. It was silly for me to think you were ready for a new relationship—that *I* was ready for a new relationship."

He shifts his chair so that he's facing me, not the view. "Oh, Ada, but I *am* ready for a new relationship. I only told you about my past so you'd know the truth about me. I hoped you wouldn't be frightened by it, but I guess I should have expected that."

I shake my head. "I'm not frightened by it. But I know you still love your ex." I can't bring myself to say her name. "And as long as you still care about her, well, I don't want to come between that."

He looks confused. "What do you mean that I 'still love' my ex?"

"I heard you talking on the phone to her," I say. "I understand."

"At the restaurant?"

I nod.

"Yes, it was Kellie who called, but she put my daughter on the phone. You must have heard me talking to Gracie."

I shake my head silently as my eyes well up with tears. I think of Ella then, her dark hair, her smile with a missing front tooth. "You have a *daughter*?"

"Yes," he says softly. "It's what I was trying to tell you, before the phone rang, before you left."

I tuck my hand into his. "Oh, Alex."

"Kellie was pregnant when she left me," he says. "She didn't tell me about Gracie until she was three. I suppose in some ways I didn't deserve to be a father then. I had to work through my issues, and I did. Kellie finally introduced me to Gracie, though, a few weeks after her fourth birthday, and it was love at first sight. Part of me will never forgive her for keeping my daughter from me for so many years. It kills me to think of how much of her life I missed. But another part of me understands her reasons. And I guess all that matters is that I'm a part of her life now. My relationship with Kellie is rocky. We don't always agree on parenting decisions, but we're trying. We both love our daughter very much, and we're committed to being the best parents to Gracie." He takes a deep breath. "Ada, you'd love her. She's eight years old, and the spunkiest little thing you'll ever meet. She loves animals and anything pink, and won't leave the house without her Dora the Explorer backpack."

I wipe away a tear. "I can't wait to meet her. That is, if you want me to."

He squeezes my hand. "I do," he says. "Very much."

I take a deep breath and think of my precious little girl and her adoring father. I think of the perfect life that I lost, and I realize that Alex and I have more in common than I could have ever anticipated.

# Chapter 19

PENNY

I'm relieved when I don't see Dex's shoes by the front door the next morning. I slip into the house and shower. I lather the soap over my body, caressing my skin the way Collin did last night. I feel guilty, and yet I feel cherished in a way I haven't been in so long. I hear the sound of the front door opening and freeze. Is it Dex? Collin? I wipe away the fog on the shower door when I see the bathroom door opening.

"Oh, there you are," Dex says.

"You're home," I say flatly. "I didn't think you'd be back for a while."

"I wanted to surprise you."

I turn off the water and reach for the towel on the hook. I wrap it around myself and step out. Dexter pulls me to him and kisses me. "I'm sorry I couldn't take you to the concert last night," he says. "Did you go?"

I nod. "Collin took me."

"Oh, good," he says. "I'll have to thank him. But first, I have a surprise for you."

"Oh," I say, feigning interest. I imagine he's bought me a gift. Something cashmere. A bracelet from Tiffany, maybe. It's his pattern. Disappointment, then pretty present tied up with a ribbon, repeat. But there is no box in his hand.

"We're going on a trip," he says.

"A trip?"

"Yes. To California."

I shake my head. "I don't understand."

"I thought we needed a little getaway," he says. "See some palm trees. Stay in a five-star hotel. Feel the sand between our toes."

"I suppose this was your psychiatrist's idea," I say, making no attempt to hide the annoyance in my voice.

He looks startled for a moment, then the smile returns to his face. "No, it was actually my idea," he says, taking my hands in his. "Pack your bags. Our plane leaves this afternoon."

At first I feel irritated. How dare he just waltz back here and tell me to pack my bags? And then the guilt sets in. I remember where I was last night, how Collin made me feel. I look at the floor, and Dex lifts my chin up to face him. "Let me make it up to you. Please?"

Because I don't know what else to say, I nod and say yes.

Dex carries our luggage up the dock, and I look straight ahead, hoping not to see Collin as I lock the door to the houseboat. I pray he isn't there. I can't bear to see him, not now, not after the night we shared. What would he think? What would I say? But then I see him ahead. He's walking toward us on the dock holding a vase of pink roses. There's a ribbon tied around the vase, which looks freshly selected from the front window of the little florist down the street. Dex would never settle for premade bouquets. He has a personal florist who knows his style—"loose, careless," I once overheard him say over the phone while ordering flowers for his sister after the birth of her son.

Collin holds the vase in his hands awkwardly. I know the roses are for me. I know they're a symbol of the love that blossomed between us last night. I run my eyes over the pink roses, and my heart nearly seizes. I want to run to him. I want to let him hold me again, kiss me. But Dex tucks his hand around my waist and I freeze, unable to say or do anything. I just stand and pray that Collin can read my eyes. They plead with him to understand.

"Hello there," Dex says to him. "Got a date?"

Collin looks at me, then back at Dex. I can tell he doesn't know what to say. I don't either.

"We're off to California," Dex says, filling the void.

"California," Collin parrots back. He looks at me dumbstruck. How could I be going away after last night? After . . .

"Dex surprised me," I say, hoping he'll understand that I have no other choice.

Dex kisses my cheek territorially and I pray that Collin sees my displeasure. "Thanks for taking my sweetheart out last night," he says. "I'll have to think of some way to repay you."

"No repayment necessary," Collin says. He looks wounded, and I want to reach my arms out to him. I want to nuzzle my face into his neck. But I can't. I can only stare ahead. I can only stand beside my husband. My *husband*.

"I have a meeting with a new patron in Los Angeles, and I decided to buy an extra ticket to take Penny along." He leans toward Collin playfully. "This is my very earnest attempt to get my wife into one of those bikinis all the women wear out there in California."

Collin forces a smile. "Well, I hear it's beautiful out there."

"Who'd you say the flowers are for?" Dexter asks.

"Oh, I, well, Lenora," he fumbles. "She's ill."

"I'm sorry to hear that," Dexter says. "Give her our best."

Collin nods, and this time he looks directly at me. "Have a wonderful time in California."

"We will," Dexter says.

My legs feel leaden as we walk to the cab waiting on the street above. I can't look back to the dock. I can't bear to see Collin again for fear that my heart will break in two.

"Don't you love it here?" Dex says, leaning back on the bed at the Chateau Marmont.

"It's beautiful," I reply, walking out to the balcony. He joins me a moment later. "You're prettier than any movie star in Hollywood, you know?"

"Stop," I say, as my lips form a reluctant smile. "You're just saying that."

He turns me around to face him. "It's the truth." He begins kissing my neck, but it doesn't feel right. Not now. Not after last night. I'm relieved when I hear a knock at the door. Dexter opens it for a porter who holds a tray with a bottle of champagne, two glasses, and an envelope.

"Did you order room service?" I ask, walking toward him.

Dexter doesn't reply. He tears open the envelope expectantly, like a little boy opening a present on Christmas morning. He pulls out a card, and I lean over his shoulder to read the flowery handwriting.

"To our monthlong artistic collaboration!—Lana"

I shake my head. "Who's Lana?"

"I was going to tell you over dinner tonight," he says. "I thought if I could get you out here, you'd see what an exciting opportunity this is for me."

"Dex, what are you talking about?"

He sits down on the bed. "Listen, Penn, I don't know how it happened, but Lana Turner saw some of my work at a gallery in Los Angeles, and her people contacted me. She wants me to work on a mural in her home."

"In her home? Lana Turner? *The* Lana Turner?"

"Yes," he says. "And she's offered to let me be an artist in residence while I work on it."

"An artist *in residence*?" I shake my head. I've seen her movies. I know how beautiful she is, and I've read the headlines about her many loves and divorces. "Doesn't that seem a little tawdry, Dex?"

"Honey," he says, "I know how it must seem. But I wanted you to come out with me so you could meet her, so you could feel comfortable with the arrangement." He takes a deep breath. "I'm going to be here for at least a month."

"Dex, really?" I should be relieved. I can fly home and spend all the time in the world with Collin. I should be happy. But instead I feel a clench in the pit of my stomach.

"I'll work fast," he says, kissing my wrist.

"I imagine she's paying you a lot of money."

He nods. "Yes. But Penn, it's not about the money. I don't know how to describe it, but since Lana reached out to me, well, it's like someone lifted a dark veil that was covering my eyes. I feel happier; I feel like I can work again."

"Good," I say. "I want that for you."

"It'll mean more commissions," he says. "Lana says that when I'm done with the mural, I'll have all of Hollywood courting me.

We could move out here, maybe. Get a little home in Beverly Hills. You'd like that now, wouldn't you?"

I shake my head. "But I love our home. I love Seattle."

"Then we'll keep it. We'll have two."

"I don't know, Dex."

"Please, come with me. Meet Lana tonight. You'll fall in love with her; I promise you will." Somehow I sense that it's Dex who's already done just that.

The maître d' pulls out my chair, sliding it in place as I take my seat. I look around the large dining room with its glitzy decor. An older man escorts a young blonde on his arm at least twenty years his junior. She wears a sparkly silver dress that's cut low on her chest. Her champagne blond hair is pulled back and piled high on her head. I feel plain and unglamorous in comparison and tug at my emerald green dress. It never fails to wow in Seattle, but somehow it feels frumpy and schoolmarmish now.

"Do you know who that was?" Dexter whispers to me.

I shake my head.

"Alfred Hitchcock," he says. Dex is clearly taken with California, but I don't share his fascination. Instead, I think of home on Lake Union. I wonder what Collin's doing right now. I wonder if he's thinking of me.

The room goes quiet, and I realize that Lana Turner has made her entrance. Dexter stands up, beaming, as she walks to our table. She's the epitome of Hollywood glamour: blond hair, curled around her face; perfectly applied lipstick; mile-long lashes; and an evening gown with a sweetheart neckline. "Darling," she says to Dex. "Thank you for coming." She kisses his cheek, then turns to me. "You must be Penny."

"Yes," I say. My voice sounds like a mere squeak compared with her deep, confident tone. She's closer to Dex's age than mine. I feel like a girl in the presence of a woman.

"I am absolutely taken with your husband's talent," she says to me. "I hope you don't mind that I'm borrowing him for a little while. I promise I'll return him in one piece."

I smile nervously. She's the kind of woman who gets what she wants. I can tell. I wonder what it's like to be that sort. To be able to order whatever you like, *whomever* you like, and have it delivered to you on a domed silver platter.

"Ladies," Dexter says, standing up. "May I fetch you drinks from the bar?"

"A Manhattan, please, darling," Lana says.

"A martini is fine, thank you," I add.

Lana lights a cigarette, then turns to me. "I've just been through the most horrific divorce," she says. "The third wasn't a charm, so I thought the fourth would be." She inhales, then blows smoke in my direction. "But, no luck." She's hard not to like, even though I'm wary of her allure. She looks toward the bar, where Dex stands. "He's quite a catch," she continues. "How did you meet?"

I can't believe she's actually interested in the story, but her eyes remain fixed on mine, so I tell her about Miss Higgins Academy, how Dex pulled his car over in the rain. Lana smiles. Her face is animated.

"Care for a cigarette?" she asks, noticing me tugging at my fingers.

"No, I don't smoke."

"You're young, aren't you, dear?"

"I'm twenty-two."

Lana smiles. She must be at least thirty-nine, forty maybe. "Can I ask you something?"

I nod.

"Your heart is elsewhere," she says, blowing smoke into the air. "Where?"

I shake my head. "I don't know what you mean."

She smiles knowingly. "I'm not going to tell. We girls have to keep these things to ourselves. And, honey, I know a thing or two about love. Hell, I've been unhappy in love most of my life. I learned the hard way not to hinge my happiness on a man."

"But I don't—"

"I don't mean to upset you, sweetheart," she says. "I just saw something in your eyes, that's all. Your husband is a fine man. But don't lose sight of who *you* are." She winks. "That's all I'm saying. I know because I've done it, and it doesn't work."

"But you seem so happy," I say.

"My dear, I've spent so many years chasing happiness," she explains, smiling to herself. "But happiness doesn't help you to grow. Only unhappiness does that."

A moment later, Dex returns with the drinks, and I try to take in what she's just said.

I board a plane home to Seattle the next afternoon. Alone. I never did see Lana Turner's home, nor did I want to, really. I decide it's better that way. And on the plane, I try not to think about her offering Dex a cocktail. I try not to think of him admiring the curve of her hips.

"Care for a drink?" the stewardess asks, jarring me from my private thoughts.

"No, thank you," I say. Instead, I think of Collin. I think of the way he held me just hours ago, the way he ran his fingers through my hair. I think of the way he made me feel. I recall the longing in his eyes. I shake my head. How did it come to this? I imagined a happy marriage, with babies in the nursery, a little garden, and lots of love. I have none of these things. I watch a couple in the seats to my left, across the aisle, share a brief kiss, and I shudder to myself.

I don't see Collin on his deck when I arrive back on the dock. I steal glances out the window as I'm making dinner or sorting the laundry, but there's no sign of him, not even the flicker of light from his houseboat. I put on a record and pour a glass of wine. Was he hurt when he saw Dex and me leaving for California together? He must have known that I had no idea the trip was happening. Surely he'd understand. It's getting late, so I change into my nightgown and wrap my pink silk robe around me. It's floor-length and trimmed around the hem and cuffs with fluffy pink fur.

I hear footsteps outside my front door. My heart flutters. It must be Collin. He saw the light on. He knows I'm home and he wants to see me. I rush downstairs and open the door.

"Jimmy," I say, surprised, hoping he doesn't see the disappointment on my face. I cinch my robe tighter. "Isn't it a bit past your bedtime, honey?"

He's wearing blue-and-white-striped pajamas. He has a teddy bear tucked under one arm. "I can't sleep."

"Oh," I say, craning my neck toward the dock to make sure Naomi isn't in hot pursuit. "Well, then, you might as well come in and let me make you some warm milk."

He follows me inside and climbs up on a barstool at the kitchen counter. I select a small pan, fill it with milk, and turn on the stove.

"What happens when we die?" Jimmy asks.

I raise my eyebrows. "That's an awfully deep question for nine o'clock on a weeknight."

He shrugs. "Mama says when you die, nothing happens. She says you just close your eyes, and it's over. But I don't know." He plants his elbow on the counter and sinks his cheek into his palm. "I think there must be more to it."

I wink at him. "I hope you're right."

"So you believe in heaven?" he asks.

I nod. "I do."

"Do you pray?"

"Yes," I say honestly. I said a prayer on the plane that very day, in fact, not that I pray very often. There was something about soaring over the earth at ten thousand feet that made me feel closer to the Almighty—that and the fact that I feel so lost.

"Mama and Daddy are atheists," Jimmy continues. "What is that?"

"Well," I say, choosing my words carefully. I'm not exactly one to talk. I became a Sunday School dropout long ago. "It means they're people who choose not to believe in a creator, a god."

"Oh," Jimmy says.

The milk is boiling now. I skim off the top, then pour some in a mug for Jimmy. "Careful," I say. "It's still hot. Cinnamon?"

He nods his head expectantly.

I smile, reaching for the cinnamon jar. "My mama used to sprinkle cinnamon on my milk every night before bed."

Jimmy takes a slurp and smiles. "I'm not an atheist," he says suddenly.

"Oh?"

He nods. "Because on the night of my fifth birthday, I prayed for an angel to watch over me." He slurps his milk, then looks up at me with a milk mustache. "And God brought you to the dock."

My eyes well up with tears then as I watch him turn back to his mug.

I don't see Collin at all the next day, and by evening, I'm beginning
to get worried. Did he go somewhere? Did he leave that morning
after seeing me go to California with Dex? I make a batch of corn
muffins and pace the living room floor while they bake.

When night falls, I put on a record, then slip on a sweater, and
sit out on the deck. A half-moon dangles high in the sky, and I
think of all the people looking up at it right now. Just then, I hear
footsteps behind me, and I turn around quickly.

"Hi," Collin says softly. His voice is timid, expectant.

"Hi," I say, standing up. "I thought you'd gone away."

"I thought *you'd* gone away," he spars back.

"Listen," I say. My heart is beating fast. "I didn't know about
the trip to California. It was Dex's idea. He's there now. Painting a
mural for an actress in Beverly Hills."

"Oh," Collin says. He takes a step closer. "So you're alone?"

"Yes," I reply. The music from the record player drifts out to the
deck. "Dance with me?"

He walks toward me and wraps his hands around my waist,
and for a moment, everything is right with the world.

# Chapter 20

## Ada

The phone rings, and I open my eyes. "Hello?"

"Ada, it's Joanie. I have news."

I rub my eyes as my surroundings come into focus. "Sorry," I say. "I must have dozed off." For a moment I'm confused. *What is she talking about?* And then I remember the articles I read about Penny Wentworth's disappearance before falling asleep.

"Penny Wentworth," she says. "She disappeared from her houseboat on Lake Union on July 29, 1959."

I sit up and stretch my arms. "I know," I say. "I found the date in an article online."

"Seems like they suspected the husband, Dexter, first," Joanie adds. "The police interrogated him. I found the transcripts. From what I can tell it ruined him. He stopped painting. Left the lake. In the end, they closed the case, saying Penny likely drowned in Lake Union. But they never did find a body.

"A producer from *Unsolved Mysteries* actually inquired about this case," she continues. "I found a note in the file online. So I put a call in to the show, because I know a guy who works there.

Interestingly, it looks like the estate of Penny Wentworth declined to be interviewed or to cooperate."

"The husband?"

"Yes, Dexter Wentworth."

"Either he's the shy type or—"

"The guilty type," she says. "But the husband wasn't the only suspect. There was some character named Collin McCleary. It says here that he was wanted for questioning but the cops could never find him."

My eyes widen. Jim mentioned someone named Collin. But who was he? "Joanie, what if she didn't die? What if she just *left*?"

"I suppose it's a possibility," she says. "She didn't have children, did she?"

"No, I don't think so."

"So there wouldn't be anyone holding her back if she did want to leave. It's not clear what happened, but I've worked for the police department long enough to know that this story has a strange vibe to it."

I nod. "You might be right. I just keep hoping that she's out there somewhere, living the life she always dreamed of with the man she loves." I pause for a moment. "Did you find an address for Collin?"

I can hear Joanie typing before she responds. "Well," she finally says. "Looks like there is one. He used to live at 2203 Fairview Avenue Number 9, in Seattle. Do you know where that is?"

My heart beats wildly as I walk to the window. "Yes," I say, my gaze locked on Alex's houseboat. "I'm looking right at it."

I venture out to the dock before dinner and see Jim ahead. He's holding a hose and spraying down the dock after a morning visit from a gaggle of Canadian geese. I wave to him.

"City folks have pigeons," he says. "Houseboaters have geese." He kneels down to turn off the water spigot.

I smile to myself.

"Well," he says, looking up at the clear sky. "Nice day. I was thinking of taking the boat out. Would you like to join me?"

I've been admiring the *Catalina* since I arrived. "I'd love to," I say quickly.

He tosses me a life vest, and we walk toward the end of the dock. The old sailboat is worn, but well kept and regal-looking, like a seventy-five-year-old woman whose beauty shines through her wrinkles. Jim climbs aboard, and I follow, taking a seat on an upholstered bench at the front of the boat. I watch as he unties the ropes and tugs at the little motor to start the engine.

"We'll just motor out to the lake, then set the sails up there," he says.

I nod as we gain momentum. It's easy to feel free out here, easy to let go of your worries. I wonder if Penny felt that way living here.

"Jim," I say cautiously, "may I ask you something?"

"Shoot."

"I'm trying to figure out who Collin was. The man you mentioned."

He looks up at me as if the question has startled him, then kills the engine, so all we hear now is the sound of the lake lapping against the side of the boat. "Yes," he says after a long moment.

I'm not sure if I'm about to broach a sensitive topic. He already seemed a bit cagey when I inquired about Penny before. But why? "It's just that, well, I did a little investigating, and I learned that after Penny Wentworth's disappearance, there seem to have been two suspects—her husband, Dexter, and a man named Collin. I'm just trying to make sense of it all."

Jim looks lost in thought. His eyes drift out to the horizon. "Penny loved him," he says. "Even as a boy, I could tell. You can see the way people look at each other." He shakes his head. "But their timing wasn't right."

"Collin, you mean?"

He nods.

"She was married when she met him, wasn't she?"

"Yes," he says, standing up to adjust the sails. I duck my head to make room. "They were going to sail away together that night, the night of—"

"The night of her disappearance?"

"Yes," he says, looking out at the lake longingly, as if he hopes to steer the boat through the locks and out to the open water just then. "But Penny never did join him that night."

"What did he do, Collin?"

"He stayed away a long time," he says. "It was years before I saw him again on Boat Street, and when I did, I hardly recognized him. Just a shadow of the man he once was. Hollow cheeks. Ashen eyes. He didn't speak of what he'd gone through, but I knew it must have been harrowing. He secured the *Catalina* on the slip at the end of the dock and knelt down to where I was sitting. 'Can I ask you a favor, son?' Of course, I was eager to help him in any way I could. I'd watched Collin building the sailboat, sometimes for hours at a time. He used to let me sand the boards before he put them in place, then I'd take a cloth and rub them with teak oil. 'I need you to look after the *Catalina* for a while,' he said. 'I need you to keep her right here for me.' I beamed. It was the greatest responsibility anyone had ever given me, and I almost pinched myself in that moment. My parents wouldn't agree to a hamster, but here was Collin entrusting me with a ship.

" 'Will you come back for her?' I asked. He looked startled, as if my question had stirred a pot deep in his heart. Will you come back for *her*? I knew he was thinking of Penny then, just as I was. It had been years since her disappearance. The night was a blur to me then, just as it is now. But we both looked out to the lake that day as we always did—hopeful that she'd come sailing in on a boat with puffed sails, eyes sparkling, apologetic for staying away so long.

" 'No,' Collin said solemnly. There was more finality in his voice than I was comfortable with. Surely he'd return for the *Catalina*, his pride and joy. I couldn't understand his reasoning. Collin was a man with sea legs. He was best suited to the water. I'd even heard my mother make an offhand remark about him seeming weaker on land and positively Triton-like in command of a boat. I knew that giving up the *Catalina*, for him, would be like giving up his right arm, or one of his senses. He'd be crippled without his boat, without his life on the sea. And yet, when I looked into his face that day, I knew there was no talking sense into him. He'd already made up his mind. He was leaving the *Catalina* with me, and he was leaving Boat Street, forever perhaps.

" 'Just promise me one thing, Jimmy,' he said. It was impossible not to see the sadness in his expression, the regret. 'Take her anywhere you like. Sail around the world if you decide, but please, bring her home to Boat Street. She belongs here.'

"I nodded as he took a final look at the sailboat, then the former home of Penny and Dexter, before he patted my shoulder and turned toward the dock. I watched him walk up to the street above until he was gone. That's the last time I saw Collin."

"Wow," I say. "And you've kept the *Catalina* here ever since?"

Jim nods. "Yes. I took her to Mexico and back, and I spent a great deal of time in the San Juan Islands, but just like Collin said, I always brought her home."

"Why do you think he was so adamant about bringing her home to Boat Street?"

Jim reaches for a rope tied to the mast and pulls it tighter. "For Penny, I suppose. I think in the back of his mind, he retained some hope that she would return."

I place my hand over my heart in sympathy for Collin. "That's so romantic. He must have loved her so much."

"Yes," Jim says. "We all did."

"You said you never heard from him again," I continue. "But did you ever learn how he spent the rest of his life? I'm assuming he—"

Jim shakes his head. "Never knew. And I s'pose part of me doesn't want to know. I saw him walk away that day. He was in bad shape. He'd probably aged more in those years away from Boat Street than he did in his entire life. I don't know that he had the strength to keep going after that. But I like to think he found his way." He runs his hand along an edge of the *Catalina*'s cream-colored sail, and I imagine how Collin might have stood in this very place, showing a young Jim, Jimmy, the run of a sailboat the way a father might teach a son. I think of Gene and his dementia and wonder if they had that kind of relationship.

I make a mental note to search for more information about Collin. I have to know what happened to him and if he's still alive. I then turn my thoughts to Penny again. The residents of Boat Street may know what happened to Penny the night of her disappearance, but I've made little headway with them. Now that Jim is opening up, will he reveal more information about that fateful night? "What do *you* think happened to Penny, Jim?"

"Listen," he says quickly, "I was just a boy."

I nod. "Of course. I'm sorry, I just—"

"Whatever happened to her, Collin had nothing to do with it."

I think about Collin's love for Penny, the way Jim described his sadness. They shared a love of the sea and possibly more. But Penny was married to someone else. Could Collin have snapped? Could he have killed her somehow in a moment of intense jealousy? "You're sure?"

He looks momentarily exhausted, as though he and every other longtime resident of the dock have carried this burden for far too many years. He sighs. "Collin's world orbited around Penny. He was willing to risk everything for her. You only do that when you love someone."

His words pierce my heart, because I know just what he's talking about.

## Nine years prior

James presses his ear to my bare belly as if he can hear Ella talking to him. I'm only twenty-two weeks along, but after our last ultrasound showed our little girl on the screen, we decided to name our baby.

I'm lying on a hospital bed in the radiologist's office. A massive amount of ultrasound gel covers my belly, and every time I move, the protective paper cover crinkles beneath me. The radiology tech has just finished the exam, but she's prompted us to wait for a moment. Her eyes dart around nervously. She wants the radiologist to come in to see something, she says. We're not sure what this "something" is, but James doesn't seem to be worried, so I'm not either. "They're probably blown away by the size of her brain," he says. "Clearly, takes after her daddy."

I give him a gentle shove as the door opens and a middle-aged man enters the room. "Hello, Mr. and Mrs. Santorini," he says. "I'm

Dr. Hensley. I'd just like to have a closer look, if you don't mind."
The tech hovers behind him. Her face looks pinched, concerned.
She clasps her hands behind her back. My heart begins to beat rap-
idly. I turn to James and he squeezes my hand.

The doctor deposits another glob of gel on my belly and then
firmly presses the imaging device to my skin. Seconds later, I see
Ella again. Her legs are kicking back and forth. "That's our girl,"
James says proudly. "Feisty like her mama."

The doctor doesn't seem to hear him or share our sentiment. He's
focused on the screen and rubs the device against my belly again and
again, trying to get a closer look at something on the screen.

"What is it?" I finally ask. I know something is wrong.

He increases the size of the screen, then freezes the image. I
stare at the mass he points to, and I want him to press Play again. I
want to see Ella kicking her sweet little legs. I want to go back to the
moment when everything was fine.

"What's wrong?" I ask again. "Is my baby OK?"

He sets the device down and peels off his gloves. "Ms. Santorini,"
he finally says, "the baby is fine."

I exhale deeply.

"It's you I'm concerned about."

"What? Why?"

"There's a very large tumor growing on your left ovary."

"A tumor?" James says, shaking his head.

The doctor takes off his glasses and rubs his brow, then puts
them back on again. "I want to be as direct with you as possible.
This looks like cancer."

I sit up instantly, gasping. "I don't understand. How can I have
cancer? I feel fine. I, I . . ."

"When ovarian cancer is detected in pregnancy, we have to act fast," the doctor continues. "The pregnancy hormones can make it grow and spread faster than usual." He looks at James, then at me. "We'll need to do a biopsy, more tests." He clears his throat. "We'll obviously have time to discuss this with the oncologist, but I want to be frank with you. It's not too late for termination."

"Termination? You mean . . . ?" I'm suddenly speechless. One moment I was looking at my baby girl kicking her legs on the screen, and the next we're talking about terminating the pregnancy. Ending her life.

"No," I say, before anyone can say anything else. "No, I won't." I reach for some tissues and wipe the gloppy goo off my belly, then pull my sweater down.

"Ada," James says. He reaches out to me, but I push his arm away.

"Mrs. Santorini," the doctor continues, "you will risk your life if you don't at least consider termination in the event of—"

"I refuse to discuss this," I say, standing up. "James, let's go."

⚘

"You OK?" Jim asks.

I shake away the memory and turn to face him. "No," I say. "But I'm trying."

He doesn't ask me to elaborate; he just tugs at the sailboat's rigging as it glides across the lake, and nods. "Me, too," he says.

# Chapter 21

PENNY

Two weeks after my return to Seattle, a postcard with a palm tree on the front arrives. "Having the time of my life. Wish you were here. Lana sends her love. Love, Dex." I toss it in the wastebasket. He doesn't really wish I were there. If he did, he would have asked me to stay with him. No, he'd always see me as a nuisance, a distraction from his work, his creativity. I stir the batter in the bowl and watch it change from glops of flour, sugar, eggs, and butter into a perfect creamy smoothness. But some things can't be beaten into submission.

I squeeze in the lemon next, breathing in the tartness of the rind, and stir again. I try not to think about Dex now. I try not to dwell on what's to come, because it frightens me. All I can think about is today, and today Collin is taking me downtown.

A half hour later, the oven timer sounds. I reach for the pot holders, then pull out a pan of lemon bars. Collin mentioned that his mother used to make them for him, so I've decided to surprise him. After they cool slightly, I slice them into squares and set them out on a white platter that Dex's sister gave us as a wedding gift. I step back and look at them on the cold dish, then shake my head and transfer them to a paper plate that I find in the cabinet.

Collin peers in the back door an hour later. He's carrying a picnic basket. "I thought we could have lunch in the park, maybe see a little of what they're doing downtown to get ready for the World's Fair."

Seattle is preparing to host the World's Fair in 1962, if the selection committee approves the city's bid. Collin said once that he'd like to take me up on the Ferris wheel. I've never been on an amusement park ride, and the very idea exhilarates me. Besides, and perhaps more important, the date, three years hence, is an unspoken promise of our future together. He'll be leaving this summer, after the boat is finished. But he'll come back. Collin would never leave me forever; I know that. That fact quiets the fear in me. It makes me feel safe, somehow.

We catch a streetcar from Fairview Avenue, and Collin nestles beside me in a seat toward the back. "I hope he stays in California forever," he whispers into my ear.

My neck erupts in goose bumps. Part of me wishes for Dex to linger too, of course. But it's a delicate subject, one I don't quite know how to navigate, so I don't say anything; I just smile, and when he kisses my neck twice, I close my eyes and let myself float in the deliciousness of this moment. A moment when my heart is full and I feel deeply loved.

I straighten in my seat when I notice an older woman staring at us from across the aisle. She wears a dark dress and a gray pillbox hat with a short netted veil. Her gaze is disapproving, and I panic for a moment, worrying that I've seen her before. Is she a friend of Dex's? A patron? After a few moments, I still can't place her, but my concern lingers.

"What's wrong?" Collin whispers. He has an uncanny ability to acutely sense my distress.

I fold my hands together. "It's nothing," I say, forcing a smile. But the woman's presence is disquieting, like a sticky burr lodged in my stocking.

When the streetcar deposits us on Mercer Street, I take a deep breath once we start walking. It's a pleasant day, not more than seventy degrees, but my forehead has erupted in beads of sweat. Collin tucks my hand in his and lifts it to his lips.

"Train sick," I lie. I decide not to let my paranoia put a damper on this beautiful day. "Those streetcars always make me feel woozy."

He lifts the basket. "Let's go find a patch of grass to have lunch."

I nod, and we walk along a paved pathway beside the construction zone for the World's Fair. We pass colorful signs and billboards illustrating what's promised to be "the greatest show on earth." In one, children are depicted smiling, clutching cotton candy and giant lollipops, holding the hands of smiling adults. All around is space-age-looking architecture, and red gondolas dot the horizon. At the center of the image stands an enormous tower that reminds me a little of the Eiffel Tower in France, or at least the photographs Dex showed me from his trip to Paris years before he met me. "What's that?" I say, pointing to the structure.

"The Needle," Collin says casually. "Well, the Space Needle." He takes a step closer to the illustration. "See here?" he says, pointing to the base of the tower. "You'll be able to take an elevator to the top and even have lunch up there."

I gasp. "It'll be like eating on the moon."

Collin grins. "I guess sort of like that," he says, kicking a pebble beneath his feet before looking up at me again, wide-eyed. "I'll take you."

I wrap my arm around his waist. "You will?"

He nods, then spreads the picnic blanket out over a patch of grass behind us. I open the basket and pull out the ham sandwiches he packed, wrapped in waxed paper. I tucked in sliced apples and a lemon bar for each of us before we left.

"These are good," Collin says, sinking his teeth into a lemon bar after polishing off his sandwich.

"Thanks," I say, watching a group of seagulls peck at a bit of bread I tossed over to them.

I've hardly noticed anyone around us, but then a young man in uniform—navy, I think—stops suddenly in front of us.

"Leary?" he says, his face brightening. He shakes his head, astonished. "Is that you?"

Collin freezes. "You must be confused," he says, regaining his composure.

"But Leary—I mean," he says, shaking his head, "sorry, it's just that you look an awful lot like a guy I knew, in Korea."

"I'm afraid I'm not the person you remember," Collin says.

The man stares at him a moment longer and shakes his head in disbelief, then finally nods, saluting him before walking on.

"That was strange," I say a few moments later.

Collin flashes me an unsettled smile. "It happens all the time," he says, his usual confident expression again intact. "I must have a familiar face."

"A handsome face," I say, grinning.

"Oh, look," Collin says, pointing ahead to a crowd of people near the sidewalk by two long cafeteria tables.

"What's going on over there?"

"Let's go see," he says. We tuck the remains of the picnic back in the basket, brush off the blanket, and head over to see what the commotion's all about.

"I want to paint mine pink, Mommy!" a little girl squeals.

"Oh," Collin says. "I read about this. Seattle citizens are invited to paint a tile for the walkway for the World's Fair."

I eye the table of white square tiles stacked in foot-long piles. A docent in dark horn-rimmed glasses stands behind the table passing out one to each person. "Collect your tile here," the woman says, "and then proceed to the table to the right to paint them."

"Want to paint one?" Collin asks.

I remember the time I borrowed one of Dex's canvases and some paints and surprised him with a painting of my own. I tried to capture the lake in the morning, just after sunrise, when it's as smooth as glass and fog lifts up like steam. But it displeased him greatly. My composition was all wrong, he said, and I had wasted a perfectly good canvas.

I sigh, feeling awkward in the presence of art. "Why don't you paint one for both of us?" I say.

"All right," Collin says, collecting a tile from the docent. I watch him set it down on the nearby table and reach for a brush. He selects a bit of red paint and squeezes it onto the palette in front of him.

"What will you paint?" I ask.

He grins. "You'll see."

I watch as he dabs his brush into the red paint. I can't remember feeling such anticipation when I've watched Dex paint. Besides, he never lets me watch him. For him, the process of creation is deeply private, which is why he spends so much time alone in his studio.

Collin makes a simple heart inside the little square tile, and I smile. Next he selects a smaller brush, and he begins painting a message inside. The words flow from his brush freely: "Forever my love."

I clutch my hand to my heart. "It's beautiful,"

"I thought we could come back here," he says, looking up at me timidly, "years from now, and see our tile, and remember how we felt today."

I smile as he fills in the edges of the tile with red paint, then hands it to an apron-clad man behind the table. "Thank you," the man says. "This will get glazed up and then embedded in the pathway that we're forming for the World's Fair."

We walk back to the park in silence. My mind is a jumble of thoughts, and my heart is filled with emotion. *Forever.* He wrote the word *forever.* I haven't dared to think so far into the future, and now that I have, it feels wild and wonderful at the same time. But a voice gnaws at me from a place deep inside. *You belong to someone else*, it says. *This is wrong. You're breaking your word. You must go home. You must not let this continue.*

Suddenly Collin stops. He turns toward me. His face looks intense and desperate, as if he's on the verge of expressing extreme joy or sorrow, or maybe both. He drops to his knees and looks up at me with yearning. "Run away with me," he says.

"But I—"

"Don't think of him," he says. "He hasn't been good to you. He doesn't deserve you."

"Collin . . ."

"I'll make you so happy. I'll love you every day, every night. I'll show you the world. Just the two of us, traveling from port to port. I'll give you the life you always wanted."

The world appears to be spinning around us and I feel unsteady, but Collin's grasp is like an anchor, keeping me here, keeping me safe.

"But I'm married," I finally say.

"What does it matter?" Collin replies. "You'll divorce him."

Divorce. I haven't ever factored that in. Mama didn't raise me to be a woman who gets a divorce. She'd never be able to forgive me. And could I forgive myself?

I close my eyes. "I don't know. . . . What about . . . ?" Why
didn't I meet Collin that day near Miss Higgins Academy instead
of Dex? Why wasn't it Collin who drove up beside me on the
sidewalk?

"Penny, he's with another woman now," Collin says. It's the truth,
but the words sound harsh and vulgar somehow. "Don't you see?"
His eyes are bright and urgent; they plead with me to understand.
"Don't you see that you deserve so much more?"

Tears spill from my lids, and Collin swoops in to dab them with
the handkerchief from his pocket. I've longed to hear him say these
things, to profess his love to me, the same love I have for him, but
now, standing in the face of it, I don't know how to respond; I don't
know how to behave. The situation calls for a next step, but I've
forgotten how to walk. I can't even crawl.

"I'll give you some time," he says. "I know it's a lot to consider.
But promise me you will consider it."

"I will," I say softly. A drop of water hits my cheek, and at first
I think it's a tear, but then I notice that gray clouds have rolled in
overhead.

I hear the streetcar's bell in the distance. "If we're fast we can
catch the trolley home," he says.

I didn't bring an umbrella or even a scarf to cover my hair.
"Let's go," I say, taking his hand.

We don't say anything on the ride home. I just look out the
window, listening to the clickety-clack of the trolley. I have Collin's
heart in my hands, but it comes at a very high price.

Gene's outside smoking a cigarette as we walk down the dock. He
tips his head at us as we pass, then extinguishes the butt under his

foot and kicks it into the lake. "Collin," he says, "there were two men in suits here looking for you a moment ago."

Collin's eyes widen, and Gene regards him curiously. "Anyone you were expecting?" Gene asks.

"No, no," Collin fumbles. "I, I'll just go see." He glances back up to the street as if he's considering whether to dart back to the trolley. My chest feels tight. I want to place my hand on Collin's arm and ask him what's concerning him, but Gene is watching us closely.

"Well," I say. "Collin was just walking me home."

Gene nods at us as we make our way down to my houseboat. As we turn to my deck, I steal a glance toward Collin's houseboat. As far as I can tell, no one's standing there.

"What was Gene talking about?" I say. "Who would be looking for you?"

Collin shakes his head. "Don't you worry," he says, kissing my forehead quickly. "It's probably nothing."

But I can tell by the look in his eyes that "nothing" is far from the truth. A dark shadow has fallen over Boat Street, and I shiver as I slip my key into the door.

# Chapter 22

ADA

The next day, I decide to sort through the contents of the chest in the living room again. Maybe I've missed a clue to Penny's story. I open the lid and look carefully, which is when I notice a flap on the side of the velvet lining that I didn't see before. I tuck my hand inside the fabric and pull out a black-and-white photo of a beautiful blond woman. She looks like a Hollywood actress, and then I realize that . . . she is. Signed in the right-hand corner is the name Lana Turner.

How strange. Were the Wentworths friends with Lana Turner? I open up my laptop and do a Google search for "Wentworth" and "Lana Turner," and I gasp when something comes up. It's a scanned article from *The Hollywood Reporter*, dated 1959. "Seattle Artist Paints Iconic Mural in Home of Lana Turner." I squint at the grainy photograph that accompanies the article and make out the actress in a light-colored dress (or is it a nightgown?) with her arm tucked around Dexter Wentworth.

*Poor Penny. She must have been so lonely here, so sad, knowing her husband was having an affair.* I remember a black-and-white Lana Turner film I watched while on bed rest during my pregnancy with Ella. James had brought home a stack of old movies and Chinese takeout after work. I'd been on the couch for four months, and my scheduled C-section was only days away. To think that the doctors had encouraged me to abort. My cancer was stable, and the tumor would be removed during a full hysterectomy after Ella's birth. I turn back to the autographed photo of the glamorous actress. Cancer almost seemed like easier competition than a Hollywood star. Is that why Penny disappeared?

I look up when I hear a knock at my back door. I see Alex on the deck, and I smile, instantly wishing I'd taken the time to freshen up after my paddle that afternoon. "Hi," I say, opening the door.

"Hey," Alex says. "Am I interrupting?"

"Oh, no," I reply. "I was just looking through some old things from Penny's chest." I hold up the photo. "I think her husband was having an affair with Lana Turner."

"Lana Turner, huh?" he says, kneeling beside me. "Marilyn, too?"

I shrug. "Who knows? The guy appears to have been quite the playboy."

He sits down on the floor beside me, examining the contents of the chest, before picking up a scrap of paper I've disregarded until now. "Look," he says. "It looks like a notice to Seattle residents about the World's Fair of 1962."

I scan the flyer, eyeing a sketch of what is now Seattle's most iconic image, the Space Needle. "Come make history as the Mayor of Seattle cuts the ribbon to break ground in preparation for the Seattle World's Fair."

"I wonder if she went to this?" I say. "Why else would she have put the flyer in the chest?"

"Maybe," Alex says, leaning against the couch. "Have you ever been to the Space Needle?"

I shake my head.

"Then I'm taking you."

I grin. "Really?"

"Tonight," he says. "I have a shoot this afternoon, but I can be back by six to pick you up."

"It's a date," I say, smiling. As he walks out the door, the word *date* reverberates in my ears. *Date.*

I step out onto the dock in heels and a black skirt. It's a warm night, so I've left my sweater and opted for the sleeveless top that Joanie insisted I buy after I tried it on at Macy's last spring. I remember how she leaned against the fitting room door and smiled at me the way a proud big sister might. "You have to get it," she said. "It looks amazing on you."

"Why?" I grumbled. "I'll never wear it." It was silky and fitted, plus it sparkled a little. I'd never wear it to work. No, it was one of those tops I might have worn on a date night with James. Unlike some of my friends' husbands, he *noticed* when I dressed up, and I loved that he did.

Joanie could read my mind; I knew it. "Buy it for you," she said. So I obeyed, taking the top up to the counter and relinquishing my credit card, even though I really didn't see the point. It hung in my closet, with tags still on, until I packed for Seattle. I threw it in at the last minute, then zipped up the suitcase before I could change my mind.

I tug at the top a little nervously as I face Alex. His eyes are big and curious. "You look beautiful," he says, and instantly my confidence blooms.

He takes my hand as we walk along the dock. I worry that my heels will wedge into the grooves of the planks, and I'm grateful that he's there to steady me when the spike of my left stiletto gets caught. We both laugh as we pass Jim's houseboat, and then I see Naomi, watering the potted plants on her front deck.

"Oh, look at you two," she says. "Going to dinner?"

Alex looks at me and smiles. "I thought I'd take our new neighbor to the Space Needle."

She gazes at us nostalgically, as if she wishes she were thirty-five again, on the arm of a handsome man like Alex, who looks sharp in a sport coat and white button-down.

We wave to her and walk to the end of the dock, where I notice a light on in the houseboat where the mail was piled up just yesterday. I wonder if Esther Johnson has returned.

Up on the street, Alex points to a gray Audi sedan, and the lights blink once when he presses the button on his key chain. "I have to tell you, that woman gives me the creeps," he says, opening the passenger door for me.

"Jim's mother, Naomi?"

"Yeah," he says. He walks around and opens the driver's side door and climbs into the car. He starts the engine, and David Gray's "Sail Away" drifts through the speakers. I listen for a moment and wonder if Penny ever wanted to sail away. Maybe she simply wanted to cut her losses and leave her adulterous husband, her critical neighbors . . . leave Boat Street forever.

I think of Dr. Evinson for a moment and his warning about running. But what's the harm in running if you run to something better, somewhere where it doesn't hurt so badly?

"Sorry," Alex says, fumbling with the volume dial, "the music's a little loud."

"Don't turn it down," I say. "I like it."

"Me, too," he says. "When things got really bad for me a few years ago, I thought a lot about getting a sailboat and just casting off."

"Why didn't you?" I ask.

He shrugs. "I think I'd get sick of myself. All that alone time out in the middle of nowhere." He glances at me then. "I might have gone if I'd had someone to sail away with."

I smile and look away. I don't ask him about Kellie or his daughter, and how they did or didn't fit into his plans.

Alex pulls into a parking spot, and we step out to the sidewalk. The Space Needle towers overhead. It looks so much bigger up close, like a flying saucer on enormous steel stilts.

"We have a little time," he says, eyeing his watch. "Want to walk around the Seattle Center for a bit?"

"Sure," I reply.

He offers me his arm and I take it. Even in New York, I didn't walk long distances in heels. I was one of those unashamed Manhattan women who wear sneakers with skirts, changing into heels only in the lobby of my office building. A podiatrist once stopped to congratulate me on my sensible choice of footwear. Joanie had a good laugh over that one.

He points to a pathway that leads through a park at the base of the Space Needle. "The city's getting ready for the fiftieth anniversary of the Needle," he says. "They're collecting thousands of tiles made by the residents of Seattle in the late fifties and laying them in the ground over there to make a pathway."

"That's sweet," I say. "Where were they before?"

"I think the article in the *Seattle Times* said something about their being found in a storage facility in the city's administrative building."

"Look," I say, pointing ahead beyond the caution tape. I walk to the tape and kneel down to see a tile clearly painted by a child. Another features the name of a woman, Bethanne, painted in cursive handwriting, with squiggles and stars surrounding the letters. And then I notice a tile in the distance, with just three words painted inside a heart. "Forever my love." Simple, and yet the statement of love pulsates with the poignancy of a Shakespearian sonnet.

"That one's beautiful," I say.

Alex nods. "It is."

I shiver, and Alex drapes his coat over my shoulders. "Let's walk to the restaurant now. Our table should be just about ready."

We board an elevator at the bottom of the Space Needle and travel upward. Alex weaves his fingers into mine, and my heart leaps. The forty-three seconds it takes to get to the top feels like forty-three minutes, in a good way. I don't let go of his hand as we step out into the lobby. And when we're seated side by side at a table that faces directly out one of the windows, he reaches for my hand under the table, and I don't pull back.

We order, and the waitress brings me a glass of wine and Alex an iced tea. I take a sip and feel warm all over.

"What do you think?" he asks.

"It's beautiful up here," I say, looking out the window. "You can even see Boat Street."

"It looks microscopic down there, doesn't it?"

I nod. "We're all just like little ants, bickering and squabbling."

"The way God sees us, I guess," Alex adds.

I look away and don't say anything for a few moments. *God. Did he see Ella and James on the day of their death? Did he know what was about to happen? If so, why didn't he stop them? Why didn't he send an angel down to swoop them out of harm's way? Why did he take them and make me watch every excruciating detail?*

"What are you thinking about?" he asks.

I bite my lip. "Sorry. I was . . ."

"You're carrying such a huge burden," Alex says, his eyes piercing mine. "You must be staggering under the weight of it."

I want to shake my head and say, "No, James and Ella are not a burden. They are the loves of my life, and I will keep them with me forever!" But he's right. My burden is heavy, and my pain is all-consuming. At any moment I'm liable to stumble, to crack under its weight. And I fear I can't hold on much longer. It's as if someone's put me in possession of an enormous, rare crystal vase and told me to carry it for the rest of my life, but every day, every second, I'm on the verge of letting it slip from my hands, watching it shatter into a dozen jagged pieces, and I with it.

"You know what they say in church?" he says.

I shake my head and inwardly roll my eyes.

"They say that God can carry our burden for us if we ask him to."

I think about that for a moment and decide not to be annoyed by Alex's statement. He's only trying to help.

"I can't tell you much about religion," he continues. "I don't have all the answers, far from it. I still have a lot to learn, but I can tell you that this is a pretty kick-ass benefit from the Almighty. He says, 'Here, I'll take your worries, your worst fears, and deal with them for you so you don't have to anymore.'"

I smirk. "I wish it were that easy."

"It is," Alex says confidently. His eyes narrow then, and he looks at me tenderly. "I know you're hurting. You may always be, and that's OK. I just want you to know that you can find comfort if you seek it. And you can learn to be happy in the midst of it. You deserve that, Ada."

"Well," I say shyly, taking his hand in mine, "you should know something, then."

"What?"

The edges of my mouth turn upward slightly. "I feel happier than I have in a long time."

"I'm glad," Alex says.

"What about you?" I ask, turning to him. "Are you happy?"

He takes a sip of his iced tea. "Yes," he says. "More so now that a certain someone has moved to the dock."

I grin.

"I've thought a lot about happiness over the last few years," he continues. "If you were to ask me a while back, I might have told you I'd given up on it entirely. I was in a really bad place for so long. I swear, I thought I had a rain cloud hovering over my head."

I don't ask him about his demons. If I learned anything in therapy, it's that it's best when someone elects to share of their own accord, not by prodding.

He scratches his head. "You know, things fall apart. You grieve. And then you sit around and wait for things to somehow get perfect again. But they don't. They never can. There is no perfect. There's just different. But different can be wonderful." He smiles to himself. "If I would have realized that a lot earlier, I'd have saved myself a lot of grief."

"What finally made you realize?"

He leans back. "I was out in the kayak, alone, in the middle of the lake. It was a cold day in November. It was clear when I set out, but it clouded up and started to rain. Heavy rain, you know. Bone cold. I decided to paddle back. I was cursing the sky for ruining my morning row. I cursed everything back then." He grins to himself. "But then I noticed something. I looked up at the sky, rain falling down, and the birds—they were all out flapping around, flying this way and that. I never noticed before that moment how rain doesn't affect birds. They couldn't care less about it. Sure, maybe they bristle a little when it hits their feathers. Maybe they decide to fly back to their nests and settle in until the clouds pass. But do they squawk and curse and protest? No. They roll with it. They chirp and sing the way they always do. They don't let a little storm ruin their days, their lives." He sighs, and turns to me. "Maybe this sounds crazy to you, but that day on the lake, I realized I wanted to be like a bird. I wanted to stop being so affected by the circumstances that were dragging me down."

"Wow," I say. "That's beautiful."

"That's not to say that some things aren't worth grieving over. I mean, what you've gone through, Ada . . ."

I nod.

"There's a time for grief," he continues. "I've gone through it. But I just didn't want my life to be characterized by it."

"Me either," I say.

My eyes well up with tears, and he wipes one away, just as fellow diners around us begin cheering and clapping. We look around, oblivious to what has just transpired near us, and then notice a young couple at a table embracing. The woman holds up her left hand, and I see the sparkle of a diamond.

I think of the way James proposed, at our favorite New York City restaurant. He'd tucked the ring in his pocket and gotten down on one knee. Simple, perfect. I feel the familiar pain creeping back, and then I remember what Alex said. I know I may always ache for the past, for the two greatest loves of my life, but I want to be a bird now. I want to flap my wings through the rainstorms. I want to start my day with the earnestness of the morning glory, the way its blossoms open with the sunrise, ready to shine no matter what.

My eyes meet Alex's and moments later, he presses his lips against mine. I'm hungry for his kiss, his embrace, just as he is for mine.

"Alex," I whisper. "I want to tell you about my past."

I feel like opening up for the first time in a long while. I want to tell him about everything, every painful detail. I want to lay it all out for him to see, like found rocks and jagged shells on the beach that he can pick up and examine and turn over. I want to be transparent again. I want him to see me, for all that I am.

He leans in closer, ready, open, waiting, and listens intently, as if I'm the only person who matters in the world.

# Chapter 23

PENNY

Dex returned from California with tan skin and a bottle of perfume for me from Lana Turner. He said she had cases of it from a photo shoot she did for Macy's, which made the gift seem even less special than it was.

"Did you miss me?" Dex says, taking me into his arms.

"Yes," I lie, prying the cap off of the perfume bottle. It smells bold and sickeningly sweet, like the type of women at the art shows who always brush up alongside Dex with their low-cut dresses and lipstick-stained champagne glasses.

"Oh," he says, disappointed. "You don't like it?"

"It's fine," I say. "I guess I'm just not used to such strong scents."

"It's what all the women are wearing in Beverly Hills," he says authoritatively, as if he may have personally sniff-tested every female on Sunset Boulevard.

I spritz a bit onto my neck, and it pleases him. "I'm sure it just takes some getting used to," I say. But now that the scent is on my skin, I feel a little nauseated.

He takes a step closer to me and unclasps a pin in my hair, and then another. My body still responds to his touch, and a chill immediately trickles from my neck, down my arms.

"Let's change your hair," he says, sweeping my bangs across my forehead the way Lana Turner wore hers the night at the Chateau Marmont. "Like this."

"I don't know," I say, pulling my bangs out of my eyes. "I much prefer to wear my hair up."

He looks momentarily wounded but then shakes it off as if none of it matters—my hair, me. "I'm going to spend the afternoon in the studio," he says. "Lana wants a few paintings for her guesthouse."

"Oh," I say without emotion.

"I'll be home tonight. For Bach on the Dock."

I almost forgot. The night in July that everyone on Boat Street looks forward to. "Yes," I say as he grabs his bag and heads out the door.

"Mama," I say with a trembling voice on the phone later that day.

"What's wrong, sweetheart?" she says.

I feel the cramp in my belly then, the type I've been having for a few weeks. I haven't yet gone in to see Dr. Roberts. I don't need him to tell me what I already know. "I'm going to have a baby."

"Oh, honey!" she exclaims. "Really? This is the most wonderful news. Have you told Dex?"

"Not yet," I say guardedly.

Of course, I haven't told Collin my news either.

"I'll talk to your aunt Sue," Mama says. "We'll have a baby shower for you, invite all your old friends from the neighborhood."

"Mama, no," I say quickly. "I'd really rather not have a shower.

Please, don't bother. If you don't mind, I just want to keep things quiet for now."

She doesn't seem to hear me. "Does Dex have any sisters who I should send invitations to? I can't recall if I met any at the wedding. And do you want to invite any neighbors, any friends from Miss Higgins Academy? We really ought to invite Miss Higgins. She'll be tickled pink with this news. Her prized pupil is having a baby!"

"Mama," I say, this time more firmly. *"I don't want a shower."*

"Don't worry, dear," she says. "We'll have it in your second trimester, when you're a bit farther along. And you needn't worry about miscarriage. Nobody has those in our family. Your grandmother delivered seven healthy babies, and I would have had a half dozen if I'd found the right man."

What I don't tell her is that I won't be around for a shower. If all goes as planned, I will be leaving tonight with Collin. He just finished the sailboat, and instead of him selling it to his client, it will be our home. Together we'll sail the world, have breakfast in the Bahamas, dinner on the coast of Maine. The world will be our oyster, as Collin says. But most important, we'll be together. Forever.

Dex's return has put a damper on our plans, but we won't let that stop us. I'll sneak out after Dex falls asleep, pack my bag quietly, and leave a note before boarding the sailboat that we've spent the past week stocking to our liking. Canned food, blankets for when it gets cold. Plenty of kerosene for the lamps. Stacks of books to read.

It wasn't easy to come to this decision. It was my view that the end of a marriage, even a bad one, would leave me brandished with a scarlet letter. Part of me wanted to continue to play along—Dex with his secrets, I with mine. As disjointed and dysfunctional as our marriage has been, there's comfort and security in the ebb and flow of our lives, where a kiss on the cheek after a week apart erases the ice between us, the deception. And isn't this the arrangement that some women long for? A life of independence, where I can come and go as I please, with a husband who does the same? But that isn't the marriage I bargained for. I married for love and togetherness, not long stretches of silence and then a blue box from Tiffany & Co. three weeks later.

No, I couldn't continue on like this, nor would Collin. And while I'd miss the comfort Dex provides, I wanted Collin more than I wanted comfort. Besides, the writing was on the wall. On the night I made my decision, I found a shirt of Dex's that had slipped behind the laundry machine. When I went to put it in the wash, I noticed a stain on the collar. At first I thought it was paint. Deep red, it had the tinge of a tube of burnt umber acrylic. But then I took a closer look, and I saw it for what it really was: a smudge of lipstick. I could even smell the perfume lingering on the fabric. I shook my head then, deciding instantly that I would no longer participate in a marriage built on deceit.

I'd write Mama, of course. I'd explain everything to her in a letter. She would be hurt. She'd never understand how I could leave a man like Dexter Wentworth. It wouldn't make sense to her, but it would to me. And that's all that mattered.

After I hang up the phone, I glance out the side window to Collin's houseboat. I hope to catch him before Bach on the Dock to let him know that Dex has returned. I don't want him to worry. Nothing will change our plans. But I don't see any trace of Collin, and then I realize the sailboat's gone. At first, I panic. Where did he go? Then I take a deep breath and consider that he must have taken it out to make sure everything's shipshape for our departure. *Our departure.* I bite my lip, realizing, perhaps for the first time, that I am really going through with this. And the thought of the two of us sailing out of Lake Union tonight makes my heart beat faster.

# Chapter 24

ADA

I look up at Alex seated beside me at the restaurant table. The Space Needle has rotated a full 360 degrees, and now it's turning our view toward Elliott Bay, where a ferry is sailing out of the harbor, perhaps to Bainbridge Island to the west. Alex's eyes are big and attentive, and he waits for me to speak. I don't know if I feel brave enough to tell him, but somehow I know I must. I hear Joanie's and Dr. Evinson's voices in my ear. I hear James's and Ella's voices, too. I feel that they're near. Alex waits patiently.

*Two years prior*

I'm sitting on the bed in our room at the Waterbrook Inn, typing on my laptop. I have two hundred more words to write and I'll have a first draft, and then I can finally play a little on this working vacation. James and Ella have been saints, keeping busy with trail walks and other activities while I work. *Sunrise* sent us here to scope out what is quickly becoming known as the hottest family destination on the East Coast. With its enormous property and access to the falls, I've decided that it definitely lives up to the reputation, and the article is shaping up to be a favorable one.

Ella bounds into the bedroom and leaps onto the bed. Her pigtails are lopsided, so I straighten them. That dark, silky hair. She's an Italian beauty, like her nonna. "Mommy," she says, smiling to reveal a missing front tooth. "Daddy says we can go out for ice cream."

"Oh, does he?" It's only an hour past breakfast, and I feel a little annoyed with James. He spoils her, and he has no plans to change his ways. I love this about him, and yet at times I feel like the odd woman out—the naysayer, the party pooper, the one who's always eschewing fun for the practical. I sigh. So what if he says yes to ice cream more than I'd like? At the end of the day, I know that Ella's the happiest little girl in the world because James is the kind of daddy who says yes. And I wouldn't have it any other way.

Ella nods and jumps up and down. Her pink tutu flounces beneath her. "I want chocolate," she says. "With sprinkles."

I save the draft of the article in progress, then turn around to face her again. "Sprinkles, huh?"

She pulls my arm. "Come on, Mommy. Let's go."

I shake my head. "I can't. I have to finish this article."

"Mommy," she whines. "You always have to finish an article."

She's right. And I feel the familiar pang of guilt that I've felt since the day she was born. The one that sneaks up whenever I'm doing anything but being her mom.

"Just give me twenty minutes," I say. "I'll finish this up and we can all go out together."

James appears in the doorway. He's wearing a long-sleeved white T-shirt. A recent trip to Mexico has turned his skin a deeper shade of olive, the way it did on our honeymoon in Italy. He grins at me. "You coming?"

"Give me fifteen?"

Ella runs to James and he scoops her into his arms. She's small for her age, petite in stature but not spirit. "Mama said I can have sprinkles," she says.

I fold my arms. "Did I say that?"

Ella smiles, and James sets her back down. "Wait, I have to go find Aggie."

When Ella was three, she saw an old carved wooden sailboat in an antiques store in Monterey, on a press trip I'd been invited to. We had no idea why, but she fell in love with the little boat. Its varnish had long since worn off, but red lettering on the side remained: "Agnes Anne," now "Aggie."

She wouldn't let it go, so James bought it for her. She slept with it that night, and every night after that. "Aren't little girls supposed to love dolls, or teddy bears?" James asked. We had to stifle our laughter while watching her cuddle the boat on that first night. "It could have been worse," James said. "She could have fallen in love with your curling iron."

Ella isn't like other little girls. She's inquisitive and curious, with a heart that senses others' emotions with the precision of Doppler radar. She drops coins from her piggy bank into the outstretched hands of the homeless in Times Square, frets over the plight of hurt animals on the roadside, and two Christmases ago, organized a coat drive at her school when she saw a little boy shivering on the playground.

"You know," James says, "what in the world are we going to do if she ever loses Aggie?"

I sigh. "We'll have to find another one."

"There is no other Aggie," he says. "Have you seen the way it's carved? It's an original. It was all hand-done. There's no way it could be re-created."

"Well," I say with a smile, "then we can't lose her."

James nods as Ella returns with the little sailboat under her arm. "I'm ready," she says, looking up at her dad.

"Let's give your mommy a few more minutes," he says. "Then we'll all go together."

I finish the article as planned, just as my cell phone rings from the bedside table. I groan. It's my editor. "Hi, Suzanne," I say, motioning for James to shut the door.

"Oh, good, I caught you," she says. "The photographer we hired for the shoot bailed. Did you bring a camera?"

I glance at James's camera on the desk across the room. "Well, yeah, but—"

"Then you can add another piece to the story," she says. "We just need some candids of families near the falls. Kids and parents hiking together, out in nature, that sort of thing."

"Suzanne, I'm a writer, not a photographer." I recognize the annoyance in my own voice, but I don't apologize or try to mask it. Suzanne already assigned this trip at the last minute—the week of Ella's birthday, no less. I had to cancel a party at Princess Beatrice's Tearoom. And there were tears. Lots of tears. And now Suzanne is asking me to bring back photographs, too?

"Oh, don't be such a diva," she says. "They don't need to be perfect. Candid is fine. Remember, that's what Juan likes. The type of stuff people post on MySpace. You just take some snapshots. He'll make it work."

I sigh.

"Hey, aren't you there with your husband and daughter?"

"Yes," I say reluctantly. I can almost hear the wheels in her mind turning.

"You could photograph them together," she says. "In front of the falls."

"I'll see what I can do."

"Great," she says. "I know you won't let me down."

I hang up the phone and throw on a jacket, then tuck James's camera into my bag and walk out to the front room, where James and Ella are playing a game of Uno.

"Ready?" James asks, looking up.

"Yeah," I say. "But we have a slight detour before ice cream."

Ella groans.

"Suzanne needs me to get some family shots of the falls."

James smiles. "Good. We can walk up that trail we found yesterday."

Ella folds her arms across her chest. "Do we have to, Mama?"

"Sorry, love," I say. "I promise, it will be quick. And you and Daddy get to be my models."

She grins and runs to the door.

The waterfall is farther away than we thought. By the time we get to the ninth switchback, James and I are winded.

"C'mon, you guys!" Ella calls out from ahead. "I can hear the waterfall!"

We catch our breath, then trudge on. "It's beautiful out here," James says to me. He stops and reaches for my hand. "You know, we wouldn't be getting to see all of this if it weren't for you." He kisses the top of my hand. "Am I married to the greatest woman on earth, or what?"

I smile. He's never complained about my career, choosing only to see the positive side of all of it. I love that about him.

"Look!" Ella calls from around the bend. "I see the waterfall!"

"Ella!" I shout. "Be careful."

James and I jet ahead and find Ella standing precariously close to a rickety railing that looks like it might have been constructed in 1892. "Honey, come back here, right now," I say.

"Oh, Mama," she says in a voice that tells me she has the potential to be quite the teenage drama queen. "I'm *fine*."

"It's my job to worry about you," I say, wrapping my arm around her shoulder.

"Can we go for ice cream now?" she asks.

"Soon," I reply, digging the camera out of my bag. "OK, let's get a few pictures first." I point to the railing, with the waterfall just beyond. "James, don't let go of her," I continue. "I don't trust that railing."

He grins, scooping Ella into his arms, before dangling her upside down. "You mean I can't hold her over the edge?" She giggles and he puts her down.

"OK, you two crazies," I say, looking through the viewfinder. "Stand together now. Smile like you're having a good time on vacation." James and Ella simultaneously stick out their tongues.

I frown, thinking of Suzanne's reaction. "Please?"

They grin, then smile properly just as the flash goes off. "Perfect," I say. "Let's just get a few more, just in case. James, can you turn toward the falls, maybe, and point like you're showing her something?"

James nods and takes a step closer to the railing. He steadies himself for a moment when his foot gets caught on uneven ground. "I'm fine," he says, kneeling down and pointing up toward the waterfall.

I notice it for the first time through the lens, and it is truly majestic. Such power. Such force. I snap a picture, then another, then
key through the images on the camera. "These are good," I say,
grinning at the way Ella smiles at James in the final frame, but I
freeze when I hear Ella's scream. I look up just as it happens, the
moment the world goes from a beautiful dream to a horrific nightmare. The railing has given way, and Ella is falling backward.
James turns to reach for her, and he slips forward.

I run toward the edge, where the two most precious people in
my world have disappeared. The voice that lurches out of my lungs
is shrill and high-pitched. *"James! Ella!"* I can't breathe. I can only
hover over the edge. It pulls me like a magnet. I want nothing more
than to join them, to throw myself into the moist, foggy air, to be
with them for eternity. I close my eyes, doubling over in terror,
shock, when I feel a firm grasp on my arm. "Miss," a man says. He's
wearing a brown park ranger uniform. "I saw what happened. I'm
so very sorry. Let's get you down and we'll call an ambulance."

My eyes brighten momentarily. "Yes," I say. "James is a great
swimmer, and Ella has had swim lessons since she was three—"

"No, ma'am," he says gravely. "I'm very sorry. There's no way
anyone could survive that type of drop. I'm calling the ambulance
for *you.*"

# Chapter 25

## PENNY

The evening's festivities are the final hurdle to our plans. We'll go, we'll smile, all the while secretly planning to sail off together when the residents of Boat Street are fast asleep or simply sedated by one too many martinis.

I haven't been able to find Collin all afternoon. The sailboat is still out, but I don't fret. He won't let Dex's return disrupt our plans.

I put on a yellow gingham dress, and when I cinch the belt around my waist, I think about the new life inside. I'll wait till we're safe in each other's arms, gazing out at turquoise water, before I'll tell Collin. It will be better then, I tell myself.

I glance at my reflection in the dressing table mirror, and as I'm powdering my nose, I hear Dex on the stairs. A moment later he stands behind me and leans in to plant a kiss on the back of my neck. At first, I bristle at his touch. But I must play along so as not to arouse any suspicion. I don't want a fight. And most of all, I don't want a scene. Not on Boat Street. Not in front of the neighbors. I couldn't bear the shame of it.

"How could I stay away so long?" Dex asks, turning my chin to him. "How could I leave such beauty behind?"

I smile briefly, then turn back to the mirror, busying myself with my mascara, but Dex doesn't relent. He unzips his trousers and I watch in the mirror as they fall to the floor, revealing his strong tanned legs. He presses himself against my back, and I feel the pressure against me as he reaches his hand into the bodice of my dress. I close my eyes, reveling in the feeling of his touch, as it might be the last time his strong hands caress my skin. Like a skilled violinist plays and plucks his instrument, Dex has always been able to manipulate my body with symphonic skill. I hesitate as he turns me toward him, but I am putty in his arms. I think of all the times I craved this attention from him, the times I longed for him to come home from his studio and pull me toward him exactly like this. But now? I peel his hands off my chest, and shake my head. "I have a lasagna in the oven."

"Let it burn," Dex replies, pulling me toward the bed. I want to give myself to him. After all, I am still his wife, and yes, part of me still loves him, and may always love him. But I climb down the ladder to the kitchen. I belong to Collin now, every inch of me.

Dex and I walk out to the dock at five. Collin's sailboat is docked in its place now, and I breathe a sigh of relief. Maybe he saw that Dex was home and didn't want to come over? I hoped to talk to him before Bach on the Dock, to solidify our plans, and mostly to promise him I'd be there this evening, like we planned. I'll find him at the party. I'll reassure him.

I place the lasagna on a card table set against Naomi and Gene's deck. She flashes us a plastic smile. "Oh, Dexter," she says, ignoring me. "You're home from California!"

He gives her an air-kiss. "Yes, flew home this morning."

Gene walks over to shake Dex's hand. "Nice night for a party," Dex says. But Gene doesn't reply. Instead, he turns to me. "How are you, Penny?" He's smiling, but I can tell something's bothering him. His left eye twitches a little.

"Oh, fine, thanks," I lie. I watch Dex weave from one person to the next, ever the social butterfly. Naomi disappears into the house and returns holding a plate of pastries. She looks at me, then sets them on the table. "Dex," she calls. "Your favorite."

Naomi hands him a chocolate éclair, and he takes a bite. "Did *you* make these? They're out of this world."

She nods self-consciously. "They're nothing special, just a recipe I picked up a from a French friend."

I look around for Collin but don't see him anywhere. Lenora and Tom and the others filter in. They ask how I am. But they mostly channel their attention toward Dex, who recounts his time in California, segueing into a story about a pool party at Lana's where Cary Grant and Lauren Bacall were in attendance.

I can't listen. It's as if I've become immune to his bravado. I look away and catch a glimpse of Jimmy. He peers around the corner in jeans and a pair of tennis shoes, one with the laces untied. He smiles at me before Naomi shoos him back into the house. He turns around with slumped shoulders.

I think of the child growing in my belly, and I promise never to view him as a nuisance but always as a great blessing. I place my hand on my stomach and look at Dexter. His face is animated. He speaks further about California, and the little crowd on the dock erupts in laughter. I could never be Mrs. Dexter Wentworth without losing myself in his shadow. I know that now.

"What's wrong, dear?" Lenora asks a few minutes later. Everyone's hovering around a makeshift bar that Naomi and Gene have set up.

"Oh," I say, looking up quickly. "Nothing."

"You look a little pale," she continues.

I do my best to smile. "I suppose I'm just a bit tired."

"Here," she says. "Let's get you a drink."

She takes my arm and we walk to the bar. Naomi hands me a martini, but it tastes bitter. Later I pour it in the lake. A green olive bobs in the water until a female mallard swims over and scoops it into her beak.

I hardly notice that the music has begun when Dex finds me a little while later. "Come on," he says, reaching for my hand. "Everyone's dancing." I take his hand obediently as he leads me closer to the little trio of musicians led by Gene on the violin. I don't recognize the song. It's stiff and classical. Dex wraps his arms around me, and I look up at the fairy lights overhead. My head is heavy, and I instinctively lean it against Dex's chest. At first I don't notice Collin standing a few feet ahead, but then I hear Naomi say his name. I lift my head as we make eye contact. Naomi hands him a martini, and he takes a long sip, throwing nearly the entire martini back in one fell swoop. He stares straight at me, just as Dex's hands drop lower on my waist. Too low. I see the look in Collin's eyes. Betrayal. My eyes plead with him to understand. Can't he see that I must play along? Can't he understand that Dex's return changes nothing, nothing at all? We'll sail away together, just like we planned. But Collin doesn't stay to hear my explanation. Before the song ends, he's gone.

By ten, Dex has had too much to drink. He's more animated than ever, and Tom doesn't even mind that he's dancing with Lenora and clutching her waist in a way he'd never have dared before five martinis.

Disgusted, I walk to the end of the dock in front of our houseboat. Surely Dexter, in his state, wouldn't notice if I packed my things and left early with Collin. But Collin isn't there, or anywhere. And the sailboat is gone too. I feel a twinge of worry then. The once-waterproof plan we'd forged now had leaks in it. Did he leave without me?

I hardly notice Jimmy sitting on my deck, and I quickly dry the tears in my eyes so he won't be frightened.

"Hi, honey," I say, sitting beside him. "What are you doing up so late?"

"It's too loud to sleep," he says with shrug. When he looks up at me, I can see tears on his cheeks.

"Sweetie," I say, "what's the matter? You've been crying."

Jimmy sniffs and wipes his nose on his sleeve. I can tell he's trying to be strong, trying to be a man, but the mere fact that I've asked him about his pain seems to have the opposite effect on him, and now tears spill freely onto his freckle-dotted cheeks. He reaches into his pocket and pulls out a wadded-up piece of paper, then hands it to me.

"What is this, honey?" I ask, unfolding it carefully.

"My comic strip," he says. "I found it in the trash can."

I think of how proud he was of his sketches. I remember the way he showed it to me so timidly and how I encouraged him to show it to Naomi and Gene. I thought they'd praise him. I only wanted Jimmy to feel some sense of happiness, some sense of worth. Here is a boy who aches for approval from his parents, especially his mother, and my meddling has only made things worse.

"Honey," I say, searching for the right words. "It must have been a mistake. Surely your parents wouldn't throw this away." I smooth out the page, smiling at the way he drew the comic strip, trying so hard to keep his lines straight. "Look at how nice your printing is in the thought bubbles. And see how you drew the farm animals here? It's magnificent." I hand the comic back to him, but he shakes his head.

"I don't want it," he says.

"Well," I say, "then *I'll* keep it. I won't let you, or anyone else, throw something so excellent away. Besides, you'll want it back someday."

"I will?" Jimmy asks, puzzled, but the idea intrigues him.

"Of course you will. When you're a famous comic strip artist."

The corners of his mouth turn up briefly, but his smile fades fast, and he folds his arms across his chest. I worry that it doesn't matter what I say. The wound is too deep, and I fear it will scar this time.

"Want to rest on my couch?" I say. "It's quieter down here."

"It's OK. I'd rather just look out at the lake."

"Me, too," I say, hoping that at any moment I'll see Collin sailing up, just like we planned. I'll run inside and get my suitcase and then jump aboard. We'll wave to Jimmy as we cast off. I might not even leave a note. "Bon voyage," I'll whisper to Jimmy. He'd keep our secret.

But the sailboat isn't anywhere in sight, and a moment later, I detect movement on the deck in front of Collin's houseboat. It's dark, but the porch light on his back deck illuminates two figures in the night. Two men in dark suits.

# Chapter 26

ADA

Alex drives me home from the restaurant and walks me back to my door. I invite him in and he follows me to the living room. He hasn't said a lot since I told him my story at dinner. I wonder how it's affected him, and I worry.

"You're really brave, you know," he says, looking deep into my eyes.

"No," I say honestly. "Really, I'm not."

"But you are," he insists. "Coming out here, forging a new life for yourself. That takes guts."

I sigh. "I wish I could tell you that it was my strength that got me on that plane, but it wasn't. It was fear. I had to get out of New York. I felt that I had to escape all my memories. All my guilt."

He turns to face me. "Guilt? Why would you have guilt?"

Tears sting my eyes. "Because I brought them to that godforsaken waterfall," I say. "It was my stupid job and nothing else. If I hadn't taken that assignment, they'd still be alive." I'm making a fist now, shaking it into the air, and Alex calmly tucks it down on my lap.

"You did what you had to do," he says. "Your work isn't the reason for their deaths. You must believe that."

I look down at my lap. I don't know what to say.

"When I was fourteen," Alex begins, "my father died. He was an alcoholic. He wasn't home a lot of the time when I was young—in fact, hardly ever. But the year before his death, he got sober. And it was the best year of my life. I finally had a dad around who was coherent enough to play catch with me, to help me build those model rockets I loved. But it was too late, almost. A fourteen-year-old doesn't want to hang out with his dad all the time. By then, I wanted to go to my friends' houses after school, hang out at the mall—anything but be at home. I always worried that my distance hurt him. And then he relapsed, in a bad way. One night he drove home from the bar and hit a tree head-on."

"Oh, Alex."

"I hated him for a long time after that. I was so angry. But mostly I was angry at *myself*. I thought I could've prevented it from happening. If I'd played that game of Monopoly with him that evening like he wanted to, if I'd stayed home instead of going to my friend John's for a sleepover. If I'd been a better son. But one day I just let it go. I stopped blaming myself. I stopped being angry. His death was tragic, but I couldn't let it define my life. And most important, I didn't cause it."

I nod. "I wish I could get to that place."

"You will," he says. "Be patient with yourself. Promise?"

I nod. "I'll try."

Joanie calls the next morning at seven. It's ten New York time, so I don't mind that she's calling so early. Besides, I woke up at four unable to sleep and spent an hour on the deck watching the white morning glory buds open with the sunrise.

"I tried calling you last night, but your phone went straight to voice mail," she says. "Is everything all right?"

"Yeah," I say. "I had company."

"You were seeing what's-his-name again?"

"Alex. We went out to dinner at the Space Needle and then came back here and talked until midnight."

"Uh-huh." Her voice is teasing, and I can imagine the look on her face.

"Stop," I say. "We've only kissed once."

"And? Is he a good kisser?"

"Yes," I reply, feeling my cheeks warm a bit at the thought.

"So are you seeing him again today?"

"No. He's on a shoot in Portland." It occurs to me that he could be with Kellie. I failed to ask whether they still work together. But I don't let my mind dwell on the thought, especially after all he shared with me.

"Hey, I almost forgot," Joanie says. "I found something that might be helpful in your search for Penny."

"Oh, what?"

I hear the sound of her sorting through papers. "A deposition given by a little boy named Jimmy. I was only able to obtain the first few pages, because a psychologist ordered him mentally unstable for trial."

"You said his name was Jimmy?"

"Yes. I'll e-mail you a PDF."

❦

That afternoon, I decide to go for a walk to Pete's Market. It's a cool day, so I put on a light sweater, and I grab my purse. An hour later

I return with a bag filled with groceries. As I step onto the dock, I notice that the empty houseboat on the left seems to be inhabited. The windows are all propped open, as if someone's just come home and is airing the place out. Just as I'm passing, an older woman appears in the doorway. Her gray hair is short and curled, the way my grandmother's is. But she has a youthful smile, and adventurous eyes that hardly match her eighty-some years. "Honey," she says, "can I talk you into helping me for a moment? I've just come home from an extended trip and I think I may have vermin living behind the dresser."

"Oh no," I say, setting the grocery bag down. "Of course."

I step inside her houseboat. It's small and clean. It has the look of a place that's more of a stopover than a home. There are no pictures on the walls or personal items about. Just a suitcase on the floor and a coffee table and sofa with no throw pillows.

"I'm Esther," she says, extending her hand. "You must be new here."

"Yes," I say. "Ada Santorini. I moved in recently. I'm renting the houseboat at the end of the dock."

"Oh, the old Wentworth residence," she says, looking me over. "And how are you liking it?"

"Very much. It's lovely here on the lake."

"It is and it isn't," she says, turning back to the dresser and making a displeased face. "So many critters."

I smile. "How long have you owned your home here?"

"Oh, forever, I guess," she says. "I came here in the 1940s. I left a bad marriage."

"I'm sorry."

"It was a hard time," she says. "I had to leave my darling daughter behind on Bainbridge Island and start over. In those days women didn't stand a chance in divorce battles, so I just threw in the towel. I didn't want to fight."

I can't imagine ever feeling that way about my marriage or my daughter. If the circumstances arose, I'd fight for her. And yet, I don't know the extent of Esther's story, so I don't pry. Besides, there's a look in her eyes that tells me she had no other choice.

"At the time, a houseboat was all I could afford," she continues. "The lake wasn't fancy like it is now. I bought it for five hundred dollars, and now it's worth five hundred thousand. Some investment, don't you think?"

I smile. "Quite."

"I was tempted to sell over the years," she says. "Especially after that movie came out."

"Movie?"

"*Sleepless in Seattle*. For a few years, it was like a pilgrimage. Folks came out here from all over the world wanting to live the lifestyle they saw in the movie."

"I loved that movie," I say.

Esther shrugs. "I never did see it."

"You should; it's really good."

"Well, no amount of money could make me sell," she says. "I travel frequently and I need a home base. I also left a big part of my heart here."

"Your daughter?"

"Yes," she says. "And a man."

"Oh?"

"He lives in a retirement home in Seattle. We haven't spoken since 1943. But sometimes I'll watch from the sidewalk when he's out in the garden."

I gasp. "You still love him."

"I always will," she says matter-of-factly. "I gave him my heart as a girl, and he's still in possession of it."

She must sense my confusion. "Listen, my dear," she says. "My life has been convoluted and complicated, certainly anything but conventional. But I'm happy with it just the same."

"But don't you wish you could know him now, this man you loved so much? Don't you wish you could have had a life with him?"

"Of course I do," she says, sitting down on the sofa. I take a seat beside her. "But that wasn't how our story was meant to be. You see, some love stories are different than others. Some last but a moment; others a lifetime. I was fortunate to have the latter; I just didn't have the privilege of spending every day with him. It doesn't mean our love was any less significant. Our time together had to end, but our love lived on."

I think for a moment about James, about our short, sweet life together. And I know that no matter who else my heart encounters in this life, it won't ever change what we had together.

"Well," Esther continues. "Listen to me rambling on."

"Why don't you go see him?" I ask. "Don't you want to visit him after all these years?"

She nods. "I do, terribly so. But I haven't found the right moment. Honestly, after so much time, I'm a bit frightened. What if he doesn't feel the same way? What if time has erased his love for me?"

I shake my head. "You have to go—before it's too late."

She nods.

"What's his name?"

"Elliot," she says. "Elliot Hartley." She looks deep in thought, as though imagining a moment they shared long ago.

I hear a scratching sound in the direction of the bureau on the wall.

Esther looks at me. "Did you hear that?"

"Yeah," I say. "What do you think it is?"

"A rat," she says, standing. "Here, help me pull it out from the wall. We'll shoo it away."

I nod, placing my hands on the right side of the mahogany dresser.

"On the count of three," Esther says. "One, two, three."

Together we pull the dresser away from the wall, and immediately see the intruder, a squawking, feather-covered . . . duck.

"Well would you get a load of that," Esther says. "It's a duck." She kneels down to level with the bird woman to woman. "Honey, what in the world are you doing in my houseboat?"

The mallard gives a defiant quack, then waddles out to the dock.

"That must be Henrietta," I say.

"Henrietta?"

"She lives on the dock, with her husband," I explain. "Er, duck husband. His name is Haines."

"Oh," Esther says. "Yes, I do remember Jimmy saying something about a couple of fighting ducks."

It's funny to hear her speak of Jim as Jimmy. "Oh, before I go," I say, standing up, "there's just one thing I'm hoping you can help me sort out."

"Of course," she says. "What is it, dear?"

"Do you recall a man named Collin who once lived on Boat Street?"

Her eyes close and open again. "Oh, yes," she says. "How could I ever forget Collin? He was special. They don't make them like that anymore."

"So you knew him?"

"Yes," she says. "Briefly. He was a boat maker. He made extraordinary wooden boats." I think of the *Catalina*, but I don't interrupt her stream of memories, for fear they'll cease. "He was only here on the dock a short time. He was running from something. I knew what that was like. I was too."

"What happened to him?"

She sighs. "I wish I knew, dear. I came home from a trip to Europe and he'd already gone. That was after Penny vanished too. I like to think that they're together. That they sailed off into the sunset and that was that." She shakes her head. "But I'm not so sure it ended that way."

"Why not?"

She peers out to the dock to make sure no one's listening before continuing. "Because of *the pact*."

"The pact?" I instantly recall Alex saying something similar.

She nods. "Those who were here the night that Penny vanished vowed never to divulge what they knew."

"Why?"

She shrugs. "I can tell you I never did find out the truth, and I don't think I ever will. The secret will die with all of them. They're stubborn that way, houseboaters."

I don't tell her that I've vowed to find out what happened to Penny, to drag the secret from the depths of the lake if that's what it takes. "Well, I should be going," I say to Esther. "It was so nice to meet you."

She winks. "You, too, dear."

❦

I don't see Henrietta when I walk out to the dock, and I hope she's reunited with Haines—for Jim's sake, at least. I return to my houseboat and unload the groceries. I remember what Joanie said about finding pages of a deposition from young Jimmy, and I'm eager to see if she's sent it.

I open my e-mail and see a new message from Joanie. I click on it with anticipation. "Here you go," she writes. "Read the last line. It's creepy."

I pull open the document and wait for it to load. A moment later a scanned page from a typewritten police report appears on my screen:

TESTIMONY FROM JIMMY CLYDE,
SON OF MR. GENE AND MRS. NAOMI CLYDE,
OF 2209 FAIRVIEW AVENUE EAST, SEATTLE.

OFFICER CLAYTON: Son, please state your name for
the record.
JIMMY CLYDE: Jimmy Clyde, sir.
OFFICER CLAYTON: Please state your age.
JIMMY CLYDE: Nine years old, sir.
OFFICER CLAYTON: Now Jimmy, please share with us
how you came to know Mrs. Wentworth.
JIMMY CLYDE: You mean Penny?
OFFICER CLAYTON: That's right, son. Penny
Wentworth. Don't cry, son; there's nothing to be
afraid of.
JIMMY CLYDE: But I . . .
OFFICER CLAYTON: What is it, son?
JIMMY CLYDE: Will she come back, sir? Will she ever
come back?
OFFICER CLAYTON: That's why we're talking to you,
young man. We're trying to make sure she does. Now
tell us how you came to know Mrs. Wentworth,
Jimmy.
JIMMY CLYDE: She lived near me. She was always so
nice. Nicer than anyone I've ever met.
OFFICER CLAYTON: Did she ever talk about anyone
being unkind to her, Jimmy? Anyone who wanted to
hurt her?

JIMMY CLYDE: No, sir. But she was sad a lot.

OFFICER CLAYTON: Oh? How do you know that, Jimmy?

JIMMY CLYDE: Because I saw her crying. He made her cry.

OFFICER CLAYTON: Who, Jimmy? Come on, now, you can tell me.

JIMMY CLYDE: Mr. Wentworth.

OFFICER CLAYTON: And why did Mr. Wentworth make her cry?

JIMMY CLYDE: I don't know.

OFFICER CLAYTON: Help me understand, Jimmy.

JIMMY CLYDE: Mother says he's better than her. But that's not true. Penny was the nicest lady in the whole wide world. Maybe he told her that. Maybe it hurt her feelings.

OFFICER CLAYTON: Now why would your mother say that about Mrs. Wentworth?

JIMMY CLYDE: I don't know, sir.

OFFICER CLAYTON: Please, Jimmy, you have to help us here. You were one of the last people to see Mrs. Wentworth. Any clue you can give us will help our case.

JIMMY CLYDE: Will it help bring Penny home?

OFFICER CLAYTON: We hope so, son.

JIMMY CLYDE: Then I'll tell you.

OFFICER CLAYTON: What is it?

JIMMY CLYDE: On the night she disappeared, Mr. Wentworth was angry at her. I heard him shouting, and it frightened me.

OFFICER CLAYTON: Jimmy, what did he say?

JIMMY CLYDE: I can't remember, sir.

OFFICER CLAYTON: Please try, son.

JIMMY CLYDE: Why did he hurt her, sir? Why? She
was an angel. She was an angel sent from heaven. I
know it. And he had to go and hurt her.
OFFICER CLAYTON: Please, don't cry, son.
Everything's going to be all right.
JIMMY CLYDE: But it won't. And you know that.
Because she's never coming home.
OFFICER CLAYTON: Let the record show that Jimmy's
parents have submitted an injunction, which I'm
holding in my hands now, halting any further
interrogation of the child on the basis that he is
mentally incapable of answering questions in a
factual way.

❧

I open my laptop and pull up my memoir in progress, but all I can
think about is Penny and why any of the residents of Boat Street
would have wanted to silence the truth.

# Chapter 27

PENNY

"There they are again," Jimmy says, pointing to the men on Collin's deck.

"You've seen them before?"

"Mama says they're the police," he says. "She says that Collin is a criminal."

"That's nonsense," I say quickly, though it occurs to me that Collin has told me so little of his past.

Jimmy shakes his head. "He doesn't seem like a criminal."

"I assure you, honey, he's most certainly not."

"Then why do these men keep coming to look for him?"

"Maybe they just want to talk to him." I say. The men notice us then, waving at me and gesturing toward the dock.

A few minutes later, they appear in front of us on the dock. "Excuse me, miss," one says. "May we have a word with you?"

I stand up. "Of course," I say, hoping they don't detect the quiver in my voice.

"I'm Colonel Everett, and this is my colleague," he says. I recognize military stripes on his jacket. "We'd speak to the others on the dock, but, well, they appear to have had a bit too much to drink."

I remember the way Dex was slurring his words, and I nod. "How can I help you?"

"You see," the man says, "we're looking for a Mr. Collin McCleary. Do you happen to know him?"

I nod. "Yes," I say honestly. "He is the neighbor on the next dock."

"You see, miss," the man continues, "Mr. McCleary is wanted for a serious crime against the US government."

I gasp. "What do you mean?"

"He is wanted for treason."

I notice Jimmy's eyes go wide beside me, and I realize that I can't let him hear a word more of this exchange. "Honey," I say to him, "go on inside until I'm finished talking to these gentlemen, all right?"

He obeys and walks inside. When I hear the door close behind me, I turn back to the officer.

"I don't understand," I say. "Treason?"

"It's a serious offense, and we want him for questioning."

"But what has he done?"

Colonel Everett looks at his partner, then turns back to me. "He defected from his unit in Korea. He's been living under an assumed name."

I shake my head. *This can't be happening.* "You mean Collin isn't his real name?"

"No, ma'am, it isn't."

I don't want to know his real name. I don't want to know any of this. In the period of a minute and a half, these men in their dark suits and their lapels full of military insignia are threatening to change my view of Collin, and I don't want to hear another word of it.

"Well," Colonel Everett continues. "If you see him, please call this number." He hands me a stiff white business card.

I nod despondently, and then they turn to leave. Jimmy tiptoes out to the deck a moment later. He must sense my worry, because he tucks his hand in mine. "Are you afraid?" he asks.

"I'll be honest with you, Jimmy, darling," I say, kneeling down so that my eyes meet his. "I am, a little." I think of Collin's love for me, and I know that even despite the setbacks—the moment on the dock, the unknown men who seek him so relentlessly—things will be fine. We'll be fine. I smile. "You see, even grown-ups feel afraid sometimes." I smooth his hair with my hand. "I wish someone would have told me that a long time ago. When I was a little girl, I thought that perfection was waiting at the end of growing up. But it hasn't happened that way for me."

He nods, but I know that true understanding of my words might be years away. I sigh over the painful passage of time and look out to the lake, desperate to move the seconds forward. I'm all but certain that the light brightening the nighttime horizon is Collin, my knight on a white sailboat, coming to take me away.

❦

It takes some persuading, but I finally convince Jimmy to go home. I stay out on the deck, alone. There is no sign of Dex. The sound of music and laughter continues up the dock, so I know the party is still raging on. So I wait. And then, just after eleven, the faint light I've been so hopefully tracking is suddenly upon me. I see the sailboat motoring in from the dark water, the dim light of the moon reflecting on Collin's face. He's seated beside the tiller, and he kills the engine, letting the sailboat creep in quietly.

I rise to my full height, and wave to him with open arms.

Neither of us speaks, but I can see his expression ease. A minute later, he secures the boat to the dock, and he leaps out to stand beside me. The tension between us burns. The slightest touch is certain to generate a spark, or perhaps an electric shock.

"You came," I say, sinking into his embrace. The elation lasts but for an instant, dulled at the thought of the men who were standing on the dock just hours prior.

"Collin, we have to talk about something important."

He looks startled and then frowns. "You still love him, don't you?" Before I can answer, he continues. "I saw the way you were dancing with him tonight."

"No, I—"

"I want your whole heart for my own," he says, "but I suppose that's more than you can give. That's why I stormed out." He looks at his feet, before turning his gaze up at me again, expectantly. "Penny, I'd be happy if I just had half of it."

"Oh, Collin," I say, squeezing his hand reassuringly.

His eyes brighten.

"There's something else," I say, letting go of his hand. "Two men have been looking for you. Collin, they told me that you're being charged with treason."

He looks silently out to the lake.

"So, it's *true*?"

He raises his hands to the back of his neck and lifts off the silver chain that holds his military dog tags. I studied the metal plates on nights we were together, and held them in my hands, listening to the way they clinked together on Collin's bare chest. I asked him to tell me about his time in the military, but he was always silent. Until now.

He opens my hand and sets the silver chain, still warm from his skin, in my palm. "They're not mine," he says. "I never wanted to join the military, but when I turned eighteen, my father marched me down to the station and told me it was the honorable thing to do. I wanted to make him proud, but I didn't realize I was actually signing my life away."

I nod and continue listening.

"At first I thought it would be adventurous, shipping off to Korea, but when I got there, I realized I had made a horrible mistake. I knew how to build boats, but I never wanted to use them to kill people. Penny, I saw death and destruction all around. Women, children were cut down by bombs and bullets. I held a little Korean boy in my arms after our attack took out his village. I held him as he took his last breath."

I look away. This picture of war is more than I can bear.

"When my unit was hit, we were miles away from our base, on leave for the night," Collin continues. I'm not ready to hear his story, but he needs to tell me. I hold still. "A man was badly burned. Unrecognizable. His name was Collin, and he was on his last tour. He was heading home to Washington the next day. That night I had two choices: Find my way back and continue fighting that miserable war, or take the chance to start a new life for myself."

"So you took his dog tags," I say. "You took his identity."

"I did," he says. "Penny, I'm not proud of what I did. But I have to live with my choices. And because of them I will always be running."

"And what about his family? Do they simply think he's missing in action?"

"When I made it home," he says, "I went to see his folks. I told them the truth. They didn't take it very well. They wanted their son buried properly, instead of beneath a tombstone mismarked with my name. But I gave them every cent I had, which at the time was quite a bit. I'd made four boats and assisted in the building of dozens more, so I had money saved before the war. It only seemed fitting to give it to them."

"And that kept them silent?"

"I hoped it would," he says. "But I guess they've finally gone to the authorities. I knew they would when the money ran out."

"And you're running now?"

He tucks his hand in mine. "Yes. Hopefully with you."

"But . . . what you've done—it's fraud. I don't even know your real name."

"It's Sam," he says. "Sam Leary."

The name sounds strange and foreign.

"I can't call you that," I say.

"Then don't."

"How can I even be sure I know you?"

He takes my hand and presses it against his chest. "You know my heart; that's how."

I wipe a tear from my cheek. "Then what happens next? What are we supposed to do?"

He nods urgently. "Come away with me."

I look back to the dock, where I hear the sound of Dexter's deep laughter, before turning back to Collin hesitantly. "But, I—"

Collin takes a step back. He's injured by my hesitation; I know it. But he forces a smile, determined to lighten the moment. "You still have your ticket, don't you?"

"Yes," I say, grinning as I remember the ticket stub he gave me as passage onto the boat. I've kept it alongside a few other prized possessions in my old chest in the living room.

Collin rubs his head and looks at me cautiously, as if considering whether to make a revelation or to keep it to himself. "There's something else you should know."

I think of the client who'd commissioned Collin to build the boat. "Collin, he's not still expecting the boat is he? You don't owe him—"

"I don't owe him anything," he says. "I get my payment when I deliver the boat. That was our arrangement."

"Oh," I say, relieved. But the troubled expression lingers on Collin's face.

"Penny, the client, the man who commissioned this boat, is someone whose name may be familiar."

I shake my head in disbelief. "Who?"

"Robert Wentworth."

"But that's . . ."

"Your father-in-law."

"Does Dexter know?"

Collin rubs his brow. "No."

"Because Dex hasn't spoken to his father in years." The revelation is making my head spin. Dex has refused to accept financial assistance from his wealthy family during our marriage. And yet, I've always wondered. I think about the checks sent to our home from an anonymous patron—well, Dex's biggest patron. The checks are from a corporation I don't recognize, but the handwriting . . . all I know is that I've seen it before. There's something unique about the way the sender loops his $p$'s and elongates his $y$'s. But I stop thinking of Dexter's art then, and instead I think of Collin's lie.

"Why did you keep this from me?" I ask.

"I, I . . . listen," he continues. "I swore I wouldn't say anything. For all I knew, he just wanted to buy a boat."

I cast him a skeptical look. "From a boat maker who lives across the dock from his son?"

Collin nods. "Listen, it's natural for a father to want to know about a son who has cut off all contact."

I smirk, suddenly feeling protective of Dex. "And I suppose he paid you a pretty penny for all of your convenient updates."

"Penny," Collin pleads, "don't be angry. Don't let this change things between us." He climbs into the sailboat and waits for me to follow. His expression is urgent, pleading. "Come away with me. This sailboat is ours, yours and mine. We'll start a new life together, just as we talked about."

I walk closer to the sailboat, then turn back to the dock, before returning my gaze to Collin. "I need more time," I say. "I—"

Collin holds up his hand, as if to say, "Don't tell me. I can't bear it."

The truth is, I don't know what words are about to cross my lips. I love Collin; it's true. But I can't deny that the revelations of the investigators have clouded my decision making now. *Dex.* I close my eyes and rub my brow. I made a vow, and at this moment, I am not ready to break it. My past indiscretions are only temporary. I look at Collin, so strong, so sure standing aboard the sailboat. Yes, he has my heart, and I'm having his baby, but if I left tonight, it would mean forever. It would mean the end to everything I have with Dexter, and I'm not sure if I'm ready for that. It doesn't feel fair to Dexter, to the vow I've made.

I run my hand along the smooth, varnished railing. In blue letters on the rear of the boat is the newly painted word *Catalina.* I smile through my tears, and he catches my eye.

"I named her for you," he says. "You said you always wanted to go to Catalina."

"Yes," I say, wiping a tear from my cheek. "I didn't think you remembered."

"I thought it could be the first place we sail to," he says.

I shake my head. "I just need more time." My voice sounds agitated, frantic.

He unties the rope from the cleat and my heart begins to race. "Collin," I cry. "Collin, no, please don't go. Not yet. Not like this."

My heart is in my throat as he pushes off. I stand on the dock, straddling two lives—the life I live with Dexter on Boat Street and another with Collin on the sea. But Collin is slipping away now.

I reach my hands out to him, pleadingly. I haven't meant to hurt him. "Come back for me," I cry, this time louder. I don't care if anyone hears me; I want *him* to hear me. "I love you, Collin. I will always love you."

I watch him drift off into the darkness of the lake, and I collapse onto the dock, burying my face in my hands.

Collin will return. He has to return. I feel desperate as I pace the floors of the houseboat. I reach for a suitcase and throw it on the floor. I could pack and get into the canoe. I could go after him. I shake my head. I'd never match his speed.

I sit down on the sofa. My hands are trembling. All I can do is wait. Collin will come back for me. He just needs time. He'll return—tonight, even. And when he does, I'll be ready.

I walk out to the deck and fix my eyes on the lake. Every passing kayaker could be Collin. Every boat. Every duck in the distance. I don't take my eyes off the lake. I don't want to miss him.

# Chapter 28

## ADA

It's after nine when Alex knocks on my door the next night. He wraps his arms around my waist and kisses me softly. "I thought you were going to be staying over in Portland tonight," I say.

"I decided to drive back so I could see you."

I can't contain my smile. "Really?"

"Really." He walks into the living room and plops down on the sofa. "What are you working on?"

I quickly close my laptop. I may have told him about my past, but I'm not quite ready for him to read my private memoirs, at least not yet. "Just a little writing project."

He nods. "Going to Bach on the Dock tomorrow night?"

"Is it already tomorrow?"

"Yeah," he says. "Naomi always makes a point of inviting me, even though I'm not an official resident of Boat Street."

"I'm glad you'll be there," I say. "Frankly, with all the stuff I'm finding out about Penny, and the investigation, I'm starting to get a little creeped out by this dock."

"Oh, don't let it get to you," he says. "These folks are a harmless lot. Quirky, but harmless. You should see the way Gene plays the violin. They used to have a full quartet; now it's just him."

"Are we supposed to bring anything?"

"Bring an app and a bottle of wine and you'll be golden."

The wind has picked up since this morning, and I hear it whistling in the eaves of the houseboat, which is swaying gently now. "Storm's coming," Alex says.

I hear a rattling sound upstairs in the direction of my bedroom, and I freeze for a moment. "Did you hear that?"

He nods. "Probably just the wind."

"No," I say. "It sounded like someone was opening the porthole in the bedroom."

Alex stands up. "Want me to go check it out?"

I nod cautiously, then follow him upstairs. At the top of the ladder, I breathe a sigh of relief. "See?" Alex says. "No boogeyman."

Then I notice the porthole is open. "Alex, something's not right." I walk over and pull the little window shut. "I always leave this window closed."

I can tell he's startled, just as I am, but he puts on a brave face. "It might have been the wind," he says. "Look, it's really rocking the boat out there." I look out and see the *Catalina* bobbing on the lake, but we both know the wind wouldn't be able to blow a solid metal porthole open.

"Want me to stay for a bit longer?" Alex asks once we've climbed down the stairs.

I nod.

"I could sing you a lullaby," he says teasingly. "But you wouldn't want me to, because I can't sing."

I grin. "James used to sing to Ella every night. She had colic as a baby, and singing was the only thing that calmed her down. Well, that and the vacuum cleaner." Alex grins. "But there was this one song—it's not even a lullaby—she loved most. He'd sing it over and over again to her, and it became their special lullaby, even as she grew up. He sang it to her the night before she died."

"What was the song?" Alex asks tenderly. I can tell he wants to be a part of my memories, and yet like a person touring someone's private garden, he's careful not to trample the tulips.

" 'Puff, the Magic Dragon,' " I say quietly.

I nestle my head into his shoulder, and when my eyes begin to get heavy, I can hear James singing somewhere very far away.

"Morning," Alex says the next day. I look at the clock. It's after nine.

"Did I really fall asleep on the couch?"

"Sure did," he says, filling a mug with coffee and setting it on the chest in front of the sofa. "And you talk in your sleep."

The sunlight is bright, and I rub my eyes. "Oh no, what did I say?"

"Something about a deadline and a motorcycle."

"I have no idea," I say, smiling.

"Sounds like quite a dream," he says, sinking into the sofa beside me. "I just hope I was in it."

"Thanks for staying over last night."

"You sure you didn't leave the window open?"

"Maybe I did," I say.

"There are so few incidents of theft on the docks, I don't think we need to worry about intruders."

I nod. "You're probably right," I say, stretching. I want to put the incident out of my mind as much as Alex does.

He squeezes my hand before standing up. "I've got to run some errands, but I'll be back at five and we can go to Bach on the Dock together."

He kneels down and presses his lips against mine, and I pull him closer to me.

"Do you have to go?"

"I do," he says. "But I'm going to think of you every second today, now that I know how cute you are in your sleep."

I smile as I watch him walk out the door.

That evening, Alex returns with a takeout antipasto plate he's picked up from Serafina's. Together with my baguette and bottle of wine, we leave for my very first Bach on the Dock. It's a party, of course, but it feels a bit like a baptismal ceremony—my acceptance into the houseboat community.

We walk out to the dock together. Colorful Chinese paper lanterns are hung along the string lights. Someone's hooked up a stereo and speakers, and jazz wafts in the air. I feel a little out of place, like a new girlfriend being introduced to a larger extended family who isn't exactly keen on newcomers. Still, the neighbors smile warmly, and someone hands me a glass of red wine. I remind myself to smile back.

"Oh, good," Naomi croons when she sees us. "How nice that the two of you could come together."

"Gene," she says to her husband, "you remember Alex, and our new neighbor, Ada."

The old man nods vacantly as we set our provisions down on the table. He looks tired, and his mind is elsewhere.

"It's just like the old days," Naomi says, taking my arm. "We used to do it up big back then. A quartet, a full bar, the works. Those were the days."

I wonder if her life has turned out the way she anticipated. She's still married after all these years, and her son lives nearby. It all adds up to the picture of a happy life, and yet there is a sadness that lingers behind Naomi's eyes, and I long to know why.

"So Boat Street was quite the place in its heyday?"

"Indeed it was," she says. "It had an energy that practically *pulsated*." She stops beside the potted plants in front of her deck as more guests arrive and mingle on the dock.

"I suppose it still does," I say. "The spirit is still alive."

Naomi shrugs, kneeling down beside a terra-cotta pot and pulling out a sprig of morning glory. "It's not what it was." She tosses the little vine into the lake, and I watch its white bud drift away helplessly. "The soul is gone."

As different as we are, her words resonate with me then. I know how it feels when the soul has left a place. After the accident, it was as if the warmth had been sucked straight out of my apartment in New York.

She stands up and brushes a bit of dirt from her hand. "But some things never change, like this deplorable morning glory."

I think about the soul of Boat Street, and I can't help but wonder if it left the dock the night that Penny disappeared. If so, why?

"Naomi," I say seizing the moment, "I've been meaning to ask you something, about a young woman who lived here—"

"Oh, look," she says abruptly, walking ahead. "Lenora's here. I'll go and greet her."

Alex walks over to me. "Is it my imagination, or do people seem a little tense tonight?"

I nod. "I know what you mean. Have you seen Jim?"

"No. Gene said he wasn't feeling well."

"That's strange."

"I know," Alex replies. "He never misses these houseboat events."

We all look up when we hear the sound of violin music. Gene stands alone at the top of the dock, and he plays a sad, slow version of "The Way You Look Tonight." I've heard it sung by Frank Sinatra and others, but never played this way on the violin. Its notes sound sad and pensive, and when a gust of wind blows through the dock, I shiver and wish I'd brought a sweater.

Later, Alex and I sit on his deck as the stars twinkle overhead. He's left the radio on, and I can hear it in the distance. "Is the music bothering you?" he asks.

"No," I say. "It's nice. In this age of iTunes and OnDemand, it's sometimes nice to be surprised."

He nods, weaving his fingers through mine.

"What did you think of the party tonight?"

"I don't know," I say, thinking of my prickly interaction with Naomi and her unwillingness to speak of the past. And yet, who am I—a newcomer—to dig around so openly? I can almost understand Naomi's reticence. I shrug. "The people here have one thing in common, and that's their collective love for the dock."

Alex nods. "Strange that Jim wasn't there, wasn't it?" He's lowered his voice. We have to be careful on the water. Sound carries.

I nod. Alex and I stopped by his house to check on him, but he was terse with us, speaking through a crack in the door. "I wonder what's bothering him?"

"Maybe it's his dad," he says. "Gene's not doing well."

I hear the interlude to a song on the radio, and I instantly recognize it. "Here's to Life," by Shirley Horn. "I love this song."

"Me, too," he says, standing. "Dance with me?"

I stand up, and he wraps his arms around me. We fit perfectly, and he holds me with ease, as if we've danced like this a hundred, a thousand times.

I listen to the song's lyrics: "No complaints, and no regrets, I still believe in chasing dreams . . . " I sigh. "I hope I can look back on my life and feel that way when it's all said and done," I say.

"Me, too."

I close my eyes tightly, then open them again and search Alex's face—so warm, so anchored to this moment, to me. The tears fill my eyes again. "I want to live again, *really live*."

He holds me tighter. "Don't you see?" he says. "You're doing that now."

Our eyes meet for a moment before he cups my face in his hands and pulls me toward him passionately. I close my eyes. I feel like I'm floating. I can see James, suddenly, in the distance. It's dark, and I can't make out his face. I open my eyes and step back.

"What's wrong?" he asks. He sounds a little injured, and it makes me feel terrible. For a moment I wonder if I'm worthy of his affection. If he gave me his heart, could I be trusted with it?

"I, I . . . I don't know," I say. "I don't know if I can do this."

He looks down at his feet. "Oh."

I take a step closer to him and take his hands in mine. "I want to, so much," I say, shaking my head. I'm a mess. I'm afraid. "I need a sign. I need a sign before I can take the next step. I need *him* to give his blessing."

James. I feel him. Is he seeing me now? I've often thought that Alex and James would hit it off. They share a sense of humor, a deep humanity. Beneath each of their surfaces, there are so many layers to experience. So many beautiful layers. But would James approve of his wife walking into the arms of a man who possesses the advantage of being alive when James is not?

We face each other for a moment, in silence, as the waves lap against the houseboat. And then a new song comes on the radio. At first I don't recognize the melody. It's folksy, and there's the strumming of a guitar. And then Peter, of Peter, Paul and Mary, is singing. I shake my head, astonished. "Puff, the Magic Dragon, lived by the sea . . ."

Tears sting my eyes. We don't need to say anything. We know. I nestle my head into Alex's chest and he holds me as we listen.

I look up at the sky. "Thank you," I whisper into the night air.

# Chapter 29

PENNY

An hour passes, and then two. And shortly after one in the morning, I hear Dexter walk into the houseboat. "Penny?" he calls out.

There's no sense hiding from him. "I'm out here," I say.

"Why is there a suitcase in the living room?"

I began packing and then gave up. "I, um, well, it's Mama," I say. "She hasn't been feeling well. I thought I might go over and stay with her for a day or two."

"Why don't you let me drive you?" Dex offers sweetly.

"No," I say. "You've had too much to drink. I'll just catch a cab."

"At this hour?"

"Sure," I reply, turning back to the lake. "It's no trouble." He kisses me and I can smell the piney scent of gin, lots of gin, on his breath. "Besides, you've had a lot to drink. You'll want to rest."

He smiles. "Won't you come to bed? Just for a little while?"

"I really should go take care of Mama," I say.

He clears his throat. "There's something I've been meaning to tell you."

"What is it?" I think of Collin's revelations about Dexter's father and I feel a pang of sorrow, regret. Instead of the forty-three-year-old man standing before me with his handsome, chiseled features and a shadow forming around his jaw, I see a young boy, lonely, lost, a little sad. I bite the edge of my lip. *Damn the Wentworths.* If his father loves him so much, why doesn't he come here himself instead of using Collin as a go-between?

Dex rubs his forehead nervously and stumbles to his left, losing his balance. "Honey," I say. "Sit down."

"Penny," he begins, "I've decided something. I'm not going to keep things from you anymore. From now on, it's you and me."

I don't know if it's the alcohol talking or if this sentiment is genuine, but I gulp, and listen. I nod expectantly.

"I want you to know that I haven't been honest with you, about . . ."

I think of Lana Turner, then remember the woman who answered the phone at the studio. Do I really want to know what he's about to divulge? Do I want to hear it? Collin might sail up in an hour, in a day, in a month, and maybe it would be better to leave things as they are. Dex with his secrets, I with mine.

But Dex continues, and I am forced to hear his confession whether I'm ready for it or not. "There's someone I need you to meet."

I shake my head. "Who?"

"Her name is Roxanne. She's eighteen years old."

*Eighteen.*

"She's my daughter, Penny."

I gasp. "Your daughter?"

"Yes. She's not much younger than you. I worried what you might think. Also I . . . listen, I made a lot of mistakes in my last marriage, and I'm not proud of myself. You've talked about us having children, Penny, and the truth is, I'd make a terrible father."

I open my mouth to speak and extend my hand to his arm, but he continues before I can say anything.

"I abandoned my first family for reasons that were entirely self-ish," he goes on. "You can see why I decided never to have children again."

"Dex, please, I—"

"It isn't in my genetic makeup to be a good father," he continues with a firm nod. "My father, my grandfather—both were lousy at the gig. So imagine my surprise when Roxanne appeared at the studio. She forgave me." He wipes a tear from his cheek. "She actually forgave me and gave me a chance to know her. I don't deserve it, but God, do you know how I have longed for that?"

I stare ahead. I don't know what to say.

"When I was with Lana, she—"

"Please," I say. "I can't bear to hear of your affair."

"My affair?"

I shake my head in disbelief. "Dexter, you're telling me that you didn't . . . ?"

He takes my hands in his. "Penny, my darling, would you actually think that I would do that to you?"

My tears are hard to stop now. I can see the look of shock on Dex's face, the honesty in his eyes. I've misjudged him. I've misjudged *us*.

"All this time," I say, my voice faltering, "I thought you were having an affair." I feel overcome with guilt and regret.

"I haven't been perfect," he says honestly. "There was a—"

"I don't want to know." For some reason the hint of his indiscretion, any indiscretion, makes my guilt more palpable.

He looks down at his feet, then back up at me. "Well, you'd love Roxanne, Penny. She's been staying at the studio until she starts at the University of Washington in the fall."

I listen to him talk for the next few minutes. We'll go to California this fall for a new installation. Lana Turner's hosting the after-party. New York in the spring for a new art gallery opening. Maybe Roxanne and her new boyfriend can join us. A foursome. I look out at the lake, empty except for a pair of ducks gliding by close to the dock. Collin is gone. I feel slightly dizzy, then overcome with a wave of nausea. I run to the bathroom and throw up.

"You OK in there?" Dex is standing outside the bathroom door. He sounds sweet, attentive, the way he used to in the early days of our marriage. I stand up, dab tissue to the corners of my mouth, and look at myself in the mirror. I've lost weight. My cheeks are hollow and colorless. I place my hand on my belly. It's plausible that the baby is Dex's, of course.

I walk out to the living room, where I can see the lake. Dex sits beside me on the sofa and nestles his head into the crook of my neck, then reaches for my hand. He holds it up and kisses each finger as if he's reuniting with every inch of me.

I wonder what I'd do if Collin appeared by the dock now. There he'd be, standing at the front of his sailboat, like a gallant sailor in the night, coming for me. Would I stand up and go to him or stay here with Dex? I feel a panicky flutter in my stomach as Dex stands and pulls me up toward him. "Sleep Walk" has just come on the radio. I first heard the haunting instrumental in California in the lounge at the hotel. It holds new meaning now. Its melody, so sad and dreamlike, lulls me into a trancelike state. Dex holds me strong and sure.

"Dance with me," he says.

He always feels amorous when he's been drinking, but it's different now, more intense, somehow. It could be the first day of the rest of our lives, or the last day of our life together.

I don't protest as he pulls me toward him. "It's been too long," he says, breathing into my neck. My mind wants to argue, but my body welcomes his embrace.

When the song ends, he pulls back and looks out to the deck.

"What is it?" I ask, a little startled.

He shakes his head. "I thought I saw something. Probably nothing." He resumes his hold on my waist.

For a moment, I think I see a shadow—a sailboat?—but it's just the ripple of the lake.

I know it then. I *feel* it. Collin isn't coming.

Dex kisses my hand and pours two glasses of wine, handing one to me.

"No thanks," I say, shaking my head.

"Why not?"

Suddenly I have a vision, of Dex holding a baby, gazing at him lovingly, then back at me. Could a child fix us? Is that all we need? I ache for Collin, but if he isn't coming, I'll have to go on. I look at Dex smiling at me now. My Dex. He hasn't always been a perfect husband, but he loves me in his own way. I could tell him about the baby. I could tell him right now. He'd be ecstatic. He'd swell with pride.

Dex watches me as I stare out to the lake. "What are you looking for out there?"

I turn back to him quickly. "The stars are out tonight," I say, thinking of Collin. He's probably through the locks now, casting off into the Puget Sound and out onto the ocean, heading south. Without me.

"There's something I need to tell you," I say.

"What is it?" Dex kisses my cheek as I feel a cramp in my belly.

"Dex, we're going to have a baby." The words tumble out of my mouth without my permission, but I feel better once they do. The secret is out in the open now for him to see, and hopefully accept.

He coughs, spraying wine onto the rug, then sets his wineglass on the kitchen counter. "What in the world do you mean?" He shakes his head, and the look on his face frightens me.

I force a smile. Every man gets a little jittery when he learns he's becoming a father, I tell myself. "I mean, I'm pregnant. You're going to be a father, Dex. Well, a father *again*." I smile nervously and take a step toward him.

He looks as if he's just gotten the wind knocked out of him. He sits down and stares at a spot on the rug.

I remember a time the month after we were married when a woman at a department store walked up to us and plopped her nine-month-old boy into Dexter's arms. "Hold him for just a moment?" she asked. "I left my handbag at the counter at Fredrick and Nelson and carrying Bobby all the way to the end of the shopping center is like lugging a ton of bricks." I noticed a bead of sweat on her brow. "Please, hold him just for a moment. I'll be back in ten minutes or less."

I looked around the lobby where we stood, and we were the only people nearby besides a teenage boy and a woman with toddler twins and a five-year-old boy who was in the midst of a raucous tantrum. I could see why she'd asked us.

Dex nodded nervously, extending his arms mechanically.

"Here," she said, plopping the large baby into his arms. Dex looked stiff and uncomfortable as we watched the woman bustle off out the door and down the street.

I tried not to laugh. He looked so cute standing there with this rosy-cheeked baby in his arms. "Look at you," I said. "You're a natural."

The comment made him stiffen even more, and the baby began to whimper, which soon turned to a blood-curdling scream. "Take him," Dex pleaded, handing the child to me.

"There now," I said, propping the baby on his stomach and leaning him against my shoulder. I rocked him in my arms the way I'd done with children I'd babysat after school, and within a minute, his eyes became heavy and he nodded off.

"See?" I said. "Babies aren't that scary. You just have to know how to handle them."

Dex stared at me with a horrified expression. "No," he said. "No babies."

I shook my head. "What do you mean 'no babies'?" I didn't understand how he could be so hard-and-fast. We'd hardly discussed parenthood. I mean, he knew, vaguely, that I wanted to have children—someday—but we'd never broached the subject head-on.

"I mean I don't want to have children," he said bluntly.

"But Dexter," I said, as little Bobby reached a sleepy fist in the direction of my nose. "You can't mean that. Give it time. One day we'll want to—"

"No, Penny," he said. And then he turned toward Third Avenue. "I have errands to run. Do you think you can catch a cab home?"

"Sure," I said icily.

I watched him walk away, all tense and angry. The woman came back ten minutes later, as promised, and recovered her baby boy. And I was left standing alone wondering if Dexter's insistence about not wanting children symbolized something deeper about his past, or if it was simply that he didn't want children with *me*.

"Well," I say, disappointed, pushing the memories deeper into my mind. I place my hand on Dex's knee, but he stands up, bristling at my touch. "I guess I thought you'd be a little more . . . pleased."

Dex rubs his chin and paces the floor in a way that makes my heart beat faster. "My Penny," he says finally, smiling in a strange way. He doesn't look like the Dexter I know. His expression is mocking and his eyes are wild, like they've been lit with a torch. "I never even suspected it." I hardly recognize his voice.

"Don't be afraid," I say, hoping to calm him down. After his revelation about Roxanne, of course he'd be nervous about becoming a father again. That's only natural. I'll have to ease his fears. I'll have to convince him that he's up for the job. "Darling, you'll be great with the baby. This is fate's way of giving you a second chance at fatherhood. You can get it right this time. Maybe he'll be an artist like you." I giggle nervously. "We could get him one of those little easels for children. Can you imagine, Dex? A little boy painting beside you in the studio?" I feel a surge of happiness then. The thought of a child, my child, fills me with deep contentment. No matter what, I will not be alone. I will have a purpose.

He laughs to himself. "You really think you can try to deceive me?"

I shake my head. "Deceive you?" My heart is racing now. *What is he saying?*

He stands up and walks to the door. "I should have known. Tom told me that his mother-in-law saw you on the streetcar, that you were with someone and the two of you couldn't keep your hands off each other. It was only fair that I'd grant you one indiscretion, given all of mine." He laughs to himself again.

*All* of his indiscretions? What about the sentiments he expressed earlier? "Dex, but I thought you—"

He looks at me like I'm a stranger. "A tryst? Fine. A midnight fling? Sure. I've had them. But darling, you've gotten yourself *pregnant*." He shakes his head. "This is unforgivable. You see, my dear Penny, I had a vasectomy before we were married." His words are cold and searing at the same time. "Let me spell it out for you, love: I can't have children anymore." He shakes his head at me, then smiles again, an angry, intense smile. "But whoever the lucky chap is, be sure to give him my congratulations."

The door slams closed and the sound reverberates in my ears. Tears sting my eyes. I don't know what to feel, what to do. The cramping in my abdomen is more intense now, and I double over. Mama never said that pregnancy *hurts* so much. I lean back in the chair until the pain subsides a bit. I need some air and decide to sit on the back deck until I figure out what I'll do. When I open the closet to reach for my sweater, Dex's coat falls to the floor. A prescription pill bottle rolls out of the inside pocket. I collect it and read the label: "Take twice daily for depressive episodes." I'm not surprised that his psychiatrist would prescribe medication for his depression. He needs it. I've lost count of how many days I've seen him hover in the darkness before sunrise, weeping, lost in his sadness. My eyes widen when I see who the prescribing psychiatrist is. "N. Clyde." I gasp. *Naomi Clyde. My God, he's been seeing Naomi all this time.*

In the next moment, I piece together what should have been obvious all along. The looks. Her coldness toward me. All the talk of his psychiatrist. Of course they're having an affair. I shiver and slip my arms through the sleeves of my wool sweater, pulling it tight around my body.

I don't realize that I've been crying until I step outside for air and see Jimmy sitting cross-legged, alone, at the edge of the dock.

He should have been asleep hours ago. But then I hear the sound of laughter and loud music coming from the top of the dock and realize that the party is still going strong.

"What's wrong, Penny?" he asks, walking toward me. He's holding a rubber ball, and his face is clouded with concern.

"Oh, it's nothing," I lie. He's too young to hear of my troubles. I can't begin to tell him the mess my life is in. Instead, I stare up at the stars sparkling overhead, and I think of how foolish I am. I stayed for Dexter, but he scorned me, and now the man who loves me—the man who loves me so much he promised to love me even if he had only half my heart—is drifting out alone to sea, without me.

Jimmy keeps his eyes fixed on the horizon. "You're sad like me, aren't you?"

I nod. "I guess so."

"What do you do when you're sad?" he asks. His eyes look like two big full moons.

"I daydream," I say honestly. "I think of where I'd like to go someday." In that moment, I envision Catalina Island with Collin. I think about us walking hand in hand on the beach. I think of the baby growing inside me, toddling along the shore. Dex's words were painful to hear, but they made things clear.

"Me, too," he says. "I'd go to Australia and see koala bears."

I smile.

"Where would you go, Penny?"

"Catalina Island," I say, looking out to the lake as if I can see my future in front of me. "There'd be turquoise blue water and sunshine. And a big sailboat that would take me anywhere I like."

"That sounds nice," he says, bouncing his ball on the dock. He's quiet for a moment, then turns to me. "Can I go with you?"

If it were only that simple.

I think of Naomi then, with her arms wrapped around Dex, whispering sweet nothings into his ear, and I feel the onset of nausea. I hate thinking of them together, and yet I don't have the right to be sad. I gave that up the night I let Collin take me into his arms. But the loneliness I feel now, well, it taunts me. "Jimmy, what would your parents think if you just up and left? They'd be sad."

He shrugs. "I don't think they'd really miss me."

"Of course they would."

I drape my arm around his shoulder. We sit together like that for a moment, until something bright floating in the lake catches my eye. I lean over the dock gently to pick it up. It's a little sprig of morning glory, the flowering vine Naomi bemoaned.

"If you left, everyone would miss you," Jimmy says softly. "Everyone would be sad. But not me. No one even cares that I'm here."

"That's not true," I say. "I'd miss you."

He smiles.

I hold up the little vine I've rescued from the lake. A drop of lake water falls from one of its white blossoms onto my dress. "Every person, every *thing*, has a purpose in this life. You, me, this little morning glory. We're all interconnected." Jimmy pauses to look at the flower in my hand. "It's our job to remember that and to realize how it all works together, even when it feels like the puzzle pieces don't fit." I think of my own life then, and how the puzzle pieces not only don't fit, but they're hopelessly scattered. Some are missing. Will my life work together the way I promised Jimmy about his? I stand up and tuck the root of the morning glory into a pot near the house. "There," I say to myself, patting the soil down around it.

I clutch my belly when I feel another surge of pain.

Jimmy leaps to his feet. "Are you OK?"

"I think so."

He turns back to the ball he's been bouncing on the dock between his legs, then tosses it into the air, but instead of landing in his lap as he intended, it bounces into the lake.

"Oh no," Jimmy cries, throwing his arms out as far as they'll stretch. "I can't reach it."

"Let me try," I say, reaching unsuccessfully for the little ball.

Jimmy shakes his head. "We could take the canoe out."

I shake my head. "Not at this hour, honey. It's too dark."

Jimmy thinks for a moment. The current has wrapped its tendrils around the little blue ball. It's drifting away. "I have a stick at my house," he says. "I'll run and get it."

I nod.

A moment later, Gene appears. "Oh, there you are," he says, walking toward me from the dock.

I'm a little startled to see him. I wonder if Dex has told Naomi about my condition. I wonder if he knows about his wife and my husband.

"May I sit down with you?"

"Sure," I say. Gene is a good man, his one fault being that he loves Naomi and is blind to her ways.

"I guess we're in the same boat," he says rather vaguely.

*He does know.* I wonder why he didn't tell me. But the fact of the matter remains: Our spouses are having an affair. He knows. I know.

"I feel like a fool," I say. "What are we supposed to do?"

Gene smiles as if to spare my feelings. Yet the tragedy and ruin, for so many lives, is inescapable. Nobody wins.

"Well, the way I see it there's only one solution," he says. His eyes flash, and I hardly recognize him for a moment. He looks bold, determined in a way I have never seen before. I look over my shoulder. Jimmy's coming back soon. I don't want him to overhear our conversation, the ugly details about his mother and my husband.

I feel another deep pain in my belly, and I double over. A boat motors by in the distance and I hear footsteps behind me. Both are faint in comparison to the surge of pain I feel deep inside, a ripping in my abdomen. Then I feel hands on my neck. I try to catch my breath, but I can't. I look right, then left. I can't breathe. I can't see anyone. I just feel pressure around my neck, fingers grasping tighter. I feel the cold of the lake next and nothing else.

# Chapter 30

ADA

I've agreed to go to church with Alex on Sunday morning, and I can hear the church bells of Saint Mark's Cathedral from our parking spot a few blocks away. "I forgot how much I love that sound," I say, stepping out of the car.

"Kellie's supposed to drop Gracie out front," Alex says. He looks a little nervous, but I try not to read into it. The truth is, I don't know how this is supposed to work either. I'll be meeting Gracie for the first time, and I'm not sure how I'm supposed to behave. Will she see me as competition for her father's attention? An obstacle? I hope not.

We walk along the sidewalk leading to the massive church. There's a crispness to the air—the earliest indication that fall is coming, and the end of my time on Boat Street, maybe. My lease is up in a week, and other than Alex hinting now and then that I should stay, we haven't had any concrete discussions about just what that might mean, nor am I ready for them. Seattle has been my big adventure, my last-ditch effort to heal. I didn't ever anticipate meeting Alex, falling in love with Boat Street, and being possessed by the mystery of Penny Wentworth. In short, I didn't expect Seattle to carve out such a significant chunk of my heart, and I'm not quite ready to part with it yet. As we walk in unison, and in silence, I remember what Dr. Evinson said: "Take it one day at a time." Yes.

A black Volkswagen sedan idles in the circular drive. I feel Alex tense as we approach, and I know this must be Kellie's car. I imagine him sitting in the passenger seat in happier times. Kellie with her hand on Alex's thigh. Alex smiling charmingly, rubbing the back of her neck.

Puffs of engine exhaust cloud the air. "I'll wait here," I say. "I want to take a look at those stained glass windows."

Alex nods and forces a smile. "Gracie's going to love you."

"I hope," I whisper, as I watch him walk to the car.

Alex opens the passenger's side door, and I can see Kellie's face. She looks vaguely annoyed. Her blond hair is pulled back, and even without makeup, she's still strikingly beautiful. For a moment, I feel a pang of jealousy. This is the mother of his child. The *mother*. I'm startled by this emotion, and I try to extinguish it as quickly as it rears its head. Kellie casts a glance in my direction and our eyes meet for a moment, but she looks away quickly. Alex speaks to her, she nods, and then he closes the door. It's clean and precise, like a business transaction, but I can't help but worry that my presence is making their co-parenting arrangement more difficult. I imagine myself in her shoes, if James and I had parted ways and he—gulp—had met someone else. I know I'd hate any woman who waited in the wings to win the affection of my daughter. I'd despise her. I wouldn't be proud to admit it, but it's true.

I forget my worries when the back door opens and a little girl in pink leggings and a magenta sweater dress barrels out. Alex scoops her up and she smiles, revealing a missing front tooth. She's eight— pretty and blond like her mom, and obviously the apple of her daddy's eye. Although she looks nothing like Ella, it startles me how much she reminds me of her. I bite my lip as Alex sets her down, and she waves in the direction of her mom's car as it speeds away. I can't see Kellie's expression, but I imagine she's looking back at us through the rearview. I wonder if she wants to be standing in my place.

I approach cautiously. "Hi," I say to Gracie. "I'm Ada."

"I know," she says. "Mommy told me about you."

I swallow hard. I have no idea what her mother might have said about me, but I try not to overanalyze. This is a big moment, and I don't want to let my insecurities overcome me. I kneel down beside her. *What would I say to one of Ella's friends in a difficult moment?* I admire the sparkly sequins on her dress. "I like your dress." Her nose is dotted with tiny freckles.

"Thanks," she says. "Guess what?"

"What?"

"I lost a tooth last week." Her voice is sweet and high-pitched.

"You did?"

She nods her head. "Mommy says the tooth fairy comes at our house *and* at Daddy's house."

I look up at Alex with a grin. "That's right," I say. "And I hear the tooth fairy is *especially* generous on houseboats."

"Really?" Gracie asks excitedly. "I'm staying over with Daddy tonight." Alex flashes me a private smile.

The church bells ring again, and he points ahead. "Come on, you two," he says. "Let's go find a seat."

We traverse the foyer and take a seat in a pew toward the back of the church. Alex watches as Gracie smiles up at me just as the first hymn begins. I don't listen to the sermon, not really. I think about my burden instead, and how I'd like to give it to someone else for a while. *God? Could I do that?* I'm not sure. But I do know that Alex was right. It just feels good to belong.

Before we're back at the dock, Alex's cell rings. Gracie and I listen to one side of his conversation in the car. He doesn't sound happy.

"That was my client at *Seattle* magazine," he says. "The layouts for the tapas feature in the spring issue came back, and they're not exactly what the editor in chief had in mind." He pulls into his parking spot just off Fairview Avenue and rubs his brow. "They want me to come in and reshoot."

"Really?" I say. "That sounds completely unreasonable."

Alex shrugs. "It's in my contract. I have no choice but to go in and get it right or else." He sighs, and reaches for his cell phone. "I'll call Kellie—"

"It's OK," I say quickly. "Gracie and I can hang out here until you come back."

His face melts into a smile. "Really?"

I nod.

He turns around to look at Gracie, and she grins. "No big deal, Daddy." She turns to me. "Can I see your houseboat?"

"I'll give you the grand tour."

I take Gracie's hand as we climb out of the car. Alex heads down his dock to get his camera, and we walk toward Boat Street. "Bye, you two," he says. "I promise, I'll only be a few hours."

As we walk up to my deck, Jim is heading back toward the

dock. He looks startled to see us. "Oh," he says, shuffling his hand through his hair. "I was, uh, just dropping by to say hello."

"Oh," I reply, remembering how he was ill the night of Bach on the Dock. "Are you feeling better?"

"Yes. Thank you." He glances at Gracie, then turns back to me. "Well, don't let me interrupt."

"You're welcome to come in," I say.

"Nah, I'd better get back. Dad's having a bad day."

"Right," I say. I wonder why he's acting so strangely, but Gracie's smiling up at me. Her big green eyes make me forget my concerns. "Do you have a bunk bed?" she asks. "I wish Daddy's houseboat did."

"I have a loft," I say. "And that's just as cool."

She jumps up and down. "Can I see it?"

"Of course you can."

Inside, I begin the tour, but soon she climbs up to a barstool. "Do you love my daddy?"

My cheeks feel hot. "Well, we haven't known each other very long, but I think he's pretty amazing."

"He is," Gracie says matter-of-factly. "Did you know he can hide a quarter in his ear and make it come out in his hand?"

"Really?"

She nods, and I instantly remember the way James did that trick for Ella. It never failed to astonish her.

"He can also tie a fisherman's knot," she says. "That's hard, but I'm learning."

"Are you hungry?" I ask, scanning the refrigerator for kid-friendly fare.

"Do you have any cookies?"

"Sorry, I don't."

"We could make some," she suggests. Her legs dangle from the stool, but she tucks them under herself and looks up at me in anticipation. "Mommy and I always make cookies."

*Of course, her mother the award-winning chef.* "Well, I did find some flour and sugar in the pantry, but I don't think I have a good recipe."

"Oh," she says, disappointed.

But then I remember Penny's little blue notebook and all the recipes inside. "Wait, I have an idea."

Gracie follows me to the chest in the living room. "Can you keep a secret?" I ask.

She nods eagerly.

"I found a chest filled with treasures from another time," I say, lifting the lid. I show her the wedding dress, the gloves, and other relics of Penny Wentworth's life before I pull out the notebook. "This belonged to a woman who lived here a very long time ago. Her name was Penny."

I hand her the recipe book, and she fans through its pages, stopping when something catches her eye. "Cinnamon cookies," she says. "Mmmmmm."

She hands me the recipe book, and I look over the ingredients. "I think we have everything here. Let's make them."

## Penny's Cinnamon Cookies

*Makes 3 dozen*

### INGREDIENTS

1 cup butter, softened
1 ½ cups sugar
1 egg

1 teaspoon vanilla
2 tablespoons molasses
2 ¼ cups flour
1 teaspoon baking soda
1 ½ tablespoons ground cinnamon

**Directions**

Preheat oven to 350. Mix butter and sugar together until smooth.
Mix in egg, vanilla, and molasses. Then, mix flour, baking soda, and
cinnamon and add to butter mixture. Form one-inch balls of dough,
and place on cookie sheet about two inches apart. Bake 10 to 12 minutes.

Gracie lets out a little squeal, then follows me to the kitchen.
Together we crack eggs and mix butter and sugar together. In twenty
minutes, the oven is preheated and we place the cookie sheet inside.
The kitchen smells glorious, like vanilla and cinnamon and butter,
and when the timer beeps, we can hardly wait for them to cool
before trying them, with a glass of milk, of course.

"These are the best cookies I've ever had," Gracie declares.

"I think I agree," I say, reaching for a second.

After they cool, I place a half dozen cookies in a Ziploc bag.
"For you and your dad," I say. "And be sure to save some for your
mom." I wonder what Kellie, the proficient cook, will think of the
cookies, but mostly I wonder what she'll think of me spending time
with her daughter.

We play double solitaire on the floor until Alex knocks on the
door and lets himself in. "Hi," he says from the doorway.

I look up after setting a card down on the stack of hearts. "How
did it go?"

He rolls his eyes. "Fine. Glad to have that over with. How's my girl?"

Gracie leaps up. "We made cookies!"

Alex grins. "I know. I could smell them all the way from the street. Can I have one?"

Gracie hands him the bag.

"Wow," he says. "These are really good."

"It's Penny's recipe," I say.

He gives me a knowing smile, then turns to Gracie. "Well, I should get this munchkin home." He pauses for a moment. "You can join us, Ada."

"No," I say quickly. "You two go ahead. I have some things to get done today."

"OK," he says, squeezing my hand. "But stop by later, all right?"

I call Joanie after Alex leaves. "I just spent the morning with Alex's daughter," I say, lying on the couch. "We all went to church together."

"Church?"

"Yeah. It was really nice."

"What was she like?"

"She's wonderful." I feel a lump in my throat. "Ella would have loved her."

"Do you think she liked *you*?"

"I think so," I say. "She braided my hair during the service, and we made cookies at my place."

"That's cute," Joanie says. "How's the investigation going?"

"I feel like I've hit a dead end," I say, laying the contents of

Penny's chest out on the floor. "No one will talk about Penny. I think I have to find her husband."

"What was his name again?"

"Dexter Wentworth."

"Sounds like one of those spoiled rich guys on the crime shows who gets away with murder because his daddy hires a hotshot lawyer." I can envision Joanie rolling her eyes on the other side of the continent.

"Don't be so quick to judge him," I say. "What if he's nothing more than a grieving husband?"

"But didn't you say that he was having an affair?"

"Well," I say, remembering what I read about Lana Turner. Of course, it was only speculation, but it was highly probable. "Yes, there's that. But that's not exactly reason enough for foul play. Lots of men in the 1950s had affairs. Think of *Mad Men*."

"Oooh, I wonder if he looks like Don Draper?" Joanie says with a squeal.

"You know, the comparison isn't that far off," I say. "In the photos I've seen, he had dark hair and that dashing look about him."

"Well," Joanie says, "be careful, all right? If he had something to do with Penny's disappearance, he's not going to like that you're poking about."

"Joanie, he's in his *nineties*."

"I know," she replies. "But it doesn't matter how old someone is. If they want to conceal the truth, they'll stop at nothing to do it."

I think about what Joanie said for a little while after hanging up the phone. But I know that I won't be able to put the pieces of Penny's story together without hearing from Dexter. So I use my well-honed reporter's Google skills and manage to find his address at the Lakeview Retirement Community. A fan of his artwork set up a page devoted to his past work, with a forwarding address to his retirement home.

I key in the number on my phone, and as it rings, I scroll through the abstract landscapes of Dexter Wentworth, at least the ones curated on the fan site. They're big and bold, with little warmth. I wonder if Dexter Wentworth the artist is any reflection of Dexter Wentworth the person.

On the third ring, an operator picks up, and I ask her to connect me.

A moment later an elderly man with a deep, gravelly voice picks up. "Hello?"

"Mr. Wentworth, my name is Ada Santorini." I'm surprised by how nervous I feel. I don't want him to hang up; I'm desperate to hear what he has to say about his wife. "Well, you see, I'm living in a houseboat that you used to own, and I'm calling to ask you something."

"You live on Boat Street?"

"Yes," I say cautiously.

"My daughter owns the property. If you have a rental issue, you'll do best to take it up with Roxanne."

"It's not about the house, exactly," I say. "It's about your wife, Penny."

He's silent for a moment.

"Mr. Wentworth? Are you there?"

"Yes," he says. "Yes, I am."

"Mr. Wentworth, I found some of your wife's belongings here in the houseboat, and I thought you ought to know about them."

"Miss . . ."

"Santorini."

"Miss Santorini, why don't you meet me this afternoon?"

"Yes," I say, my heart beating faster. "That would be wonderful."

"I live in apartment forty-seven at the Lakeview Retirement Community."

"I can be there at three," I say.

"That's fine."

I eye the leftover cookies, and decide to box them up to take with me. For Dexter. From Penny.

# Chapter 31

Alex appears on my doorstep as I'm stepping out to catch a cab to Dexter's apartment downtown. "I'm glad I caught you." He's out of breath from running down the dock; he holds a manila envelope with the flap dangling open.

"Where's Gracie?"

"She's watching a movie," he says, glancing over his shoulder. Through the window, I can see her sitting on Alex's couch. I grin. "You made her wear a life vest?"

"House rules," he says.

"I love that you're paranoid."

"Listen," he says, "I was going through some old shots I took five years ago, when I first arrived on Boat Street, and I found these."

He hands the envelope to me, and I pull out a stack of eight-by-ten black-and-white images. I flip through the first three—shots of the dock and mostly my houseboat and the view beyond—and then look up at Alex. "I don't get it. What am I supposed to be looking for here?"

He points to the corner of the frame, and I see a woman

kneeling down on the deck in front of my houseboat. I look closer. "Is that . . . Naomi?"

Alex nods.

"It looks like she's crying," I say.

He flips to the next photo, and the next. In succession, they show a woman who is doubled over in grief.

"She must've had no idea I was taking photos that day," he says. "Obviously, I didn't see her there either."

"What do you think this means?"

"I think it means she has some emotional pain associated with your houseboat, or someone who once lived there."

I take the photo on the top of the stack in my hands and touch the corner where Naomi kneels, holding her head in her hands. I can almost feel her pain radiating between my fingertips.

I step off the elevator, and in the hallway, the scent of Pine-Sol floods my nose. *What was the number again? Room 1201, yes.* I walk around a corner and then I come to the door: 1201. My heart thumps wildly in my chest as I reach out my hand.

I knock once, then again.

A moment later, the door creaks open, and Dexter stands before me. He's tall and fit. He hardly looks like a man in his early nineties. His hair is gray and clean and combed neatly to the side. "Ms. Santorini," he says, smiling. I can see why Penny must have found him so charming.

"Please, call me Ada."

He leads me through the door. His apartment is neat and tidy, and well-appointed with a modern, angular sofa and a sleek-looking coffee table. It looks like the kind of interior that's been aided by a decorator. I wonder if he's dating her. I imagine she's half his age and drives a BMW.

"Can I get you something to drink?" he says.

"Water's fine."

He returns with a small bottle of Evian from the refrigerator and sets it in front of me on the coffee table. A droplet of condensation rolls down its side.

"So," he says cheerfully, sitting in a chair opposite me. "How can I help you?"

I set the cookies down on the coffee table first. "Would you like one?"

"No, thank you," he says, indicating his heart. "I'm on a strict diet, my—"

"They're your wife's recipe," I say. "Penny's cinnamon cookies."

He looks momentarily shaken. "Did you say it's *Penny's* recipe? How did you—"

"I found her recipe book."

"Where?"

"In the houseboat, inside the chest."

"The one in the living room?"

"Yes. Her things are still there, frozen in time. Her wedding dress, some books and mementos."

I pull out the blue notebook and set it on the coffee table. He picks it up and thumbs through its pages. His chin quivers a little at the sight of the familiar handwriting.

I feel funny watching him. It's a private moment, so I look up, admiring a painting of a woman on the wall. She's beautiful, with blond hair and a low-cut dress. She's sitting on a dock looking out at the gray lake. Her eyes are sad, distant. She isn't in the moment but is looking ahead, into the future. It has to be Penny.

"That's her," Dexter says, looking up at me. "I painted it the year after she disappeared."

"She must have been so beautiful," I say.

Dexter nods. "She was the most beautiful creature I've ever laid eyes on. Even all these years later, I haven't met anyone like her."

"Were you happy together?"

Dexter rubs his brow. "We were once. But I was so consumed with my work. Too consumed. I strayed, and I'll never forgive myself for it."

I think of Lana Turner, but I don't dare ask him about her. "What do you think happened the night Penny disappeared?"

"I wish I knew," he says. "The fact is, that night's haunted me every day since. I turn it over in my mind again and again, hoping I'll recall something I missed."

"Tell me what you remember."

Dexter sighs. "It was the night of Bach on the Dock, the annual neighborhood party. We had a fight."

"What was it about?"

"She told me she was pregnant," he says.

"You must have been so happy."

He shakes his head. "I knew it wasn't my child. I was so consumed with rage, I didn't stop to consider her plight, what a difficult spot she was in. And after what I put her through? Well, she didn't deserve that kind of coldness from me. If I could do it all over again, I would have accepted her news, accepted the child."

"But you turned her away?"

"I wanted to make her pay for the pain she caused me. I stormed off. I went to Naomi's."

I raise my eyebrows, recalling the images of Naomi that Alex took.

"We were close," he says. "Listen, I'm not proud of parts of my past, especially that one."

"And when did you learn that Penny had . . . gone?"

"Naomi's son, Jimmy, was crying," he says. "His father, Gene, told us that he'd gone to check on Jimmy, and he found him alone on the deck crying. He later said that . . . well, there have been so many theories. He said his son saw her leave by boat."

"In a boat? With who?"

"I thought it must have been Collin," he says, "a neighbor who lived on the next dock. Naomi told me Penny had become close to him during the time I was away in California. I believe he was the father of the child."

I can feel his pain, even now, despite the passage of time.

"Well," he continues, "it didn't hold up. When the detectives questioned him, I learned that he and Penny were planning to go away together that night, but something went wrong. They had a fight, and he left without her."

"Are you sure he didn't come back for her?" I ask, clinging to the possibility that she might have sailed off into the sunset with her true love after all.

He shakes his head. "No. Collin had already set off for the ocean by then. He wasn't anywhere near Lake Union. So it had to be someone else, something else who lured her away."

"But who?"

Dexter throws up his arms. "The police questioned a handful of transients in the area," he says. "They developed a few theories over the years, but none ever solidified. I pray that she just left, that she simply jumped on a boat and sailed away, like she always wanted to do. But I don't think that's what happened. Her mother died in 1972 without hearing from her again, and Penny never went more than a few days without calling her mom." He rubs his forehead. "My one big regret in life is how I left her there that night. After my own transgressions, you'd think I would have been able to forgive hers."

He appears to be sinking deeper into his grief, but I can't let him leave me. Not yet.

"And Collin," I say. "What became of Collin?"

"I wondered the same thing myself," he says, looking up again. "He left Boat Street. Never did come back, except briefly when he left his sailboat in Jimmy's care."

"Yes," I say. "I know."

"I didn't find out until years later," he continues, "but Collin died."

"How?"

"On a sailboat in Key West. He had a heart attack. The Coast Guard found him after he'd already died." He shakes his head solemnly.

I think about these two men. They shared one thing, the love of a remarkable woman, and neither of them had a happy ending. "I'm sorry," I finally say. "I . . . hoped things had turned out differently for Collin."

"Me, too," Dexter says faintly. He stares at his hands. They're folded in his lap in contrition.

I wonder what Penny might think of her husband now if she were standing beside me. Never remarried, all but stopped painting— at least, according to the Web site I read—a man who carries such a heavy burden. Would she love him? Would she forgive him? My eyes wander around the room. I don't know what I'm looking for. A clue? A sign? At once, I notice a little frame on a bookshelf. It's an old-fashioned painted sign, an advertisement of some sort. The lettering is familiar, but I can't place it. I stand and walk to the side of the room, compelled to have a look.

My hand trembles a little as I take the frame and read the words "Leighton Shipping Company" in weathered gold letters. I gasp. Ella's sailboat had the very same inscription on the side. "Where did you get this?" I ask, turning around. Penny's story, my story—it's come full circle. My heart pounds inside my chest and I wonder if Dexter can hear it. To me, it sounds like a bass drum.

"My father owned the company," he says. "The truth is, even in my heyday as an artist, I never could make a living at it, well, not the type of living my family was accustomed to. It was my father's fortune that kept me alive. He was my biggest patron, even though we hardly spoke. Of course, I didn't know that at the time. I found out years later."

"But this name," I say, pointing to the lettering. "My daughter used to have a little carved wooden sailboat with the very same name on it."

"Yes," he says, standing. He walks to a buffet near the dining room table, and pulls out a near replica of Aggie. "Like this?"

"My God," I say, gasping. "That's exactly it."

"My father had a few hundred made. They sold them in the gift shop for a while. I used to take them down to the lake and let them glide out on their own. I always liked to think about where the tide would take them—through the locks, maybe, and out on the ocean. To think that one of my sailboats made it into your daughter's hands." He holds up the little boat, and smiles. "Would your daughter like this one? It's the last one I have, and I'd be happy to give it to her."

"No," I say quickly. I don't have the strength to tell him that Ella isn't here anymore, and I hope he can't see the tears in my eyes. "Thank you, but you keep it. It must mean a lot to you."

"Really," he says. "I insist." He places the sailboat in my hands, and I read the words on the side.

"The Mary Jo," I say, smiling. "My daughter had the Agnes Anne. We called her Aggie."

"They were all hand-painted," he says, "each with a different name. "The joke is that each was named after one of my father's former girlfriends."

I smile. "Well," I say, looking at the sailboat again, imagining what Ella would say if she were here. "This was an unexpected surprise."

"As was meeting you," Dexter says, smiling.

"I'm leaving Penny's notebook with you. If you like, I'll bring her chest over later, when my friend Alex can drive me. It's a bit heavy."

"I'd be ever so grateful," he says.

"Well," I say, heading to the door. I tuck the little boat in my purse, not wanting to offend him by giving it back. "Thank you, again, Dexter. Wherever Penny went, I hope she knows just how much you cared for her, how much you have thought of her since."

"Me, too," he says.

Later that evening, I meet Alex and Gracie at a crepe stand on Fairview for dinner. He orders two ham-and-provolones and I choose a goat-cheese-spinach-and-tomato. We watch as the woman behind the stand pours the batter on the round wheel and rakes it into a perfect circle with a wooden tool. Within seconds, the batter thickens and bubbles, turning a shade of golden brown. She reaches for a tub of cheese labeled "Pro 3-5," then shakes her head and tucks it under the shelf before looking up at us. "Almost forgot to toss this one. Found it in the back of the fridge. Expired months ago." She opens a new tub of shredded cheese and sprinkles it on Alex's crepe. I'm not thinking about expired cheese, however. It's "Pro 3-5" that haunts me. I know it's silly. It's an expiration date for provolone cheese, but I key Proverbs 3:5 into my phone, and read what comes back: "Trust in the Lord with all your heart and lean not on your own understanding; in all your ways acknowledge him and he will make your paths straight."

He will make your paths straight.

"What is it?" Alex asks, as the woman hands him his crepe and then passes me mine.

"Nothing." I smile, but as we walk back to Boat Street, I think of James and Ella and the lonely ache deep inside, and I say a little prayer. *Dear God, if you're out there, I beg of you, please help me find my way. I don't want to feel lost anymore.*

# Chapter 32

The next day, I pick up the phone and make the call I've been dreading for so long, too long.

"Hi Mama," I say quietly when I hear her voice.

"Ada? Is it you?"

"Yes," I say through tears. "Mama, I'm sorry it's been so long." I can see her standing there in the kitchen, in front of the big window that faces the street, where the old sycamore stands guard. Ella climbed that tree. I pushed her on the swing that I myself had swung on as a child. "I'm so sorry—"

"Oh, honey," she says. I can hear the hurt in her voice, but I can also hear the acceptance, the unconditional love, just as I would have shown Ella if she ever walked through her own dark patch. "Please, don't apologize. I knew you'd call when you were ready."

The truth is, I don't know if I'm ready, just that it's time.

"It was wrong of me to close myself off the way I did," I say. "And I want you to know that it had nothing to do with you. It was my own fragility. I was afraid that if I heard the sadness in your voice it would only make it worse."

"I understand," she says. "Your father and I just wanted you to know how much we love you. It's why we kept calling."

"I got your messages," I say. "And the letters. All of them. Mom, I was just afraid, afraid that I wasn't strong enough to talk about the accident with you." I take a deep breath. "I'm in Seattle now."

"Seattle?"

"Yes, just for the summer," I say. "I left New York, quit my job. I wanted to get away, and it's been everything I hoped it would be. Mama, I met someone. His name is Alex."

I hear her crying now.

"Mama, are you all right?"

"Yes," she says. "Yes, I'm just so happy to hear your voice, honey, that's all."

"Say hi to Dad, OK?"

"I will. When can we see you?"

"Soon," I say. "I was thinking we could have Thanksgiving together this year. Is Aunt Louise still making that awful bean casserole?"

"Her specialty, you know," she says with a laugh.

"Save a spot at the table for me, OK?"

"Should I make it two?"

"I don't know just yet," I say, glancing out the window toward Alex's houseboat.

The morning plods along, and I can't get Dexter out of my head. The sunlight streams in the window and reflects off the silver frame of the *Catalina* painting. I study the sailboat, then recall something I told Ella years ago. She'd lost Aggie, and we'd gone back to school to find the little boat, to the market, to the park. It ended up being a veritable grand tour of New York City. But after the exhaustive search, Aggie turned up at home, under her bed. The lesson?

Things are usually right under your nose. And then it hits me. I recall something I came across in Penny's chest a few days ago, and I pull it out and tuck it into my pocket, then run out to the dock, where Jim is hosing down the *Catalina*.

"I have to speak to your parents," I say, catching my breath.

"But they can't, they're—"

"Jim, I have to, and I need your blessing."

Jim's mother pours tea from a white ceramic kettle, and hands me a cup.

"Thank you," I say.

"Gene isn't well enough to join us," she says preemptively.

"Oh. I'm sorry to hear that."

Jim exchanges glances with his mother.

She crosses her legs. "Now, what can I tell you?"

"Yes," I say, pulling a photo of Penny out of my bag, one I'd found in the chest. "Do you remember this woman?"

She reaches for her glasses on the coffee table, then has a closer look at the photo in her hand. Her face is pinched and tense. I imagine that after years of asking all the questions in her practice, it must feel uncomfortable for her to be the one on the spot.

She sets the photo on the table, visibly shaken. "Yes," she says. "I do. Well, I did, a very long time ago. Her name was Penny Wentworth. She was the bride of Dexter." She pauses, as if the name has knocked the wind out of her.

"I know," I say. "I went to see him yesterday."

"You did?"

"Yes." I remember the photographs Alex took, the ones where Naomi had been doubled over in her sadness.

Her eyes are misty, and I can see the anguish brewing in her gaze, like a storm that's gaining strength over the ocean. Whatever tough exterior she has been fronting is gone now. Jim hands her a handkerchief. "It's OK, Mom," he says, "you don't have to—"

"Was he well?" she asks, ignoring her son.

"Yes," I say. "Well, for his condition."

"His condition?"

"He has a heart condition."

"Oh," she says, dabbing the corner of her handkerchief to her eye. "If you want to know the truth, I was in love with him. Madly in love."

"Mom," Jim says, "please, Father will hear you."

She holds up her hand to silence him. "It makes no matter. It's no secret to him."

Jim looks at his hands in his lap.

"Yes, I loved Dexter Wentworth. But it was all a mistake, a terrible mistake. Not just because he was my patient, but because he was married. I destroyed everything he had with Penny."

Jim stands up and walks into the kitchen as if this revelation is too much for him to take.

"She was everything I wasn't," Naomi continues. "Sweet and gentle. Innocent." She lets out a nervous cackle. "I wanted to be like her."

Naomi looks at Jim. "I'm so sorry, son," she says tearfully. "I wasn't the mother I wanted to be. Will you ever forgive me?"

"I forgave you a long time ago, Mom," he says, sitting beside her again.

"Naomi, what happened the night that Penny disappeared?"

She closes her eyes as if the memory is close, perhaps painfully so. "She and Dexter had a fight," she says, opening her eyes. "He was distraught. I took him into my arms." She closes her eyes and embraces the air as if he's kneeling in front of her. The vision seems to soothe her, momentarily, before Jim speaks.

"You told him you could never be happy unless you were together," Jim says to his mother. "It's funny, after that night, I realized that your unhappiness had nothing to do with me."

"Oh, Jim, dear, of course it had nothing to do with you." She pauses, and her eyes widen. "Wait, how did you—"

"I was there," he says. "I saw you together when I was looking for my stick. I found it and I ran back to the dock. But it was too late then. She was gone."

I cover my mouth and shake my head. "Jim, what happened?"

"I don't know," he says. "Dad was standing there. He was crying. It was the first time I saw him cry."

I take a deep breath. "So she just slipped and fell into the water? It doesn't make any sense. She'd lived on a houseboat for years; surely she had good balance."

Naomi looks pained by something. I look into her eyes. "Tell me what you're thinking about," I say.

She bites her lip. It's as if she's trying to keep the memories bottled up and hidden away, but there's a crack in the bottle now. They're seeping out and she has no control over them anymore.

"It was the best and the most terrible night of my life," she says. "Dexter told me he was leaving Penny. One minute I was elated, imagining us finally being together. It's all I could think about. And the next minute, that dream was gone, forever." She dabs her handkerchief to the corners of her eyes once more. "After . . . the accident . . . Lenora and Tom knocked on our door. I guess they knew I was inside with Dexter; maybe everybody knew. Well, they told us what had happened. I'd never seen so much pain in a man's eyes.

He ran out of the house, with his shirt unbuttoned. He didn't care anymore. He didn't care about me anymore. The only thing that mattered was Penny. I followed him down the dock and pushed through the crowd of onlookers.

"He just kept pacing the dock, screaming her name. I had to look away," Naomi continues. "It was the last night I saw Dexter. His houseboat was always rented out after that."

I nod. "Naomi, if she . . . if she was killed, who might have been to blame?"

She stares at a speck on the wall and shakes her head as if deep in thought. "I knew it when I saw him standing there crying," she says. "I could see it in his eyes."

"Gene?"

Jim looks away.

"Yes," Naomi says. "I've come to believe that he did it for me. He did it so I'd be happy."

"And is that why you forgave him?"

"Yes," she says, before a shadow of concern comes over her face. "You aren't going to have him arrested, are you?" she pleads. "Not in his condition."

It's all happening so fast. I don't know what to do. But I know that no matter what the circumstances, Penny deserves justice. "The police will want to at least take your testimony," I say. "For the record." I place my hand over hers. "Naomi, Penny was pregnant that night."

"My God," she says. "I didn't know."

"What do we do next?" Jim asks.

We've been so deep in conversation, none of us notice Gene standing in the kitchen until he clears his throat.

"Gene, dear," Naomi says. "What are you doing up?"

"I'm going to turn myself in," he says.

Naomi stands up and shakes her head. "Dear, you're not well. Go back to bed. You need—"

"No," Gene says lucidly. "I know what I'm saying. I know what I did. I need to confess before it's too late to do it. I've carried this for too long, dear."

"This is what I was trying to prevent from happening," Jim says to me. He shakes his head as if trying to sort out what to do next. "I didn't mean to frighten you, but you were asking so many questions about Penny, I worried there might be something inside your house-boat, something incriminating. Look at him. He's in no state to go to prison."

"You," I say. "It was you who was trying to break in?"

"Yes," he replies. "I long suspected this ugly truth in my family's past. Sometimes I thought it was a dream, a recurring nightmare, but deep down, I knew what I saw as a boy. That horrible image of my father's hands around her neck—it's burned in my memory."

Naomi shakes her head. "Gene, no, I won't let you do this. You don't know what you're saying. Go back to bed." She looks at Jim. "Jimmy, stop this nonsense. Take your father back to bed."

"No," Gene says, holding up his hand. "This family has suf-fered too long because of what I did. To think I had everyone on Boat Street believing that Jimmy was to blame. It's the only way they'd keep the pact." Jim looks at his feet as his father shakes his head slowly. "It's time I come clean."

"Father," Jim says. His face looks ashen. "You told them that I—"

"I'm sorry, son," he says.

Naomi is crying now. She stands up and walks toward him, throwing her arms around his shoulders. "Please," she begs. "Don't do this. Don't go to the police."

He takes her face in his hands. "I knew you could never love me the way you loved Dexter Wentworth," he says in a quivering voice. "I thought that if she were gone, he'd be too guilt-ridden to continue the affair."

Naomi shakes her head. "No, Gene. No, I won't hear of this."

"And I was right," he says. "But what I didn't know was that you'd only be half here. One part of your heart would always long for him. I didn't factor that into my plan." Gene touches her chin lightly, but she turns away.

"All this time," she says, searching his eyes, "I thought you did it for *me*. I thought you wanted her out of the way so *I* could be happy." She shakes her head. "But you did it for *yourself*."

Gene is stoic, but I can see that her words have pierced him in a place that only she can reach. He walks to the closet. "I'll just go and get my coat. Son, will you drive me to the station?"

Jim stands. "Dad," he says. "I—"

I squeeze Jim's arm. "Let him go," I say under my breath. "He needs this."

"But his health . . ."

"The police will take that into account, I'm sure," I say.

Jim nods. I watch him walk toward his father. I know it must be painful for him, for all of them. But this scene should have played out fifty years ago. The sadness in the room is thick, but there's relief, too. I see it on Naomi's face; Gene's, too.

"All right, Pop," Jim says slowly.

"You're doing the right thing, Gene," I say, standing up.

"Oh, Penny," he cries. "Will you ever forgive me?"

"Her name is Ada, Dad," Jim interjects.

Gene looks momentarily stunned, then nods. "Of course it is."

I reach into my pocket. Penny's hospital bracelet is there, as is the crumpled paper I found in the chest. "Here," I say to Jim. "Something I found in the houseboat. I think it belongs to you."

Jim unfolds the wrinkled paper and studies the comic strip he drew as a boy, with its crude figures and jagged lines. It was once a castoff, perhaps, but years later, I look into Jim's tear-filled eyes, and I can see that it might just be the greatest relic from a lost childhood. While this little freckle-faced boy may have been lost in the shuffle of his parents' own heartache, he mattered to Penny.

# Chapter 33

After Jim escorts his father to the police station, I practically race up to the street, then run down Alex's dock. I can't wait to tell him about Gene's confession, about all of it.

I stop, out of breath, in front of his door. I place my hand on the doorknob, but pause when I notice a pair of lime green flats and two adorable little girl's UGG boots. I peer through the window that looks directly into the kitchen and living area, and my heart seizes.

Kellie's standing barefoot in front of the stove, stirring something simmering in a large pot. Alex and Gracie are huddled over a picture book at the bar. Everyone's smiling. It's the picture of a happy, idyllic family.

I take a step back. How could I think that I could insert myself into their world? I can't knock on the door. I can't think about going inside. I don't belong here. I shake my head and run back up the dock.

"Joanie, it's me," I say into the phone. "I'm coming home."

"Oh, honey," she says. "What happened?"

I rub my eyes. I know she can hear my voice cracking. "Nothing, exactly," I say. "I met the man of my dreams. I fell in love. But he's a part of a family, and I can't break that up."

"Oh," Joanie says. "Are you sure you're not misinterpreting the situation? Didn't you say he's divorced, that he's over his ex?"

"That doesn't matter," I say. "I just saw them together. The three of them. You should have seen the way his little girl looked up adoringly at her mom and dad." I pause to wipe a tear from my cheek. "I can't interfere with that, Joanie. I'm catching a plane home this evening."

I spend the next few hours packing, and when my suitcase is arranged, I wipe down the counters and hand-wash the dishes in the sink. I dry the water glass that Alex used the night before, and I set it lovingly on the shelf. *It's for the best,* I tell myself.

I make the bed upstairs, then give the living room a once-over. I'll miss this place. Jim. The ducks. The lake. The way the morning glory blooms just as the sun rises. I walk outside to the deck and kneel down to pick a white flower and tuck it in my pocket. I don't ever want to forget Boat Street.

I stand up just as Kellie is walking out of Alex's houseboat. She's wearing a coat, and her purse is slung over her shoulder. She stops briefly, then waves. "Hello," she calls out. I'm a bit startled by the overture. Each of us knows of the other, and yet we've never spoken. What would I say to her?

"Hi," I reply.

"May I come over?" Kellie asks.

I nod stiffly. I don't know what to expect. Will she plead with me to stay away from her daughter? From Alex? Will there be *words*? I brace myself.

"Just a minute," she says. "I'll walk around."

Two minutes later, she's standing in front of my deck. "What do you think?" she says, pointing to her shoes. "They were an impulse buy at Nordstrom. But lime green? I'm not so sure."

I grin. "They're really cute." I'm surprised by how much I already like her. She's funny and warm and reminds me of Joanie, but I still regard her presence cautiously. "Would you like to come in?"

"Yes, thanks. I was hoping we could talk."

Inside, she sits on a chair in the living room, and I sink into the sofa. My heart is beating wildly. I feel like I'm in the principal's office. Will her smile morph into a stern expression before she warns me against spending time with Gracie? Will she confide that she still loves Alex and plead with me, woman to woman, to back off?

We both began speaking at the same time. "Sorry," I say.

Kellie smiles. "This is awkward, isn't it?"

"Yes," I reply quickly. "Listen, I don't want you to worry. I'm leaving, tonight, actually."

She looks confused. "Leaving? Why?"

"I don't want to interfere," I say. "It's best for Gracie if the two of you have the space to work things out."

"Work things out?" She lets out a little laugh. "Alex and me?"

I shake my head, confused. "But I thought . . ."

"Ada, I'm engaged," she says, holding up an enormous sparkler on her left hand. "I moved on a long time ago."

"You did?"

She nods. "Listen, we've had our past, and it wasn't always easy. We were two people who were never meant to marry, but we did anyway, and the best result was Gracie. Alex and I were in a terrible place for a long time, but we're good now. Gracie's good. She loves you, by the way."

"She does?" I feel like Jell-O. This isn't the conversation I anticipated having, and yet it's the greatest, most unexpected gift.

"Yes," she says. "And so do I. Alex told me about you, about what you've been through. Well, what I want you to know is that I welcome you into this crazy, dysfunctional family of ours. You make Alex happy, and that makes him a better daddy. A win-win."

I grin. "I can't believe I read the situation so wrong."

Kellie smiles. "It's OK. All that matters now is that you stay and give it a chance. Think you can do that?"

I nod.

"By the way," she continues, "those cookies you made for Gracie were really good. Do you have the recipe to share?"

"No," I say, "but I can get it for you."

"Please," she says. "I'm working on a cookie book in the fall, and I'd love to include it."

"I have to admit," I say, thinking of Penny, "the recipe isn't mine. It's from a woman who lived in this houseboat a long time ago."

"Oooh, history," she says. "Even better. Stories always enrich a recipe." She looks at her watch. "I have to go," she says, standing up. "My editor will be at Wild Ginger in a half hour." She leans over and rubs the back of her right shoe. "Serves me right to have to walk three blocks downtown when I wear a new pair out. You don't happen to have a Band-Aid handy?"

"Blister?"

"Yeah," she says.

I run to the bathroom and return, handing her the bandage.

"Thanks," she says.

"It took a lot of courage to come over to talk to me," I say. "I don't know that I could have done that."

Kellie shakes her head knowingly. "Yes, you could have. You're a mother to a little girl," she says, pointing up to heaven. She lowers her voice. "Alex told me."

I nod.

"We do anything for our children's happiness; you know that."

I blink back a tear. "I don't know what to say."

"Don't say anything," she says, smiling. "Go get your guy."

# Chapter 34

Jim returns from the police station at three in the afternoon, alone.

I'm sitting at the edge of the dock, where I've been since Kellie left, and I turn around when I hear the creak of his footsteps on the dock behind me. Boat Street is changing; I can feel it.

He slips his hat off and holds it to his chest. "Hi," he says.

I stand, and my eyes sting with tears. "Where's Gene, is he—?"

"They're keeping him for questioning."

"Jim, I'm so sorry," I say. "Please, believe me, it wasn't my intention to—"

He holds up his hand. "No," he says, looking out to the lake through misty red eyes. "No, this needed to happen. You should have seen him at the station." He turns back to me. "It's like a burden was lifted off his shoulders."

I think of what that might feel like—his secret, like a lead vest worn every day, peeled away—and I'm relieved for him, even if it means spending the rest of his life, however short it may be, behind bars.

"And will they make a case against him?" I ask. Penny deserves justice, but I can't help but worry about Gene's age, his health.

"The officer told me they'd look out for him," Jim says, rubbing his brow. "They'd treat him kindly."

We don't say anything for the next few minutes, and I try to imagine what Jim must be thinking about this place he's called home for so many years.

"What's next," I say, "for Boat Street? For you?"

He kicks a pebble into the lake and it makes a tiny splash. I think of Penny out there still. I think of Jimmy's hazy childhood memories, his pain.

"I thought I'd take a trip," he says, "on the *Catalina*. For Penny."

"She'd like that," I say, smiling. "Where will you go?"

Jim takes a deep breath. "Well, first Catalina Island, and then, well, I don't know. Wherever the wind takes me, I guess."

"Sounds nice."

"Truth is," he continues, "I probably should have made this voyage years ago. Guess I was worried about Mom and Dad, worried about . . ."

"Go," I say. "If Gene should need anything, well, I'll give the officers my contact information. And Alex and I will look after Naomi."

*Alex and I.* I like the sound of it.

Jim thanks me and walks up the dock to his houseboat. When he's gone, I study the planks beneath my feet, remembering how I felt when I first arrived, how I fell to my feet and wept until I hadn't a single tear left. I think of my journey, and Penny's, and this dock we both have called home. *Home.*

I look up, and I see Alex walking toward me. Gracie skips along beside him. She's wearing pink leggings, a gray sweatshirt, and those purple UGGS, which Ella would have loved. The ensemble is punctuated, of course, with a fluorescent yellow life vest, courtesy of her daddy.

"Oh, good," Alex says, smiling with his keys in his hand. He must be coming from the parking lot. "We were hoping to find you."

I look down at this beautiful child. Wisps of her blond hair fall out of her ponytail. Her smile is big and joyous, just like Ella's used to be.

"Hi, honey," I say, kneeling down.

"Ada," Gracie says, "did you know my daddy has a crush on you?"

Alex tugs at her hood. "Hey now, are you trying to embarrass your poor old dad?"

Gracie grins, then runs ahead.

"I talked to Kellie," I say.

His eyes narrow. "You did?"

"She gave me her blessing," I continue. "It's funny, but I needed that. I needed to know that I wasn't crossing any boundaries. When kids are involved, that's important."

He nods and wraps his arm around my waist. "I'm relieved," he says. "I thought she was going to warn you about my allergy to housework, which I assure you is only a part truth." I grin as we watch Gracie silently for a moment, and he tucks his hand in mine. "I know your lease is up soon," he says cautiously. "What can I do to get you to stay?"

I look away from him for a moment. It's tempting. I want to stay. I've promised Jim I'd be here for his parents. But . . . I also feel a tug at my heart. It's a restless, unsettled feeling, and I consider the fact that I might carry it with me forever. In some ways, I wish my burden were as easy to part with as Gene's. I wish I could simply confess it away.

Alex kisses my hand. "What's holding you back, Ada? Is it *him*?"

*Oh, James, can I share my heart, my life, with anyone other than you?* Naomi and Gene's houseboat is to our right; I look at her potted flowers. A green morning glory vine has wrapped its tendrils around one of the terra-cotta pots. It bursts with the white flowers I've come to love on the dock. I think of Penny then, and wonder what she would have said at the sight of the blossoms, what she would have felt.

Before I can respond, Gracie waves from the end of the dock. "Daddy!" she calls. "Look what I found."

Alex and I walk down the dock hand in hand.

"Look!" Gracie says again. She holds up a piece of driftwood with a hollowed-out center, like a boat. "It just needs a sail and it could be a sailboat! A real sailboat!"

"Honey, if you're interested in sailboats we should have Jim take us all out in a *real* sailboat tomorrow," Alex says.

Gracie grins. "A real sailboat?"

"Yep," he says, pointing to the *Catalina*. "That one over there."

Gracie sits down, cross-legged, on the dock and plants her cheek in her palm. "I wish I had my own sailboat."

I think of Ella's precious Aggie and her newfound twin, Mary Joe, in my bag. "Wait," I say, fiddling with the zipper.

A moment later, I hold up the little sailboat Dexter gave me. "Would you like to play with this one?"

Gracie's eyes are big. "Really?"

"Go ahead," I say, handing her the tiny craft. Its white canvas sail has yellowed, just like the one on Ella's prized Aggie.

I watch her as she sets the boat in the lake and leans over the edge. She pulls the little sailboat back and forth.

"She loves it," Alex whispers to me.

I nod, wrapping my arm around his waist. "It belonged to Dexter Wentworth."

Alex looks confused.

"I'll explain later."

"Daddy," Gracie says, "what does this writing mean on the sailboat?"

Alex turns to me. "Why don't you ask Ada?"

I hold the little boat in my hands and read the words painted on the side, for maybe the one thousandth time. "Leighton Shipping Company," I say. "My daughter had a sailboat just like this one, and we could never quite figure out where it came from, but we used to like to say the name." I smile. "Leighton. It's kind of a neat word to say, isn't it?"

"Leighton," Gracie says, then giggles. She's quiet for a moment, then looks up at me thoughtfully. "You have a *daughter*? What's her name? Why doesn't she live with you?"

Alex puts his hand on my shoulder. I know he's worried about me, but I feel stronger now. "Yes," I say. "Her name was Ella. She doesn't live with me now because she's in heaven, with her daddy."

Gracie looks up to the sky as if she's trying to envision Ella's face, then she turns back to me. "Are you very sad?"

"Yes," I say honestly. "And I might always be a little sad." I glance at Alex. "But I've learned that I still have so much in life to be happy about. Besides, I'll see her again." I point up to the sky where Gracie's looking.

Alex kisses my forehead lightly. "I promised Gracie ice cream," he says. "Want to join us?"

A wave of emotion rushes over me. It's thick and consuming. It makes me want to crawl back into the quiet, solitary place I existed in for so long before coming to Seattle, the cocoon I built for myself. Suddenly, I think of the day of the accident, how I promised Ella ice cream. I hear her voice. "Chocolate, with sprinkles."

I look beyond Alex, and at the top of the dock near the stairs that lead to the street, I see her suddenly, standing beside James. They're barely there, just a hologram, glimmers of their former selves. But I see them, and they're smiling. They're happy. James nods at me. He's saying, "Go ahead, my love." Then Ella waves. My eyes fill with tears, and then they're gone.

Alex looks at me cautiously. "If you're not up for ice cream, we can—"

"No," I say quickly, wiping away a tear. "I want to. I never want to be the kind of person who says no to ice cream. Not anymore."

Alex squeezes my hand.

"Look," Gracie cries. "Ducks!"

We watch as Henrietta swims by, with Haines beside her.

The three of us walk ahead. It's Monday, and there's a chance of rain in the forecast, but it's OK. And with each step along Boat Street, the old wooden dock lets out quiet creaks of approval.

I have finally found my way.

# Epilogue

## PENNY

There he is, my son, all grown up. I sit in my sailboat and watch him on the dock as it drifts on Lake Union. She's not as yare as the *Catalina*, of course, not as grand. This boat feels the wind deeper, and in a storm, air seeps into the galley. But despite her shortcomings, she's been my home, my companion, all these years. Together, we've sailed the world, and when I say that, it's not an exaggeration. I've seen the sun rise in New Zealand and watched it set on the shores of Capri. I've had a life. Mind you, not the life I imagined I'd have when I was a young bride. But I've lived a life that is mine, and mine alone.

I kill the motor and drift quietly as I look out to Boat Street. It's not the first time I've been back. I make a yearly pilgrimage, just to see it. To remember.

No, I didn't drown that night. Gene did hold me under, and I nearly gave up the fight, but then in the midst of the struggle, it was as if time stopped. And maybe it did. Beneath the dock, a little morning glory vine grew. All my time on Boat Street, I'd never seen a morning glory bloom at night. They'd always open their blossoms with the morning sun, then close them tightly by the time the moon appeared. It's true, they aren't night creatures—but that night they were. They called to me.

Gene must have thought I drowned. And I nearly did. Thankfully, it was too dark for him to see me as I floated below the dock, coming up for air in the space beneath the wooden planks. The morning glories kept me company there as the residents of Boat Street mourned me and their own transgressions.

I'm not sure how long I stayed there, clutching the logs under the dock. I shivered for a long time, until I gained the courage to swim away to the next dock, and somehow, dripping wet, I made it to Pete's Market undetected, where I dried off in the restroom.

A stranger gifted me the train fare to Portland, where I waited tables long enough to pay my passage to California, to Catalina Island. I'd miscarried by then, of course. The early pain was an indication that something was wrong. I mourned the loss of that baby, Collin's and mine. But there would be another; I just didn't know it yet.

Eleven years later, when I saw Collin again, in a marina in Key West, I thought I was seeing a ghost. His hair was longer then, his skin so dark from the sun. Despite the passage of time, I hadn't given up hope of running into him. I looked for Collin in every port, whipped out my binoculars to examine every passing boat on the sea. And then, in a moment of amazement, there he stood.

We shared a night together, the most beautiful night of my life. It gave me my son, Alex. But tragically, Collin never knew his son. He didn't even know I carried him. We planned to sail away together, from Key West onward. Where to? We didn't know. It only mattered that we were together.

That morning, Collin took his boat out to a neighboring dock for refueling (not the *Catalina*; a few years earlier, he'd bestowed it on Jimmy, thinking I had passed on). I waited for him to return, but he never did. Frightened, I contacted the Coast Guard, who found Collin collapsed over the tiller. He'd died of a heart attack on his way back to me.

That year was the most difficult of my life. Pregnant, alone on the sea. Though it broke my heart to admit it, a boat was no place to raise a baby. I'd met a nice couple in Oregon when I'd lived there briefly years prior, and I decided I'd take him to them. They were childless, and I knew they desperately wanted a baby. I'd ask them to raise mine for me.

You may think of my actions as selfish, but I knew no other way. My life was on the sea. By then, I felt more amphibious than human, understanding the tides and the seabirds better than humankind. I was a water baby, as my mother had always known. Giving my son a normal life, a stable one, seemed like the most loving thing to do. So I did it.

Alex was three months old when I dropped him off. He would be raised as their child. He'd never know of me. I agreed to this. And yet I regretted the arrangement every day of my life. I remember handing Alex, rosy cheeked and plump, with that sandy hair just like his father's, to Sandy Milstead. He reached up his little hand to her cheek, cooing as if he'd already forgotten me.

I left, but I came back. A lot. Alex never knew me, but I knew him. I stood in the shadows watching as he graduated from kindergarten. I sailed to Hawaii when his family took a trip there after his adopted father's death. I agonized when he was in Sudan, catching the news in every port of call. And then, when he moved to Boat Street, my heart bulged with pride. He was meant to be there, in his father's house. (Of course, I had a hand in that. I dropped a hint to his real estate agent, anonymously, about a certain houseboat coming up for sale. Fate did the rest of the work.)

A kayak glides by on the lake, and I nod at the couple paddling beside my boat. I no longer worry about whether people will see me, recognize me. My beauty has faded. I am an old woman now. The Penny they remember is now encased in wrinkles with a mop of gray hair atop her head.

But Boat Street is as charming as it ever was, and on this day, it positively shines. There's love there again, you see.

I smile to myself as my granddaughter, Gracie, plays with her little sailboat. I see myself in her. That spirit, those eyes.

I've come to know Ada, too, from afar, of course. I've watched her on the dock in the mornings. I've seen her weep. It tells me she's soulful, deep. And she loves the morning glories, as I did. She touches them delicately, almost speaking their language. I watch now as she nestles her head against Alex's chest. Yes, this woman loves my son. Love is all I ever hoped for him, and he has found it.

I've forgiven Naomi, even Gene. Life is too short to live with bitterness. And I think about Dexter, more often than you'd guess. Our relationship was a complicated one, but there was love there, real love. I'm thinking about paying him a visit soon, before it's too late. I look out to the skyline of Seattle. He lives in one of those tall buildings. Maybe I'll go today.

A seagull perches on the bow, just above the letters I painted below the railing. I used blue paint and outlined each character in gold trim. The paint has weathered from years on the sea, but it's still legible, still the perfect name for my sailboat: *Morning Glory*. I wipe away a spot of dried-on seaweed with my sleeve and smile to myself. No, it hasn't been the life I imagined, but it's been a beautiful life. My life. And in every port, every waterway, I've taken a bit of Boat Street with me.

# Acknowledgments

Before this novel was a real story, it was simply an idea. And there are two important people who championed it at the very earliest stages. First, Elisabeth Weed, my dear literary agent: I thank you, always, for believing in me, for being so incredibly good at what you do and just plain lovely to work with. You are the best in the business, truly. Next, Denise Roy, my editor, now on our fifth book together, you steered me back to this novel when I found myself lost in a sea of ideas. Without your gentle nudges, this story wouldn't be here. And without your immaculate editing, it wouldn't be the novel it is. Especially touching was your ability to feel the emotions of my characters and draw from your own life in our editorial conversations. Hats off to you and all you do for me and my books.

Heartfelt thanks to the wonderful behind-the-scenes people who do such excellent work on behalf of my novels. I'm talking about you, Jenny Meyer, foreign agent extraordinaire; Shane King; Dana Murphy; and the always amazing Dana Borowitz. Also, all the fabulous folks at Plume: Phil Budnick, Liz Keenan, Milena Brown, Ashley Pattison, Kym Surridge, Kate Napolitano, Jaya

Miceli—thank you all so much. (And a special thanks to Liz, who trekked all the way from New York to Seattle to spend a rainy day with me touring the places that inspired my novels and hanging on the houseboat.)

A special thanks to all of the critics, book bloggers, and booksellers whom I've come to know over the years. I'm endlessly grateful for your enthusiasm and kindness to me.

To my family and friends, as always, thanks for your unceasing support, love, and friendship. I have read that writers are a teeny bit cuckoo (truly; I'm afraid studies prove this), and I commend you for always being there for me, even when I'm in the throes of a first draft, or revising the next, or talking nonstop about the new idea that's haunting me—especially longtime friend Sally Farhat Kassab; fiction writer and partner in crime Camille Noe Pagán; Natalie Quick, who always reminds me of the importance of forgiveness; the lovely Wendi Parriera and Lisa Bach; and so many others. Also, my family, much love to you: Terry and Karen Mitchell, and you, too, Josh, Jessica, and Josiah.

And I must thank the various people who were lovely to me (knowingly or unknowingly) as I wrote this novel, including the kind Beth Farrell (it all began aboard your charming houseboat!), Gayla Field, Jason Werle, Jeri Callahan, and so many more.

Music was incredibly important to my writing process for this book, especially the voice of Karen Carpenter singing "Rainy Days and Mondays," as well as the diverse musical talents of Brad Mehldau and Pat Metheny (the song "Make Peace" was put on repeat during the writing of this novel), Frank Sinatra, Shirley Horn, James Taylor, David Gray, Sarah McLachlan, and so many others.

In addition, I must share my gratitude with the incredible, kind, good, and warm houseboat community of Seattle's Lake

Union, especially those on the dock who put up with my rambunctious boys with grace and understanding, the neighbors who smiled at us on quiet foggy mornings, and those who waved from their decks while we paddled by.

Finally, to my boys, Carson, Russell, and Colby: We had fun on the houseboat, didn't we? Your curiosity and playfulness inspired me, and I will always remember our time on the lake together. The ducks were so well fed during our stay there. And dear Jason, my husband, best friend, generous optimist, and superdad: The truest love in the pages of this novel is a reflection of my love for you. xo

154
280

# From Sarah Jio

**THE VIOLETS OF MARCH** — SARAH JIO
*A Novel*
AUTHOR OF *THE BUNGALOW*

978-0-452-29703-6

SARAH JIO — AUTHOR OF *THE VIOLETS OF MARCH*
**THE BUNGALOW** — *A Novel*

978-0-452-29767-8

AUTHOR OF *THE VIOLETS OF MARCH* AND *THE BUNGALOW* — SARAH JIO — **BLACKBERRY WINTER**

978-0-452-29838-5

NEW YORK TIMES BESTSELLING AUTHOR OF *BLACKBERRY WINTER* AND *THE VIOLETS OF MARCH* — SARAH JIO — *THE* LAST CAMELLIA — A NOVEL

978-0-452-29839-2

"Sarah Jio's writing is exquisite and engrossing." —Elin Hilderbrand

www.sarahjio.com

**PLUME**
A member of Penguin Group (USA)

IN A S[...] MMUNITY, THE
ARTISTIC SP[...] HED SINCE THE 1950s
MAY HAV[...] [...] SAVED ANOTHER

*On Seattle's Lake Union floats Boat Street.*
The farthest slip on the dock holds a houseboat sided
with weathered cedar shingles and trailing morning glory,
the white flowering vine whose loveliness is deceiving. In
the 1950s, Penny, newly Mrs. Dexter Wentworth, takes up
residence, dreaming of fulfillment as the muse to a successful
local artist destined for national renown. In present day, Ada
Santorini is drawn to the same floating home, hoping its
gentle rocking will lull the pain of the personal tragedy that
drove her from New York City.

As Ada settles in, she discovers a trunk full of mementos of
a radiant love affair that unfolded in Seattle's most iconic
locales. Neighbors reveal little about the past, only that the
beautiful and mysterious Penny had a hold on all who knew
her. The travel writer in Ada senses the journey of a lifetime.
On Boat Street, Penny's mysterious past and Ada's own
clouded future are destined to converge.

## Praise for SARAH JIO

"An intoxicating blend of mystery, history, and romance."
—*REAL SIMPLE*

"Exquisite and engrossing."
—ELIN HILDERBRAND, bestselling author of *SUMMERLAND*

"Ingenious . . . imaginative." —*THE SEATTLE TIMES*

Readers Guide available online at www.penguin.com

www.sarahjio.com

Cover design:
Jaya Miceli
Cover photograph:
Ingrid Taylar